BLOOD FEUD

by

Daniel Harris

Books by Daniel Harris

Goodbye, Dearie
Capital Crimes
Blood Feud

RoseDog❧Books

PITTSBURGH, PENNSYLVANIA 15222

The contents of this work including, but not limited to, the accuracy of events, people, and places depicted; opinions expressed; permission to use previously published materials included; and any advice given or actions advocated are solely the responsibility of the author, who assumes all liability for said work and indemnifies the publisher against any claims stemming from publication of the work.

RoseDog Books
701 Smithfield Street
Pittsburgh, PA 15222
Visit our website at *www.rosedogbookstore.com*

ISBN: 978-1-4349-7383-2
eISBN: 978-1-4349-7105-0

Author's Note

This work is fiction. All of the events, people, and places are drawn from my own experiences or from stories that were passed on to me by friends or coworkers. I borrowed liberally from both sources for the express purpose of creating a story that the reader might become a part of as he/she continues to turn the pages of this novel. In summary, this novel is a literary work whose content is produced by the imagination.

To Benny, Danny, and Sammy Harris: You bring untold delight to your parents and to us everyday.

"My name is Ozymandis, King of Kings:
Look on my works, ye mighty, and despair!"
Nothing beside remains. Round the decay
of that colossal wreck, boundless and bare.
The lone and level sands stretch far away.

—Shelley

Introduction

How did I become involved? I didn't know it at the time, but when I was a boy, I was drawn to this local food store, Dominic's, in Newton Center. Ike was President. It was early in 1960, and good independent food stores were the rule then, not the exception. Sure there was the A&P, but other than that, big, dominant chains like Stop & Shop were just beginning to emerge on the retailing landscape. I remember as kids that the big joke was that A&P and Stop & Shop would merge and become...you guessed it, the Stop & P. Humor wasn't very subtle in those days either. But Dominic's was a special place to me. Even before you entered the store, you'd step under the awning of the two front windows and be assaulted by the aromas and vivid colors of fruits and vegetables that were neatly stacked on tables on either side of the entryway. As you stepped up into the store, it resembled more of a meeting place than a food store. Several older men would be gathered around a table, watching two people compete on a game board that was neither checkers nor chess. Kibitzing was in strong evidence as one combatant or the other made a move. People stood in the aisle and chatted, and I'm guessing the store carried three or four hundred items versus the 50,000 that a chain supermarket carries today.

Help was in abundance. Every aisle had a clerk with a white apron on, and I remember that the floors were old, made of wood, and so clean that you could eat a meal off of them. More often than not someone would greet my mother by name and take her order. The place always smelled of fresh ground coffee, and the meat behind the glass counter was fresh and very red. The fish was filleted and ice chips were everywhere. The heads of the fish were displayed and peered out at me through the glass. They looked like they could still swim to me if someone would just put them back in the water. It was a wondrous place for a nine-year-old to be... remember we didn't have much TV in those days—we had to entertain ourselves. A trip to Dominic's for this nine-year-old was entertainment, a pure delight. Sure, watching the Superman serial at the cinema on Saturday or riding my bike with my friends would rank ahead of a trip to Dominic's, but this food-store trip was in my top five.

As we exited the store, I asked my mother, "Why didn't we take our groceries with us, Ma?"

She replied, "Because we've got other errands to do, and I asked Dominic to deliver them, Russell."

"When I grow up I think I'm going to work there," I said.

"Don't you want to be a fireman or a policeman?" my mother asked.

"Naw, if I can't play for the Red Sox, I think I'd like working at Dominic's."

"First thing's first, young man; you get your education and then we'll talk about what you will do."

"Yes, ma'am."

As I was to learn, my mother had priorities for her children, and the very first one was education. My dad had gone to night school to graduate from college and earned his degree eight months before his 40th birthday, while my mother graduated from high school and went to work as a secretary for a doctor in Boston. But education and the church were pretty much the top priorities. It was a little confusing to my friends: my name was Russell Riley, but I went to the Episcopalian church. It didn't confuse me that much; my mom was a Protestant, and my dad was Irish Catholic, but he hadn't been in a church since he married my mom. Ergo, we went to church at the place designated by my mother.

We were a pretty typical middle-class family. My dad sold cars in Watertown, and my mom was a homemaker, as we said in those days. I never understood why the parents of the girls I dated in high school were somewhat ambivalent about me. Now I know. If I dated a Catholic girl, that family seemed pleased about it until they found out that a guy named Riley was a Protestant. If I dated a Protestant girl, the family didn't seem all that pleased about it until they found out I was a Protestant. But then they weren't sure if I was the real deal. It should have worked for me but it didn't. Boston was heavily Catholic, Irish and Italian, Democratic to the core, and Cardinal Cushing was a hell of a lot more important in the citizens' view than either the mayor or the governor. That many days hadn't passed in this neck of the woods when shopkeepers had signs in the windows that said, "Irish need not apply." If you thought about it for a while, this was a town that was ripe for the likes of Louise Day Hicks and the busing crisis that would follow in 10 years. But Catholic versus Protestant, black versus white, Democrat versus Republican, Yankees versus Red Sox, and Ted Williams versus the "Knights of the Keyboard" were all conflicts that I grew up with in New England. We had a mayor run for office from the county jail, and we were the only state to vote for McGovern for President…including his own.

I was too young to understand global events. Like most young boys, I went to school, played sports, didn't see what was so special about girls. I tried the new fast-food place— McDonald's—where they had sold more than a million burgers nationwide. The big event at our house was that Dad received a brand-new Ford every year, and we took a spin in it while it still smelled like a new car. We lived in a small three-bedroom house in Newton Center, and every week my parents, my older brother, my younger sister, and I couldn't wait to see *The Milton Berle Show* and *I Remember Mama*. We had a DuMont TV with a magnifying glass in front of it, and it was surely one of the seven wonders of the world.

But that all changed when I was 13 years old. My dad was killed in an auto accident on Route 9 in Framingham. My mother was devastated by his death, but from a financial standpoint, she was in pretty good shape. My dad had a reasonable amount of insurance, and my mother came from a family of some means in New Jersey. With the combination of insurance and her family inheritance, we kept our heads above water.

My older brother and I both obtained jobs after school. He worked in the Chinese laundry, and I got a job at Dominic's, working for Mr. Galetti. He had to be 60 because his two boys, Joseph and Dominic, had graduated from college and were in their 20s. My jobs included cleaning floors, washing fruit, and packing out shelves with canned groceries. As time went by I was able to really study Dominic Galetti. He was definitely old-school, old country, where cash was king. He was no taller than 5'6", but he was stocky and exceedingly strong. Even at 60 years of age, I saw him lift crates with one hand that I could hardly get off the ground with two hands. For a guy who was used to doing a lot of physical work, he dressed very well. He was far from a "dandy," but he always had on a pressed shirt with a collar, pants with creases in them, and his trademark suspenders. But the thing I remember the most about him was that those creased pants were always stuffed with cash. When the bread man made his delivery, Dominic paid in cash. When fruit trucks, a wholesaler van, and a meat truck backed into the rear of his building, the transaction was always the same: cash, cash, and cash.

But it was a different era. It wasn't crime-free, but it was drug-free. People weren't as concerned about security. My mother would leave the three of us in the car with the windows open and doors unlocked when she shopped. Maybe she was hoping we'd be kidnapped. We almost never locked our house during the day. When my mother did so on a rare occasion, she'd leave a note thumbtacked to the door that said, "Kids, the key is under the mat." The inescapable conclusion was that my mother felt that potential perpetrators couldn't read.

Dominic Galetti was a businessman who dealt with his consumers and vendors face-to-face every day. His wife, Anna, never really learned English, but Dominic's English, although spoken with a heavy accent, was very good. He treated everybody the same—with respect and with personal touch. As I assumed more and more responsibility, many of the vendors would remark that they were treated fairly by the Galetti organization, something they said was a rarity for the food industry.

Chapter One: The Trap

Helen Cortez was anxious and exhilarated at the same time. She had worked her way to a third interview with McAlister, Dodd, Eden, and Lancaster, a seemingly prestigious international legal firm based in the United Kingdom. It would be a dream realized if she were offered a position with this company. And why not? She deserved it. She was born in Mattapan, educated in the Boston school system, earned a scholarship to Holy Cross, and graduated with honors from Boston College Law School. She'd won a clerkship with Judge Cleon A. Matthews, who presided on Boston's highest court. He was a minority, African-American, and only 42 years old when he was appointed. Judge Matthews had given her positive feedback on several occasions for her diligent and creative work on behalf of his court.

Cortez was tall, angular, athletic. She was the perfect combination of two cultures. Her dad was a native of Eleuthera, while her mother was Boston Irish. Helen had her dad's dark hair and lithe build, but her face very much resembled that of her mother. Her hair was shoulder-length, and it had a natural wave in it that seemed to accent her high cheekbones and hazel eyes. She had snow-white teeth, and when she smiled her eyes seemed to sparkle, captivating her audience to the point that some seemed to linger longer than they should, observing the beauty before them. It was as if they had to check her out again. Was she really that beautiful? The conclusion: she was. With large, well-formed breasts, long, exquisite legs, she was difficult not to notice. But in the overall scheme of things that were important to her, she wasn't all that taken with her looks. In fact, she seemed unaware of the stares and the heads that snapped around when she entered a room.

So what if she was poorer than a church mouse? Working for Judge Matthews was definitely prestigious, but it didn't pay a lot. She'd be able to pay back all those law school loans if she landed this job. Getting back to a positive bank balance would be a moral victory, she decided. This firm hadn't spared expenses. Her first interview was in Montreal, the second in New York City, and this one was right here in Boston at the Four Seasons. By day's end she hoped to have an offer in hand.

She had completed her work on the current case and left a folder on the judge's desk for him to peruse at some point. It was a high-profile case involving the Galetti Supermarket chain. Two brothers, Joe and Dom Galetti, had built a $2 billion-business, opening almost 60 supermarkets over the past 20 years. Dom had died prematurely and his widow, Maria, was suing Joe Galetti because she felt he had taken company stock and profits over the years that belonged to her side of the family. The newspapers and local media types were having a field day with the story. There seemed to be something fascinating to the everyday public about a family squabble where a billion dollars might change hands as a result of a court ruling.

In fact, the case was causing such a stir that it came up often during the interview process with the folks from McAlister, Dodd, Eden, and Lancaster. They were just like the curious public—they wanted to know what Judge Matthews was saying behind closed doors and what role she played in the proceedings. Helen supposed that, during these discussions, she hinted that her role was, in fact, bigger than it actually was. As a rule she was straightforward and honest, but she did "guild the lily" a little in the interview process. Not given to hyperbole often, she did tell the interviewers that she was providing precedents for the judge to study and that he asked her opinion on a number of key issues. This wasn't exactly so, as Judge Matthews rarely asked her to interpret the day's proceedings for him. But what the heck, it was only a very little white lie, she rationalized.

As businesspeople they seemed particularly interested in whether Judge Matthews favored either side or if he played it right down the middle. Helen remembered telling them that the judge tended to lean toward Maria Galetti and away from the powerbroker and business mogul, Joe Galetti. But upon reflection she knew that was really her opinion, not the judge's point of view. She made a mental note, if the opportunity arose, to set that straight in this interview.

As she entered the lobby of the Four Seasons, she was met by senior partner Mark Graceson and human resource manager Harry Tremble. She liked Graceson immensely. He was near 70 years old, with snow-white hair, and he had a large nose and the biggest ears she'd ever seen. He dressed impeccably in pinstripe suits, and his shoes were shined to a sparkling hue. *He was old-world*, she thought. Mark Graceson reminded her of Tip O'Neill.

Harry Tremble, on the other hand, was nice enough, but Helen didn't warm up to him. He was a tad under six feet tall, portly, and he sweated a lot. But it was the beady eyes that made him so unattractive to Helen Cortez. While he was saying something, Helen was constantly wondering what he was really thinking.

Mark greeted Helen with a smile and a handshake and said, "Nice to see you again, Ms. Cortez. I'm sure you'll be pleased to know that this arduous process is about to end."

"Good morning, gentlemen. Not at all, Mr. Graceson. Thanks to you, this interview process has been relatively stress-free," Helen said.

"Let's go up to the second floor," Harry Tremble said. "I've got a room reserved where we can talk in private."

They turned toward the stairs and proceeded toward the conference room. It was a beautiful room with exquisite furniture, but what captured Helen's attention was that there was a tape recorder on the conference table. As they settled in chairs, Graceson and Tremble poured coffee for themselves, and Helen made herself a cup of tea. Tremble started off leading the interview, which was a change from the first two interviews that had been led, in the main, by Mark Graceson. "Ms. Cortez, we have a confession to make. We're not with McAlister, Dodd, Eden, and Lancaster. In fact, we are part of a team that is working on the defense of Joe Galetti, the case currently pending before Judge Matthews' court."

"But I don't understand..." Helen Cortez said.

"Let me explain. My name is Arthur Modello, and I'm a private detective, and this is Nicholas Blaine, an attorney for Joe Galetti," he said, pointing to the man Helen Cortez thought to be Mark Graceson. Helen looked at Graceson but he did not make eye contact with her.

Instead, Graceson picked up a pencil from the table and twirled it in his fingers as he began to speak. "What we are doing is trying to establish with someone close to Judge Matthews—and that would be you, Ms. Cortez—that he is prejudiced against our client. In these first two interviews we had with you, which were recorded in their entirety, we believe we now have that evidence."

Helen's face flushed and she felt very hot. She was trying to control her emotions, but she was very close to tears as she said, "But this isn't fair. You established this evidence in a false manner. This is a ruse; it's a cruel hoax."

"It may not seem fair, but it is legal, and unless you appear as a witness for the defense, we will release these tapes to the press," Modello said.

Helen now had a complete understanding of the situation. She was being used to aid the defense, and there was obviously no job opportunity in the offing. She stood, gathered her briefcase and her handbag, and said, "You are the type of people that give the legal profession a bad name. I have no intent of appearing as witness for you or anybody else in this case. Good day, gentlemen."

She left the room with as much dignity as she could muster. As she descended the stairs to the lobby, tears streamed down her face. She stepped onto the sidewalk in front of the Four Seasons with only one thought: *My career as a lawyer is over...before it ever began.*

Chapter 2: What's a Galetti?

I, Russell Riley, was a lucky guy. At 38 years of age, I was the president of a family-owned supermarket business that had grown to 58 stores and over $2 billion worth of business in the 25 years since I'd joined the firm. I know you can do the math, but including working part-time, I had joined the firm at 13 years of age, just after my dad died in an auto accident, when Galetti Supermarkets had but one store. Now that I think about it, back then it would have been Galetti Supermarket, without the "s." I'd married a wonderful woman, had two children, drove a Mercedes E320, made more money in a year than I thought I'd make in a lifetime, and had a small stake in the ownership of the chain. Small, I guess, is in the eye of the beholder, a relative term, because multiplying any percentage of ownership times $2 billion makes a very interesting sum. I was the highest-ranking nonfamily member of this organization, but, in truth, I felt as if I were family.

Trip Galetti, the nephew of CEO Joe Galetti, and I were walking down the executive hallway on our way to our monthly board of directors meeting in the conference room. Trip was actually Dominic Galetti III. His granddad, the original Dominic, had started the chain, and his dad, Dominic Jr., had played a key role both creatively and with astute real estate moves in the successful expansion of the chain. If I were forced to point out a reason for our success, and there were several, store location and store format would be high on the list. And Trip, who was two years out of Dartmouth College, was not a relative who didn't contribute to our growth. I'd trained him since he was in his early teens, and he had a natural affinity for the business. Trip was about an inch taller than I at 6'2", with dark, wavy hair and a well-proportioned 190 pounds. Although he had the mannerisms of his dad, he was a dead ringer for his mother, Maria. We were chatting about a meeting we'd just left with the MASSPIRG Environment Group, as Trip said, "Jesus, Russ, those people are intense."

"Yeah and they mean well. It's kind of hard to argue against their cause on this bottle bill, but they have no concept of what it costs to actually execute their program."

"Is it a fair fight?" Trip asked.

"Hell no," I said. "The public perceives that the supermarket industry is beating up on these guys, but, in truth, they are well-organized, well-heeled, and they have very effective local and national lobbies."

We entered the conference room, wandered over to the coffee urn, filled two cups with coffee, and we each grabbed a sweet roll on the way to the conference table. The thought crossed my mind that Dominic Galetti, the founder, would have been proud of this room. It was a no-frills conference room: bare walls; comfortable but inexpensive chairs; and an oblong conference table that looked as if it belonged in a bingo hall. It made me recall his office in the original store in Newton Center. It was a six-by-eight-foot room located in a corner of the back room of the store, and it had a door made of wood on the bottom half and wire mesh on the top half. The most interesting part of that old office was that Dominic always had three to five grocery bags sitting behind his desk filled with money. In those days every supplier who entered the store with merchandise was paid in cash.

I'm sure other supermarket executives, if they ever gained entrance to this conference room, wouldn't believe this barren space was the boardroom for a company that did the annual dollar volume of the Galetti chain. But, to me, it reflected the culture of our organization. Spartan would be a term I'd use; don't get me wrong, I don't mean cheap, but unlike other supermarkets, we only expanded by using the cash we generated from our current stores. We only used banks to borrow money if we had to, and we always bought enough land at a store site to create a bank of stores around us that would allow the consumer to do more than just shop for groceries.

Joe Galetti looked over his half-glasses at Trip and me and said, "Thanks for sitting in for me with the environmental pukes; I just wasn't in the mood for those folks today."

If I didn't know Joe Galetti was the CEO of a very large company and conservatively worth several hundred million dollars, I wouldn't have guessed it. He was in his late 40s, tall, gaunt, with a thin face, a large nose, and long, thin fingers that seemed perfect for playing classical piano. He had a thatch of white hair that always seemed to be standing straight up. He wore gabardine gray slacks, a button-down shirt, and a brown sweater that buttoned up the front. It had long ago lost its shape, as it hung on his bony frame like a topcoat. He drove a seven-year-old sedan and constantly told me that my car was an extravagance. If you put Joe in a lineup and made me guess his vocation, I would have said schoolteacher or a novelist in search of a best seller. His great strength was the numbers. Years ago, when there were only four of us on the board, he was the one who kept us solvent by dictating the rate at which we could expand. His brother, Dom, his wife, Maria, and I were the other three board members always pushing to expand, but we never got by Joe's number 2 pencil and calculator until he said so. He was an introvert, conservative by nature, pragmatic, unemotional, and he always began with the worst-case scenario. His role was critical to our success, and I think we all knew it even if we didn't agree with him very often. He may have looked like a slightly mad professor, but, in truth, he was a very astute businessman.

"You're welcome," Trip responded. "Actually, they were fairly easy on us, but we both think it's because we're in the eye of the storm. The bottle bill is a done deal; it's just a matter of how long we string it out before they put some onerous version of it on the ballot. Sooner than later is my guess."

Elsie Baden spoke next and said, "You know, Joe, if we put one of their people on our board, it would be a hell of a PR move. I'd dare say unprecedented, in fact."

Elsie Baden was an outside director on our board who ran a very successful chain of high-end boutiques. My wife loved her stores but not the retails. She was a rarity; a woman on a food-industry company board of directors which, in the main, was dominated by white males over 50, mostly Italian and Jewish, with one common thread. They were all millionaires.

"That's not a bad idea," Samuel Hirshberg, the retired Shawmut Bank CEO, interjected.

Harold Soloman, our legal counsel, and Larry Linehan, the accounting guru, agreed. Only Norm Parelli disagreed because, as a construction company owner, he was always doing battle with environmentalists and planning boards. Joe took it under advisement, but no decision was made.

Joe seemed more somber than usual, but the financial report by Linehan should have cheered him up immeasurably. The conversion of the Pantry Place supermarket acquisition was done, and most of the stores had been doubled in size. The great majority of these renovations had been done for cash, with the 30 original Galetti stores generating mountains of cash to finance the Pantry Place renovations. I'm not sure if Joe had it all planned out in his mind, but what he had done was quite brilliant. He waited until his original chain was big enough to sufficiently finance the acquisition. Said another way, if we'd purchased Pantry Place when we had 8, 12, or 16 stores, the loans needed to finance the expansion would have been too burdensome. So he waited until he had a base of 30 stores that were grossing three-quarters of a billion dollars a year and then made his move, adding 28 stores by acquisition purchased, in the main, with cash. This was reflected in Linehan's summary when he said, "Within nine months every expansion store will be wholly operated by the corporation. The only difference being that we will own all the Rhode Island stores, but, of course, we don't own the accompanying shopping centers as we do in Massachusetts. Our preliminary guess is that when *The Griffin Report* next reports share of market, we will have a fifty percent share in both markets that we compete in currently."

We all broke the silence with a spontaneous round of applause. Joe got out of his chair and walked over to a slide presentation set up near a podium. This was a rarity, as our meetings were usually pretty casual. The lights dimmed and Joe began to speak as a slide of Dominic's original store came up on the screen. "It all started with my dad, Dominic, in this store in Newton Center many years ago. I can tell you one thing. If he were here today he'd do two things. First, he'd go around and congratulate everyone in the room, and, secondly, he'd spend an extra minute with you, Larry, to question you closely on the cost of the furniture in this room."

I laughed out loud at that comment, because that's exactly what he would have done. That first slide brought a rush of memories for me. I'd spent eight or nine years inside that building.

Joe continued. "Our expansion really started when my brother, Dom, and I joined the organization full-time. We were about Trip's age, and we thought we knew it all, unlike Trip, who actually does know it all. We had just completed our sixteenth store, and we'd started to be noticed by the competition." Joe was flashing up those sixteen locations while he spoke. "They are kind of like the original colonies. In fact, they have been around so long that they need to be remodeled."

He was so right. What a disturbing thought. God, at 38 years old, I was a relic. Christ, I probably needed to be remodeled as well.

Joe continued by saying, "Since that time we've added forty-two stores. These forty-two stores will represent about seventy-five percent of our total volume. So, in effect, it took us twenty years to build sixteen stores and less than ten years to add forty-two more."

Even with the acquisition, that was mind-boggling to me. Joe was telling us that the results of the past 10 years were now producing 75 percent of the volume. You just don't have a chance to reflect on this kind of perspective every day in this business. It just moves too fast as you attempt to do the things you need to accomplish that day, that week, or that month.

Joe said, "Here's a look at the empire we've built over the last ten years. I'm not going to single out anyone in this room because you've all been integral to this success. How many of you are sitting here thinking this history lesson is warming us up for our next expansion?"

We all raised our hands at once and laughed simultaneously. Joe was smiling when he said, "You'd be wrong. I think we need to take a breather. We need to reevaluate the stores, our employees, who our consumer is, and see if we are what we think we are. You know we built these stores with the idea that we would know our consumer and that we'd have the best meat, fruit, and vegetable departments in the land. Let's look at that a little closer. Our stores average four hundred thousand dollars a week, and the average consumer spends fifty dollars—that's eight thousand customers a week. This isn't Newton Center any longer, so we probably don't know our consumer like we used to. And I'm not sure those three departments are as good as we think they are. We need to ask the consumer some pretty penetrating questions and be prepared not to like the answers. I congratulate each and every one of you for our progress over the last ten years, but before we rush off to the next expansion, let's see if we can learn a little more about who we are in our current state."

Trip looked at me and I could tell he was surprised by this strategy. "What do you think?" he asked.

But before I could answer him, Joe was basically asking the same thing from the front of the room. We kicked it around for quite a while, and it wasn't a unanimous choice for a couple of reasons. First, expansion had become a way of life, something we anticipated as a part of everyday life, so just stopping didn't seem natural. The other factor, which was more controversial, was that we would have consultants measuring our progress and giving us strategic direction. I had an aversion to consultants, and I'd be the first one to tell you that it wasn't entirely fact-based. What really bugged me was, we paid these guys huge sums of money, and they, in fact, had never run a business of their own. Joe and I really got after each other on this subject, much to the delight and fascination of the rest of the board. I said to Joe, "I don't want some pimply-ass kid with an M.B.A. telling me that our strategy with the consumer is flawed."

Joe responded in kind by saying, "Hey, if I tell you we should listen to this pimply-ass kid, then we're going to listen to him. *Capiche?*"

Silence. All the rest of the board were looking at their hands or staring up in the air as the CEO and president of the organization glared at each other from opposite ends of the table.

"But, Joe, that's never been our game plan," I said. "You said it yourself a minute ago. Three-quarters of our volume and profit has come in the last ten years because of expansion. If it ain't broke, why are we trying to fix it?"

Joe was starting to dig in, almost anticipating my objection. "Listen, Russ, I know you think I'm stodgy, but I think it's time for a breather. We need to evaluate who we are and if we are satisfying our customers' needs."

"Why are these things mutually exclusive? Why can't we evaluate and still expand?" I asked.

Joe Galetti was now annoyed that I persisted and tried to bring the discussion to closure by smiling and saying, "Because I say so."

"I want it on the record that I'm opposed to this move, and I'd like to have a show of hands from the board on where we stand on this issue," I persisted.

"In this matter there will be no vote. It's been decided. And, Russ, if you don't like it, you're free to look at other opportunities."

This had escalated pretty quickly, and even I knew when to throw in the towel by saying nothing and glaring at Joe Galetti.

Joe adjourned the meeting and studiously avoided me as he and the rest of the board filed out of the room.

I walked to the front of the room and backed up the slides until it landed on the original store in Newton Center.

I can remember being in the back room of this store when a vendor from, say, a large soap company, would come in to see Dominic Galetti.

"Dominic, how are you today?" the sales representative would ask.

"Not as good as you," Dominic would counter.

"Why's that?" asked the rep.

"I just read in the paper that P&G had a record quarter, making money hand over fist on poor little merchants like me."

The rep knew Dominic was yanking his tail a little, but his respect for the man before him took another jump up. This wasn't some immigrant who wasn't aware of his surroundings or how his vendors were faring. "Yeah, our company seems to be doing okay, and it's because of people like you, Dominic. We're moving a lot of soap through your store, and it wouldn't be happening if it weren't for you!"

"Thank you, Larry, but I don't want to do too good a job for you."

"Why's that?" the rep asked.

"Because my results will get you promoted, and I'll have to break in a new guy!"

The representative laughed hard while patting Dominic on the shoulder and said, "The truth is, Dominic, that I've learned more from you in the last year about the grocery business than I ever learned from my supervisor."

"Give me an example," Dominic said.

"Well, when I first started working for the company, I was taught by my supervisor that a back room loaded with our product was a good thing because there was no room for my competitors' products. But you taught me a front-end display loaded with our product was a better idea because the customer isn't going to come back here to buy anything!"

"Hey, that's good...you were listening," said Dominic. "Now, what have you got for me?"

"Dominic, I've got a deal on Ivory Flakes, and I've got Dreft, with a drinking glass in every package," the sales rep said.

"I'll pass on the Ivory deal, but I'll take ten cases of Dreft. But, Larry, Woolworth's isn't going to like it."

"How come?" the representative asked.

"Because you are giving away things they sell in their stores."

"Oops...I don't think our resident geniuses in Cincinnati had thought of that," said the rep.

I don't know if the soap representative was aware of it, but in a five-minute conversation, I saw clearly how the battle lines were drawn between buyer and seller. But what really struck me about that conversation I heard was how aware Dominic was of things that weren't necessarily related to his store's business. He knew exactly how a large soap company in the Midwest was doing, and he instinctively knew how a noncompetitor, Woolworth's, would feel about a vendor giving away drinking glasses. This vision and scope of his surrounding environment would serve his sons very nicely in the future. They would build on this vision by owning store locations, not renting or leasing them as many competitors did, and they would become the first food store business to own the shopping center their stores were housed in. Principles based on "why pay the bank interest?" and if a Woolworth's wants to sell merchandise in a shopping center, they will have to pay rent to do it. By paying cash and owning everything in a shopping center that housed one of their stores, they reduced overhead dramatically. It was almost as if a dollar made by the Galetti Corporation was a net dollar, while the same dollar made by a competitor was a gross dollar that still had to have rent and leasing expenses deducted before it went into the bank. Being debt-free by using cash in any business is a good thing, but it's particularly good in the food business, where net profit for the industry hovers around one percent.

Dominic Galetti was not only insightful, but he also was a good man to work for when I was a young boy. I worked 20 hours a week in the store and took home $12 a week. But, without fail, every week Dominic would give me a package wrapped in white wax paper to take home. Sometimes it was roast beef, a leg of lamb, or pork chops to take to my mother. I'd always thank him but by the time I was finishing my sentence, he'd be walking away from me, saying, "It's all a part of your pay, but this way I'm sure you're not spending all your money on bubble gum."

In truth, I turned all my wages over to my mother and so did my brother. She had started an in-home sewing business that was very successful. She was a magician with that old Singer sewing machine and expanded her business to include making curtains, porch furniture coverings, doing alterations, and dressmaking. A local upholstery business used her to make slipcovers, and, as it turns out, she may have been a little too good. I'd hear that machine buzzing away long after I'd finished my homework and gone to bed.

As I entered high school, my duties didn't change that much, but I was learning a lot about a retail store in the food business. By stocking the shelves, I knew what the big sellers were in every category, as well as those items that were just taking up space. I learned where the good display spots were, as well as those places that were infrequently visited by our customers. I also learned why the food industry was a low gross margin business. The more popular an item was, the lower the gross profit. *What a crazy business*, I always thought. An item becomes popular, Dominic lowers the price and makes less money. *This is nuts; we ought to take the price up, not down*, I thought to myself.

Finally, I couldn't contain myself one afternoon and rushed up to see Dominic, who was in his little office in the back room. The room was so small that only one person could sit in it. That person was Dominic, who was hunched over his desk. On the floor in back of him were five brown grocery bags filled to the top with money. He was looking at newspapers that were advertising what his local competitors were running that week for specials. I said, "Dominic, I've got to ask you something."

"So ask," he said.

"I know what every item in this store moves in a week. Every time a new item takes off, we lower the price and lower the profit. It doesn't make any sense to me. It's not logical. We shouldn't reduce the price on these items...if anything, we should take the price up."

"That makes sense to me," he said, smiling up at me. "But you made a classic error. The fundamental rule of the food business is that it isn't logical…it's an image business, not a make-sense business."

"Huh?" I asked.

"Here, look at these ads of food stores, and tell me if you see any items that really sell well."

I squeezed behind his desk and said, "Sure…there's Tide, Maxwell House coffee, Ivory soap, Cut-Rite Wax paper, and Crisco."

"See any items that don't sell well in my store?"

"Not really."

"There you have it. So now what's wrong with your theory of taking the price up on the best-selling items?"

"The competition won't let you?" I guessed.

"Right. If I don't have competitive prices, where does your mother go shopping next time?"

"The A&P."

"Now you're catching on…it's all image. I don't have to have the lowest prices on everything, but on those things my customer knows the prices of, I have to be close. Where we have to beat the competition is in the vegetable aisle and the meat aisle. It's perception and image that sells groceries. In our case, we try to make image reality by having the freshest vegetables and highest-quality meats."

"Okay, but it seems to be backwards to me."

"I wouldn't argue with you about that. You know a lot of people think Italians know a lot about vegetables. I'm not sure why. I didn't know a vegetable from a tennis ball when Anna and I started this business, but the perception was there, and I wasn't going to try to do anything to change it. I've tried to build on it over the years."

"I think you have succeeded. Every once in a while, Ma will go to the A&P, but I've never seen her buy vegetables or meat there. She keeps saying, 'Nobody does those like Dominic.'"

"That's good. Now get out of my office and get to work; this is my nickel we're talking on."

"Yes, sir," I said as I turned to leave his office.

That was the first day I saw her in the store. Her name, I was later to learn, was Diane Dunbar. She was with her mother, and I couldn't take my eyes off her. I knew Mrs. Dunbar because she was a regular at the store, but, until this very day, I didn't know she had a daughter. I guess I wasn't the most observant guy in the world, but I knew I had never seen her before in my life. How had she escaped me? I was quite sure she didn't go to my high school, so I guessed she must be in a local parochial or private school.

She was 16 years old, and I was right about one thing—she did attend a private school. Diane Dunbar went to Dana Hall in Wellesley. She was tall, perhaps 5'9", but she seemed even taller because her posture was so good that I imagined she could balance a book on her head, and it wouldn't fall off as she moved. It added to her presence, really, which, to me, was quite intimidating. I couldn't really describe her physically because she wore a loose jumper that went right to the top of her shoes. But that wasn't actually the reason I couldn't describe her physically; the real reason was that I was mesmerized by her face. She had long, black hair, high cheekbones, and the darkest-blue eyes I'd ever seen. She was in deep conversation with her mother in the aisle when they passed me, and that was probably a good thing. I was gawking at her, and when I looked down at the task at hand, I'd stamped the same can of peas six times with my price marker.

Just at that moment Mrs. Dunbar looked at me in my confused state and said, "Good afternoon, Russell, how are you?"

It wasn't a tough question, really, but I was digging very hard to come up with an answer. Finally, I croaked, "Ahh, I'm fine."

Mrs. Dunbar smiled...I think she noticed my temporary insanity and what caused it and said, "Russell, this is my daughter, Diane. She's helping me with errands and providing good company as well."

"Nice to meet you, Russell," Diane said as she looked directly at me.

"Same here," I mumbled.

They continued down the aisle, and as they turned the corner, Diane looked back down the aisle at me, smiled, and waved as she disappeared around the corner to the next aisle.

All afternoon I replayed the scene in my mind and chastised myself for being such a dolt. *Same here, same here...now there was some brilliant commentary. Pretty impressive, Riley, man, you're about as smooth as a pricker bush. How hard would it have been to say, "Nice to meet you as well, Diane," or maybe even, "It's a pleasure to meet you, Diane. Your mother never told me that she had such a beautiful daughter." No, that would have been a little too forward, but "Same here"...that was really pathetic.* Ever the optimist, I thought to myself, *Well, it can only go up from here after this abysmal beginning.*

She made several more trips into the store, oftentimes not accompanied by her mother. I did my best to position myself in an aisle that I knew she frequented, and I was right about one thing...I wasn't as tongue-tied as the first time I'd seen her. We actually chatted as if we were friends, but I just couldn't seem to get my nerve up to ask her out for a date. It wasn't anything that she said or did; quite to the contrary, she actually made me feel very comfortable when we talked. She had this way about her that made you think that whatever you said, no matter how inane, was really important to her. She had a wonderful smile and a laugh that told you that she was really enjoying the moment.

We must have had quite a few moments because Dominic, who never missed anything, started to notice that I was somewhat distracted when Diane Dunbar was in the store. One day he said, "Hey, Mr. Riley..." He always called me Mr. Riley when he was going to ride me a little. "What am I paying you for anyway?"

Not knowing where he was going, I answered, "To work hard in your store for a very low wage?"

"I'll ignore the low-wage crack, but you got the rest of it right."

"Any complaints?" I asked, feeling as if there wouldn't be any forthcoming.

"Only when that dark-haired beauty appears in the aisle," he said.

I must have turned crimson at that comment because I could feel the blood rushing to my face. "Gotcha, didn't I, lover boy?"

"Is it that obvious?" I asked, feeling somewhat chagrined.

"Yep," Dominic replied. "And I'll tell you something else."

"What?" I asked.

"She likes you, I'm sure of it," he said.

"I know you are the world's greatest grocer, but where is the evidence that you're an expert in these areas?"

"Frequency" was his one-word answer.

"What does that mean?"

"Hey, c'mon. I taught you better than this. This young lady has been in this store twice in her life; she meets you and now she's doing her mother's shopping solo every week. C'mon, I'm old but I'm not blind!"

"You think so?" I asked, a little too hopefully.

"Yes…but God knows what she sees in you, because I missed it," Dominic said as he started to walk to the back room.

"Thanks, Dominic," I shouted, "I think."

Dominic's talk with me convinced me to take a flyer and ask Diane for a date…of sorts. The next time she was in the store, I asked her if she wanted to come see me play baseball. We were playing Needham for the league championship, and her reply really surprised me. She said, "Sure, I've already seen your team play twice, you know."

"You have?" I asked. "How come?"

"My dad said he'd read about you in the local paper, and he said you were pretty good."

"Hey, that's great. Thank your dad for me. How come you didn't come see me after the game or at least yell at me?"

"Oh, I was cheering for you, all right, but you were so focused on what you were doing that I don't think you noticed."

"I wished I'd known you were there. I would have tried to play better!" I said.

"You did okay but breaking balls were giving you fits."

"Geez, you're right about that. How do you know so much about baseball?" I said.

"Hey, you can't live in Beantown and not know baseball."

"Got that right," I said, with BoSox Nation enthusiasm.

* * *

We were playing Needham at their field, and, during infield practice, I saw Diane arrive and make her way to the stands. She was dressed in Bermuda shorts and a short-sleeved blouse, and I saw a few of my friends following her path to her seat. I can only imagine what they were saying to each other as I tried to concentrate on the game at hand. As luck would have it, I wasn't having a very good day. I made an error in the field and struck out twice. But the first half of the last inning, with two of my teammates aboard, I got a waist-high fastball right down the heart of the plate and hit it over the center field wall. It seemed pretty meaningless at the time, as we were leading 3-2 when I hit the home run. As it turned out the home team scored two runs in the bottom half of their inning and we won 6-4. So my home run meant something after all.

Before we had to get on the bus, I had a chance to talk briefly with Diane. She said, "That guy should have thrown you a curveball."

"Yeah, I'd still be swinging and missing if he had," I said.

"Never mind; all's well that ends well," she said.

"Hey, how about we take in a movie tomorrow night?" I asked as casually as I could, but I was hoping only *I* could hear how hard my heart was thumping in my chest.

"Are you asking me out on a date?" she asked.

"I think so," I replied.

"Well, you know what this means?" she asked, with those laughing eyes.

"No, what?" I asked.

"Now I won't have to take so many trips to the store to try and get your attention."

I laughed out loud as I started to make my way back to the bus. "Well, I hope you come by every once in a while, because you've supplied me with a certain amount of inspiration with your visits."

She smiled and blew me a kiss as I boarded the bus. You can imagine the riding I received from my fellow bus mates on the way back home, but I didn't care; I was riding on a cushion of air!

Chapter 3: The Brothers

Trip was standing next to me in the conference room as I returned to the present situation. As I looked up at Trip from my chair, he said, "Man, I don't know where you were, but it was a long way from here."

"Yeah, I was out there. I drifted back to that store in Newton Center that you see on the screen. Working for your granddad and watching your dad and your uncle, after just graduating from college, start to make their mark on the business."

"Have you some time to walk a store with me?" Trip asked. "I need to talk to you about something, and sometimes these walls have ears."

"Boy, do you know how to set a hook. I'll get my coat and meet you in the parking lot in five minutes."

Trip was driving and we were heading for what we all called the "Flagpole Store." The manager of this store, Larry Mussina, had the misfortune of running a Galetti Supermarket in Bridgewater, Massachusetts, the same town where our headquarters and warehouse were located. Thus the name "Flagpole" sprung up, because it was almost as close to our headquarters as the flags that flew on the front terrace of our building. I suspect it was somewhat like being a barracks in the Army that was on 24-hour inspection alert for a white-gloved colonel.

On the way to the store, Trip told me about an event that could turn my world upside down. "I'm afraid I've got some news that is pretty bad, but I thought you should know about it before the press gets a hold of it."

"It can't be that bad," I said.

"There's going to be a fight over control of the company stock, initiated by my mother."

I didn't say anything immediately. Finally, I said, "Who is Maria going to sue?"

"Uncle Joe," Trip said.

"But I don't get it. I thought they both owned an equal number of shares," I said.

"They did. But after my dad died almost fifteen years ago, Mom thinks that Joe has systematically taken some stock that belongs to her."

"Why does she think that?"

"She recently received a tax form from the state that said she generated three million dollars' worth of income. Mom took it to an independent tax attorney, who told her he didn't know the specifics, but it had something to do with selling stock."

"All of a sudden this notion of stopping our expansion is starting to make sense. He's gearing up for what could be a nasty court battle," I said.

Trip pulled into the Bridgewater store and started to walk toward the store. I told Trip I needed to take a walk and that I'd join him in a little while.

My first thought was whether or not I still owned my 25 shares of stock. But as I walked around the parking lot, my mind drifted back to Dominic, the founder, and his wife, Anna. They were both gone now, but I couldn't help thinking that they'd be shocked at this most recent turn of events.

The boys were very close. Dominic was the gregarious one, while Joe tended toward the serious side. They grew up on the Italian side of town—a stretch of land filled with three-story tenements and clothes hanging from just about every floor of every house. Garlic was the predominant smell, and most families had five children or more. Dom and Joseph had a bedroom they shared with three sisters, and maybe the most significant miracle was that they all found time to use the one bathroom and arrive at school on time. Joe would often tell me that they never felt they were poor, because they had food on the table and clothes on their backs. In fact, it wasn't just food…they were sumptuous meals cooked by their mother, Anna, that featured fresh vegetables and sauces that were hovered over all day. As a result, Dom and Joe were never impressed by the Italian restaurants in the North End of Boston. I, on the other hand, thought every restaurant in the North End served the best food I ever tasted.

Both boys were excellent athletes, and coach after coach visited the Galetti house, trying to persuade Dominic to let his boys join their soccer or basketball teams. But Dominic thought it a waste of time and sent the coaches on their way without persuading him that sports were a vital outlet for the boys.

They worked in the store when they weren't in school and, at early ages, started to run portions of it. Dom was a meat cutter, and Joe ran the produce section, and it was no accident that these two areas became the reason the consumer flocked to their store. Their customers knew day in and day out that they would pay a little more for staples at the store than at the A&P, but that was a small price to pay for the privilege of filling their baskets with the best meat and vegetables in the state.

No real surprise, they both married Italian girls from the neighborhood whom they had known since grade school. They bought houses two blocks from each other in Dover and went to work for their dad after finishing college. Dom's wife, Maria, four years his junior, was slight, dark-haired, and beautiful. She was said to have a fiery temper, and she displayed more independence than most women of this era. Dom knew he'd met his match when he married Maria, but that was okay with him. He didn't like the "wallflower type," as he would say…and, with Maria, he was surely in no danger of capturing one. Joe's wife, on the other hand, was tall and wispy—a dreamer who always wanted a large family and the house to match. Her name was Adrienne but everyone called her Alfie, and she seemed to be the total opposite of Joe. He was studious, no-nonsense, and preoccupied with his vocation, while she had a wonderful sense of humor, wasn't very practical, and loved to read poetry. It could have been an "opposites attract" thing; I wasn't sure. Maria and Alfie grew very close, and they spent much of their free time together. As the men started to grow the business, the two wives started to deliver children.

Dominic and Anna watched all these proceedings with great pride and pleasure. Dom and Joe had convinced Dominic to buy the building next door to the store, and they had turned it into an office building. Dominic preferred having his office in the store, but he reluctantly moved his stuff into the building next to the market and only after the boys had cut a door between the two buildings so that Dominic could travel from one to the other without going outside. Both boys understood the lesson their father was trying to convey with that door as well. Simply put, it was, "Don't stray far enough away from your customer that you lose touch."

A typical meeting among the three in that office was loud enough for people to hear in the store. Dominic would usually open the meeting by saying, "What have my sons—the college graduates—been up to now?"

Dom would jump in immediately and say, "Pop, we just wanted to give you an update on the two stores we've opened up in Dedham and Wellesley." Dom's responsibility was site selection and real estate. Most of the people he hired were from the old neighborhood, including the Parelli brothers, who were building a growing business in construction into a very solid operation.

"We paid too much for Wellesley," Dominic said.

Now it was Joe's turn. "You may be right, Pop," Joe said, "but the demographics look really good, and, in the long term, this store will be a winner."

"Demo what?" Dominic asked while biting into an apple.

"Demographics, Pop," Joe said. "You know, the profile of the customer, average income, age…those kinds of things."

Dominic was silent for a long time. In truth, he was pleased with what Joseph had said, and although he didn't know it was a demographic, he knew his boys had their eyes on the right target.

"But this expansion is costing us; the bank has its hand in our pocket, and I don't like it. You know the bank almost took this store away from me in the Depression, and that's the last time I ever used a bank," Dominic said with the conviction that experience brings to the table.

"We know, Pop," Joseph said. "I'm in charge of the finances, and if there is one lesson I learned from you, not the textbooks, it is that cash is king. But at least on a temporary basis we need to work with them."

"Okay, okay, but remember this, if the economy turns down—and it will—that's the time to have cash and not be in debt. People will sell to you for a song because they will be up to their ears in debt."

"It's a good lesson, Poppa...and we won't forget it, believe me," Dom said.

"What about competition in these areas?" asked Dominic.

"I won't kid you...there is a lot of it," Dom replied. "We've got the high end represented by S.S. Pierce, chains such as A&P, and the specialty meat shops that, right now, seem to be faltering. If we stay the way we are now, we'll become the victim of the chain stores too..."

"What do you mean? We've been very successful up until now," Dominic said.

"Yes, we have," Joe said, "and we'll stick with our basic strategy of having the best fruits, vegetables, and meats available, but the stores need to be larger and offer more items...."

"Where's the money coming for that, Mr. Wall Street?" Dominic asked.

And that's how each meeting went with these three men. Dom and Joe reaching for the sky, and Dominic checking for the parachute. Over time it became somewhat frustrating for the brothers, and it wouldn't be until years later that they recognized the key role their father had played while they were finding their way in the business world. He might not have known the word "demographic," but he knew the consumer, the competition, and that cash was king.

The two brothers were close, but they had very different approaches to life. Dom resembled his father. He wasn't short—probably about 5'10"—but he seemed shorter because he was built like a middle guard. Wide but not fat, Dom had huge shoulders and arms, with a barrel chest and solid, large, muscular legs. He had dark-black hair and a pleasing face, with a wide, straight nose that, proportionally, didn't seem out of place with the rest of his body. He smiled often and had this habit of thumping me on the back with his oversized hand as he went by me in the aisle. He could lift a side of beef as if it were an empty cardboard box, and his apron was always covered with stains from his work as a butcher. People just seemed to gravitate toward him for an opinion, a good word, or the latest joke that was making the rounds.

Joe, on the other hand, was tall, slight, and moved in quick, nervous strides. He towered over his brother, and when he stood in the fruit aisle holding a cantaloupe, it looked more like the size of a grapefruit or an orange because his fingers were so long. I quickly became aware of their personality differences by the first word they used in a sentence when asking a question. Dom would use the word "how." How is your mother? How are you doing in school? How's baseball going?

Joe, on the other hand, was more apt to start his questions with "what." What does that display on end number three return? What was our volume this week? What are you doing about the damaged product in the back room? What new products have you seen presented by salespeople this week?

It wasn't that completely clear-cut that Dom was the people person and Joe was the accountant, but, to the casual observer, it was pretty obvious. One thing surfaced quickly as they expanded: their need for quality personnel became apparent. They both tended to reach back into the old neighborhood and handpick people they had known and trusted since grade school. Many of these people would come to work for the Galetti brothers straight out of high school and work their entire lives for one employer. In the long run, as the Galetti chain grew and prospered, this would become a tremendous competitive advantage. These employees were fiercely loyal, and, as a result, their turnover of personnel was about half of that of the national chains. They weren't antiunion, but the unspoken code was that the Galettis would try to match or exceed the national chain rivals in salary and benefits so the need for a union would be minimized.

I was now in my senior year in high school and had been working for the Galettis five years. My role had expanded since I first walked the aisles at the age of 13. I ran the center of the store. Meat, produce, frozen, and dairy were around the perimeter of the store, with the staples and canned goods dominating the aisles in the center of the store. Nothing fancy. I still filled the shelves, made sure the floors were clean and waxed, and checked the arrival of goods in the back room to make sure the invoices matched what we were receiving. Ninety-five percent of the vendors we dealt with were honest, but it was the other five percent that could destroy your bottom line. For instance, the milk guy was a little shady in that the bottom case of a five-case stack sitting on a two-wheeler was empty, so we were being charged for five cases of milk when, in truth, we only received four cases. And sometimes rivals would do things to each other that made us look bad to our customers. We had one bread man who would walk along a row of bread of one of his competitors and poke holes in the wrapper with his pencil. Dominic wasn't a cruel man at heart; he'd rather use sugar than the whip, but those two people were lucky to get out of the store alive after Dominic was finished with them.

During my senior year, Dominic's role in the store began to diminish, and, as a result, I started to inherit some of his work. One of those jobs was seeing the salespeople. At first, I saw it as a distraction to my other work, but over time I started to realize that this was a good way to learn about the products I was pricing every day on the shelf. Perhaps the biggest benefit was that these people made me aware of what new products were coming on the market, and it was my job to try and project how they would be received by our customers. Over time I became pretty good at understanding what new items would work and which ones wouldn't do so well. It was a no-brainer to take items from a company such as Procter & Gamble or General Foods. They were going to create demand for the item by peppering the airwaves with advertising and dropping a blizzard of coupons. The people who represented these companies were as good at presenting and selling these products as the programs that backed their new items. The tough ones to judge were the smaller companies who didn't have the marketing muscle to give the product a lift initially. I made my share of mistakes. When I was presented aluminum foil for the first time, I thought it was too expensive and would never replace wax paper. Boy, was I wrong. Paper napkins, Pampers, and Hi-C orange drink were all items that I didn't think had a chance that became best sellers.

As I continued to see salespeople, I teamed up with Joe Galetti. He'd taken over the chore of picking the items to run in the weekly advertisement, so it was a natural thing to coordinate what was coming into the stores with what we advertised.

We'd meet every Thursday afternoon to talk about the next week's newspaper ad. Joe was always businesslike, stern but not unkind. He'd usually start by saying, "What did those salesguys foist on you this week, Russell?"

"Well, the P&G guy has a new sink cleaner named Comet and it looks good."

"Okay, but it'll never give Bab-o any competition," Joe remarked while doodling with his pencil on the ad item sheet.

"Don't be too sure. He gave me a demo in the bathroom sink. Side by side with Bab-o, and Comet did a better job."

"Did you buy it?" Joe asked.

"Oh, yeah, and it actually gave me a pretty good idea."

"Try me," Joe responded.

"I thought we'd feature Comet the week the coupon drops, on an end display with some of the more profitable items in the category. Things like scrub brushes, cutting boards, oven cleaners, dish towels that have a high gross profit."

"Not bad," Joe said.

"Do you have sugar on this week, Joe?" I asked.

"Yes."

"Okay, let's run Maxwell House side by side with it and add that new powdered Cremora."

"Think that stuff will sell?" Joe asked.

"Don't know. I like the real stuff myself, but it's starting to move almost a case a week."

"What else?"

"I've got a barbecue sauce that you could run in your meat ad..."

And so it went with Joe... I never really knew how he felt about the work I was doing. He never said anything negative to me, but I missed Dominic and his daily chats about things. The result of this tutelage over the past five years was that I had learned the grocery business from the ground up.

One day, on a Wednesday, Joe called me into the office. It was during the early spring of my senior year in high school. It was out of pattern, and I was wondering if I had screwed something up, because, except for our Thursday meetings, we always talked in the aisle or back room of the store.

When I opened the door to the office, Dominic, Joe, and Dom were all sitting at a conference table, looking up at me as I entered and closed the door.

"Pull up a chair, Russell," Dominic said, "and take a load off the floor!"

"Should I be nervous?" I asked.

"Russell, you're like family to us," Dominic said. "As close as family can be with a last name of Riley!"

I laughed at Dominic's comment. "Well, that's a relief. I was wondering what I'd messed up at to be called to the office," I said.

"We want to know what you are thinking about in terms of college," Dom said.

"Well, I've applied to BU and Northeastern," I said.

"Not Harvard?" responded Joe.

"No. It doesn't appeal to me, although I might have an outside shot of getting in."

"Tell me about your grades," Dominic said.

"Mostly As, a few Bs, and one C," I responded.

"What did you get a C in?" Joe asked.

"French."

"You should have taken Italian," Dom said with a smile.

"I would have but they don't offer it. But you know, I think I would have received a C in that too. Language isn't my thing."

"Why BU or Northeastern?" Joe asked.

"Well, first, they are good schools and they are local. My brother is at BU, and he really likes it. Also, they both have work-study programs, and I think I have a chance for a scholarship."

"Well, if money was no object, would you like to go to Harvard?" Dominic asked.

"Honestly, I don't think so. I think I'd be a fish out of water."

"We've got a proposition for you. Do you want to hear it?" Joe said.

"Sure, I'm all ears," I said.

"We pick up all the tab for your education. How's that sound so far?" Dom said.

I was stunned. I could feel the emotion of such a generous offer as my eyes started to blink. I was starting to tear up a little as I said, "But why would you do such a generous thing?"

"Nothing generous about it," Dominic said as his huge hand slapped the table. "You know me by now, Russell…there's a hook."

"Okay," I said, not really understanding what Dominic meant.

"We put you through school. You work here when you can for the next four years, and you come work for Dom and Joe for a period of three years after you graduate," Dominic said.

There was a silence in the room as I just stared back at the three Galettis. "Why would you want to do that?" I finally asked.

Uncharacteristically, Joe responded with a big smile on his face. "Because you were taught from the ground up by the master, my dad. You've worked for us for five years, and every time we give you a new job, you perform it with excellence. I keep telling these other two guys how much I enjoy our Thursday meetings and the degree of creativity you bring to the table. We have this idea that college will only enhance the natural skills and affinity you have for this business. At the same time as you'll be in college, we expect to expand from three stores to eight stores, and we're going to need management talent as the business expands."

That was the longest piece of rhetoric I'd ever heard from Joe. And you could have fooled me that he enjoyed our Thursday meetings. Before I could respond, Dom jumped into the conversation and said, "Look, Russell, it's a good deal for us. Look at it from our side. We could go out and hire a Harvard M.B.A. for a lot of money, and, believe me, we have the resources to do it. But, in all likelihood, he wouldn't know anything about the business, and he'd be a stranger to us. We wouldn't know anything about him. His work ethic. Would he be willing to get his hands dirty learning the business? Would he have the patience to work at retail, to understand the customer and the competition? Maybe, maybe not. With you, we know what we've got. You're bright, personable, hardworking, and we think you have a real nose for this business. Furthermore, you fit the profile of people we like to hire. Even as we expand, we want to be known as a family business that hires people who are loyal and committed to going the extra mile."

"Okay, okay," Dominic said, "for all the reasons the boys said, Russell, but here's the most important reason."

"Okay," I said.

"Because I told you to take the offer."

We all laughed at the old man, and I said, "You've got a deal."

Dominic got up, walked over to his desk, took a bottle out of the drawer, and grabbed four paper cups out of the dispenser on the wall on his way over to the table. He poured four small cups of red wine and then said, "A drink to seal the deal."

We all repeated the phrase and drank the wine. I coughed for about 30 seconds after swallowing the wine, much to the delight of the Galettis. They all stood and shook my hand, and, as I was getting ready to leave, Dominic said, "Russell…"

"Yes," I responded.

"You're going to have to learn to drink red wine if you join this operation full-time."

"Yes, sir," I said as I closed the door after me and returned to the store.

That night at dinner I replayed the scene in the office that had taken place in the afternoon. My mother had the same reaction that I had. She was stunned and tears started to roll down her cheeks. My sister, Erin, became alarmed and said, "Why are you crying, Ma?"

"Tears of happiness, my dear," she said as she patted my sister's hand to reassure her.

Then my mother looked up at me and said, "You don't suppose that nice Mr. Galetti is in the Cosa Nostra and that you're signing on for some type of blood oath or something to do?"

"Oh, Ma, you've been reading too many novels, or maybe it's the Kefauver hearings. That's the most ridiculous thing I've ever heard. And, besides, they're not going to let a guy named Riley into that outfit."

My mother smiled and said, "I suppose you are right, but I worry about you."

"That's good, Ma," I said. "I'm glad somebody has that job."

* * *

The Galetti brothers and their wives met every Wednesday night to have dinner at one house or the other. The wives were very fond of each other, and they looked forward to having dinner together. Both were excellent cooks and they helped each other with the meals. Whoever the hostess was for the evening could count on her sister-in-law bringing dessert. But the logistics were getting more complicated because Maria had now given birth to two children, with one on the way, while Alfie had three children of her own. The oldest child of the five children was four and a half, so there were cribs, baby carriages, and other baby tools of the trade in every corner of every room. Fire trucks, dolls, and toy soldiers were spread on the floor like confetti, but the four adults hardly seemed to notice. Alfie, Joe's wife, was more of the traditional wife. She reveled in being a housewife, bringing up children, and cooking the world's best sauces. She was bright and loving. One of her missions in life was trying to make her very intense husband relax a little.

Maria, Dom's wife, was driven. Her home life was fine, and she loved her children but she wanted more. She had been a high honors student in high school and an excellent athlete, and she had the urge to compete. She felt she could assume a role in the business, but Dom resisted her requests strenuously. In fact, it was probably the only thing they ever argued about. Dom loved his wife dearly; that was the major reason he didn't want to see her at work every day.

The four adults were gathered around the table, while the five children were all asleep in various parts of the house. For the moment the only noise that broke the silence was the sound of knives and forks, made when people were concentrating on their food. Dom wiped his mouth with a large yellow napkin and said, "Delicious, Alfie...you can cook, right up there with Mama."

"Thank you, Dom," Alfie said. "I had some pretty good ingredients to start with," she said with a smile.

"Damn right you did," Joe said, agreeing with his wife, "but this sauce was sent from heaven."

"I second that motion," Maria said. "What's new in the business, Dom? Fill Alfie and me in; tell us something exciting. We're busy all day cooking and taking care of these children."

"Well, we offered to pay for the Riley kid's education if he'd come work for us after he graduates," Dom replied.

"That is a new twist," Maria agreed. "Why did you do that?"

Joe jumped in and said, "Because he's a special kid who has a nose for the business, and we're going to need all the help we can get as we expand to eight stores."

Maria didn't miss this opportunity. "I'm available," she said. "I could help you menfolk if you'd let me."

"We'll think about it," Dom said. "But right now you've got bigger fish to fry," he said, not unkindly, as he patted his wife's swollen stomach.

"Okay," Maria agreed reluctantly. "But I'll be back after this child is born, asking the same old question."

"We never doubted that for a minute," Joe said with a smile.

"You could do a lot worse than to hire Maria," Alfie said, sticking up for her sister-in-law. "Did you guys ever stop to consider that ninety percent of your customers are women? It might give the corporation an advantage on your competition if you had a woman helping to make decisions on what women like and dislike."

Joe didn't say anything, but he was stunned by what his wife had said. She made an excellent point, and, frankly, it was one that seemed pretty obvious now that it had been articulated by Alfie. He only wished that, as the analyst, he'd thought of it. But he was proud of his wife. For someone who wasn't supposed to be that practical, she had uttered a very pragmatic statement that could lead to a Galetti competitive advantage.

After Dom and Maria had gathered up their sleeping children and headed back to their house, Joe said to Alfie, "Hey, that was a very good point you made about the women's touch in the food business."

"Thank you," Alfie replied. "Maria is a very smart person who won't always be happy as a stay-at-home mom. I, on the other hand, will be very happy to stay at home and raise our kids."

* * *

During the years I was at BU, Joe and Dom's families had started to grow and mature. Dom and Maria had four children—two boys and two girls—while Joe's family had one boy and three girls. They still lived in Dover two blocks apart, but as their families had grown, so had their houses. Both Dom and Joe had renovated their original houses to the point that they were both almost twice as big as the original houses. Dom's boys, Dom and Arthur, and Joe's boy, Joseph Jr., were attending the Fessendon School in West Newton, while the girls were in a private school as well.

The families remained extremely close and still met once a week for dinner. It was a good chance to get together because, at work, Joe and Dom hardly ever were together. Dom was busy scouting and securing locations, while Joe ran the everyday business. In the four years I was at Boston University, they added five more stores in upscale suburbs of Boston. They really needed to move to a new office building, but they knew that Dominic would be upset about a relocation, so they bought the building next to their office and now literally owned the whole block where the original store was located. They kept their grocery wholesalers as their suppliers, but they were now large enough to have to hire their own grocery buyer. Dominic was now fully retired, but the boys kept an office for the old man, who still came to the weekly strategy meetings.

It was the late '60s in New England, and the Galetti brothers weren't the only people expanding in the food business. A&P had always been there, but Stop & Shop, Star Market, and First National Stores were all expanding and opening stores. The independent stores that had been the backbone of the industry in the '40s and '50s were disappearing from sight with frightening regularity. They couldn't compete with the larger chains that built larger stores and priced products at margins that the smaller stores couldn't match and still turn a profit. People were moving to the suburbs from the city, and shopping centers were being built with regularity. The five-and-dime stores and specialty clothing stores such as Best & Co. were feeling the pressure too, as department stores—Jordan Marsh, Filene's, W. T. Grant, and Zayre—were popping up like crabgrass in an unattended lawn.

The Galetti brothers could see the trend clearly, as their original store, in the heart of Newton Center, was slowly losing dollar volume. But, as fate would have it, their train had left the station at just the right time. If they had stuck with the original store, they eventually would have had to look for another line of work. Instead, they followed the principles laid down so many years ago by their father. They teamed up with the Parelli brothers' construction business and built shopping centers where they owned all the buildings. In these shopping centers they surrounded their food stores with dry cleaners, package stores, and drugstores that they owned outright. And when someone came calling, such as W. T. Grant, they leased the store to a department store chain that didn't compete directly with their food stores.

Their expansion was predicated on cash flow. They used the banks during the initial start-up of a shopping center but paid them off as soon as the cash was available from a more mature shopping center. This helped them in two ways—one was pretty obvious, the other was not quite as easy to fathom. Because they operated with cash, their expansion was fairly slow—two stores a year—and, as a result, they were flying "under the radar" of the larger chains that were expanding at a faster rate on someone else's money. The more subtle advantage was that when a chain store built in a location near a Galetti store, the chain store couldn't use their size and leverage to lower prices against the Galetti store and run them out of business as they had with the independents.

The Galetti stores were wholly owned, free and clear of any overhead, and they matched the chain store prices penny for penny and beat them at their own game. The big chains saw this but rationalized that the Galettis were just "a fly on an elephant's ass," and they didn't become alarmed at this smaller but very tough competitor.

They would live to regret this oversight in time.

I wandered into the Bridgewater store and saw Trip in an animated discussion with the store manager, Larry Mussina. For the first time in 25 years of working for this supermarket chain, I thought that the potential of this court fight could once again reduce us to that "fly on an elephant's ass."

Chapter 4: Maria Galetti

I had met Maria Galetti several times at social occasions. But it wasn't until I started full-time for the Galetti family, after graduating from college, that we became friends. We were still in the office building in Newton Center next to the original store, and it was bustling with activity on my first day of work. Salespeople waited on the first floor to see buyers, secretaries moved silently through the hallways, and the door that used to lead to the store was gone.

Both Dom and Joe greeted me and made me feel right at home. After a minimum of small talk, Joe spoke to me about what I would be doing for them. Joe said, "Things have changed, Russell."

"They sure have. Who would have thought eight years ago that a single store would have burst into eight stores," I said.

Dom jumped and said, "Let me show you how that's going to change in the future." He led me to a wall that was covered with an 8- by 4-foot map of southeastern Massachusetts, Cape Cod, and the eastern part of Rhode Island. On the map were a series of different-colored tacks. "Here are our stores with the black tacks—that was Joe's idea, he didn't want to be in the red. First National in blue, A&P in green, and Stop & Shop in red. What do you think?"

"Now I know how Custer felt," I said with a smile.

Both men laughed and Joe said, "Yeah, it looks like an uphill struggle all right, but right now that's an advantage. Our read is that the big boys are too busy squaring off against each other to spend much time on us."

"How are we doing?" I asked.

"We thought you'd never ask!" Dom said.

"The original store next door is dropping in volume every month. At some point we'll close it and expand the office," Joe said matter-of-factly. "Dedham, Wellesley, Weston, and Natick are doing very well, while Sudbury, Concord, and Needham, so far, are not meeting expectations."

"Okay. Where do I fit into this puzzle?"

"That's easy. You'll have an office here, but it's hardly bigger than the broom closet," Dom said not unkindly. "Want to know why it's so small?"

"Sure, but let me guess."

"Okay," Joe said.

"Because it's my first day on the job, and I probably don't deserve an office at all."

"Not even close," Joe replied. "The reason it's small is because we don't want you in it."

"Huh?"

"You heard it right the first time," Dom said. "Your job will be out in the field; for instance, we want you to find out why we are getting our butts kicked in Sudbury, Concord, and Needham."

"That's a long way to go on my bike," I said with a straight face.

The brothers looked at each other, and Dom reached into his pocket and dropped a set of car keys on the table.

"What is this?" I asked.

"It's the keys to your car…geez, you're not too bright for a college kid, are you?"

"Hey, I went to the same place you guys went," I said.

"It's parked in the back of the store. It's a new Mercury Comet, six-cylinder, stick shift, no radio and no AC. We want you spending a minimum of time in that as well."

"Thank you very much," was all I could muster.

"You're welcome," Joe said. "Here's what we've laid out for you for a program. You'll spend the first month here in the office sitting in with buyers, attending manager and strategy meetings, and learning all there is to know about our grocery wholesaler. At some point down the road, we may buy our own warehouse, but for now we're going to use New England Wholesale as our supplier. After that you'll be responsible for getting Sudbury, Concord, and Needham up to snuff. You'll be using the same guidelines you're used to: the answer lies somewhere with the customer and the competitor. We're just starting to use the computer, and we're looking hard at planograms."

"What's a planogram?" I asked.

"It's a visual that sets up every department of every aisle. Soda, chips, toilet paper, etc. It bases space for an item on the rate that an item moves. If the item doesn't turn over, it's gone. Simple as that."

We talked for another hour and then Dom took me down to my new office. I had to laugh. It was smaller than a broom closet, but it was located right where a good broom closet should be located…adjacent to the men's room. It reminded me in size of Dominic's office in the store next door that had a door for a desktop that rested on concrete blocks. This office had a real desk, a phone, and a hook on the back of the door for a coat. It had a window but it was 18 inches wide and two feet high, and I couldn't see out of it unless I stood on my tiptoes.

"All the comforts of home," Dom said as he retreated down the hall to his office.

It may have appeared to the casual eye as a hole in the wall but I liked it. It was *my* hole in the wall, and two weeks out of college, I had an office, a car, and I was making $6850 a year. Thanks to the Galettis I had no college loans to pay off, and, fortunately for me, the VISA card hadn't been invented yet, so I was totally debt-free. As I stepped out of my office, I ran right into Maria Galetti. She saw me and said, "Hello, Russell…welcome to the jungle we call work."

"Thank you very much, Mrs. Galetti," I said.

"Are you surprised to see me?" she asked.

"I am. What are you doing here?"

"I work here," she replied.

"What do you do?" I asked, with a little more surprise in my voice than I intended.

She laughed and I felt my face turning red. "Joe and Dom thought it would be a good idea to have a woman's perspective since ninety percent of our customers happen to be women."

"You know the good ideas always seem very simple. And having you on board is a great idea," I said.

"Well, thank you, Russell. That's very nice of you to say so," Maria said.

"It doesn't seem very strange to me having a woman working here. My mom has been working since I was thirteen."

"Nice to have at least one enlightened male on board," she said.

"Tell me about something you're working on that a woman would really like."

"Flowers at a good price, that a woman could take home and put in her living room."

"I love it; and you know what else?"

"What?"

"Dominic would be jumping up and down he'd like that idea so much."

"Hey, we're going to get along just fine…maybe I can use you to sell a few ideas to my husband and Joe."

"Maybe," I said. "Where are you getting the most resistance?"

"Joe. He's a great bottom-line guy, and we're lucky to have him, but he doesn't seem to understand the consumer that well."

"Dom understands the consumer," I said.

"Yes, he does," Maria agreed. "Glad to have you here, and I'm sure we'll talk again," she said as she walked away from me.

"You bet," I said. I knew Maria was closer to my mother's age than mine, but as I watched her walk away, all I could think of was what a babe she was. Tall, dark hair, piercing blue eyes, a great figure, with the longest spike heels I'd ever seen. I sure hope Dom couldn't read minds! While I was daydreaming about Maria Galetti, I thought it might be in part because Diane Dunbar and I had started to drift apart. She had graduated from college and was touring

Europe before attending law school. The Christmas holidays were approaching, and Diane had returned for two weeks to be with her family. I spent as much time as possible with her, but between her family obligations and my work schedule, we didn't spend as much time together as I would have liked. The physical attraction between us remained strong, but her outlook on life had changed dramatically. She talked of the wonders of cities such as Venice and her exposure to the great museums and works of art that only a culture such as Europe could provide. At the same time I was involved in the more mundane work of the supermarket industry, such as devising planograms for canned beets. Worlds apart. It wasn't a subtle change, and I noticed the difference immediately, and I was pretty sure she had become aware of it as well. We were in my company car—that Diane had nicknamed "The Hotel Comet" because it was the only place where we could be alone and away from our respective families. This was the first time the thought occurred to me that having an apartment of my own would have been a real advantage, but I was still living at home. We were parked on an old, deserted road that we had frequented in high school when Diane said, "I sure have missed having your arms wrapped around me, Russ."

"I've missed you. That smile, those long legs striding at such a pace that I have to jog to stay up with you."

Diane laughed and said, "These legs are a little cramped here in the Hotel Comet, but I'd rather be here with you than in a castle with some Russian prince."

A little surprised, I said, "Ahhh, just how many foreign noblemen have we known?"

"None in the biblical sense, but, of course, I have had a few dates in the last six months."

"Of course," I said as my eyes suddenly stung. It hurt. I hadn't had a date in six months, but, in fairness to Diane, we weren't engaged and we hadn't signed an exclusivity pact. She noticed that I was silent and said, "A penny for your thoughts. All of a sudden you seem to be a million miles away."

"It's nothing, really," I replied.

"C'mon, Russ...you're talking to me, and I can tell that you have something on your mind."

"Okay. I feel as if a trust has been broken but it really hasn't. We've been going together for seven years, and I can't ever remember talking about you having another date."

Diane pondered for what seemed like an inordinate amount of time and said, "I see why you would be hurt. Haven't you had a date since I left?"

"No, I haven't," I said softly.

"Ohhh..." said Diane. "Well, maybe you ought to. I love you, I know that. But is that enough? We've been going together since I spotted you in a supermarket aisle, but shouldn't we spread our wings a little while we've got a chance?"

And before I could grab it back as it rushed out of my lips, I said, "As long as we're not spreading our legs as well."

"Russell!" Diane shouted. "That's a terrible thing to say."

"I'm sorry if you're offended, but I don't think we'd be having this conversation if you hadn't gone to Europe."

"Well, I am offended," she said. "Where does it say that I'm the personal property of Russell Riley?"

"It doesn't," I responded. "But whether you realize it or not, we're starting to go in different directions. Not to be too obvious, but while you're taking in the Sistine Chapel, I'm tossing heads of lettuce into a bin."

"Oh, Russ," she said as she pulled a Kleenex from her pocketbook. "How could that be? We've gone together for ages. You're a soul mate to me."

"Once removed right now," I replied.

"Take me home, okay?" she said.

I did as she asked. I think in our conversation that night—although I can't be sure—that I had articulated part of a thought that hadn't surfaced yet with her. She not only wanted to see the world, but she also wanted to be free to date other people. They say you can't come back to your hometown—things seem smaller and, perhaps, over time you have outgrown the environment of your youth. I felt sure this was the case with Diane, and, unfortunately for me, I was a casualty in this scenario. It never occurred to me that we wouldn't be together in the end until now. I was severely depressed about it, but I kept telling myself I'd get over it. But it was an agonizingly slow process.

I'm not even sure my mother noticed it, but if she did, she didn't say anything about it and I was grateful. I may have provided a coherent thought to Diane, but I didn't want to share my thoughts about Diane with anybody else.

The next few weeks sped by as I tried to acclimate myself from a one-store operation where everything was right in front of me to see to an eight-store chain that had more moving parts than a Rube Goldberg invention. I spent a lot of time with the buyers. They were good and they were knowledgeable, but they didn't have the rapport that Dominic had built with his suppliers. I was painfully aware of this because, when I had taken over that part of Dominic's job, I could feel that the representatives really missed the old man's humor and insight. Hell, I missed it even now. It gave me an idea that I knew Joe wasn't going to like, so I kept turning it over in my mind until I could figure out a way to present it without getting my ears pinned back at the weekly strategy meeting.

I finally decided to just float it out there as a trial balloon at the next meeting and try to get out of the way if the building fell on me. At the end of the meeting, Dom always had a session that he called "What if…" When that part of the meeting came, I started my pitch when I said, "What if we throw a party once a year for our suppliers? I'm not talking dogs and beans. A banquet in a fancy place, invite the wives, and give awards to those people that the buyers think have done an outstanding job."

"Are you crazy?" Joe said immediately. "I don't even know these people, and if I did, I probably wouldn't like them."

"Wait a minute, Joe, this is 'what if' time," Dom said. "Why would you do that, Russell?"

"Because none of the competitors do it," I responded.

"Okay, so what you're telling me is that we have an exclusive on a really bad idea," Joe responded.

"Maybe," I said, "but the idea really comes from when I used to watch Dominic handle his suppliers."

"I don't get it," Dom said.

"Well, you know I took that job over from Dominic in the original store, and I could tell the sales representatives were disappointed that they had to deal with me. You remember, Joe. I used to do the weekly specials with you back then."

"I remember," Joe said as I saw a twinkle in his eye, "and for the record, Comet is now outselling Bab-o about ten to one. But so what?"

"It just makes sense," I said. "We're smaller than the three big guys, so we have to try harder. It was the same way in Dominic's time. He only had one store but that didn't matter. They had fun with Dominic because he was always one step ahead of them, and he treated them with respect. They probably called on Dominic more than they should have, but they couldn't help themselves. Dominic was a human being and he sold insight and respect and the reps loved him for it."

"Don't our buyers treat our suppliers with respect?" asked Joe.

"They do. And they are very good at what they do. Maybe it is a nutty idea," I said.

"Wait a minute," Dom said. "It won't cost us jack shit to do this, and you know the big chains won't think of it and wouldn't do it if they did. I say we try it, and if it's a bust, we bill back the suppliers."

We all laughed at Dom, and Joe thought it was particularly funny because it was about as subtle as Dom got about his brother's preoccupation with money.

Joe knew that he was a beaten man. He looked at me and said, "Okay, okay, we'll give it a try…but, Russell, if it's a bomb, I'm putting someone else in your office with you."

I looked at Joe and said, "Okay, but you'll have to remove the desk to make room for him!"

We were all laughing when Dom said, "Meeting adjourned on that note."

I didn't know it at the time, but that was a critical advantage for our business. We weren't big enough where memos went out in triplicate to a host of people who wrote notes in the corner and shipped it off to another battalion of people. By the time everyone had seen the note, the originator had forgotten why he had written it in the first place. Not so at Galetti…six people sat around a table face-to-face and hashed things out. One of those people was

Maria Galetti, and I would bet what little money I had that none of our competitors had a woman on their strategy board.

She came right up to me after the meeting and said, "Russell, that was a big idea. Better than flowers."

"Oh, I don't know about that," I said. "We'll make a lot more money with your idea."

"Maybe, maybe not," she said.

"What do you mean?" I asked.

"Think about it. What if—to coin a phrase—a popular brand goes on allotment?"

"Okay," I said, not knowing where Maria was going.

"Don't you think we would get more than our fair share from the suppliers if we had favored nation status?"

"Good point," I said. "That's using your head for something besides a hat rack."

Maria laughed and patted my arm as she said, "Now I know why those guys wanted you to work here."

"Well, thanks. Can I tell you something totally off the subject that I hope you won't be offended by?"

"Sure," she said, looking me right in the eye.

"No other strategy board in this business or any other, for that matter, has a person on it that smells as good as you do."

"Well, thank you," Maria said. "It's a Chanel No. 5, and I'll tell you something else."

"What's that?"

"It's all Marilyn Monroe wears to bed at night."

"Wow, now that's an image, but how can we sell it?"

"Oh, c'mon, Russell...all work and no play makes a very dull boy."

"Blame it on the boys. They're pretty intense about the business."

"I hear you," Maria said with a wink as she walked out of the room.

As it turned out, both ideas were very successful. The cut flower department was the first thing the customers saw when they entered the store, and from the initial sales figures, we knew we were onto something. It needed a careful eye because once the flowers went by—much the same as the produce department—there was no returning them to the supplier for a refund. But with Maria's vigilance, this department started to build good profits, and, for the moment, we had a competitive advantage. The supermarket industry as a whole had no pride of authorship; we'd all copy something from a competitor if it worked. This was particularly suicidal in some cases, especially in the case of a merchandising vehicle such as double coupons. One chain would break with double coupons, and the consumer would run to those stores for the double up. But this competitive advantage only lasted until the next week, when all the competitors in the market would respond with double coupons of their own. The manufacturer of the coupon only paid for the face value of the coupon, so the chain was left holding the bag for the remainder of the doubling of the coupon.

This led unscrupulous chains—not Galetti, I will add quickly—to try and scam the manufacturer with all kinds of ploys. For example, one chain hired people to gang-cut coupons, throw them in a clothes dryer so they would look wrinkled and used, and then send them to the manufacturer for redemption of the face value of the coupon. I'm no expert but I think that's mail fraud and carries a pretty hefty jail term with it. Other folks would run coupons on their Xerox and submit them, but, of course, the backsides of these coupons were blank, so they were pretty easy to spot. It's rumored—but I can't substantiate it because we never played that game—that manufacturers would even pay for these devices because they didn't want to upset their rapport with their customers. In later years, if we could substantiate that a vendor was doing this with another customer, we would either discontinue their items or, if we had to carry them, we'd stop advertising those items in our weekly food ads.

But Maria's foray wasn't so easy to duplicate. This unimaginative industry would actually have to do some work to copy the flower department idea. Even to this day, some competitors haven't bothered to do it.

Our first ever vendor's banquet was a big hit. Dom, who knew a lot of the vendors, thoroughly enjoyed himself as I had expected, but the surprise to me was Joe Galetti. With Alfie and Maria at his side, the manufacturers, food brokers, and principles flocked to meet the mystery man of the organization. Joe presented a few of the awards, and he was warm, witty, and he really got into the spirit of this evening, where the buyers and sellers checked their weapons at the door and just had an old-fashioned good time.

The next day the phone was ringing off the hook at work from the attendees of the previous night, calling to thank us for our hospitality. In the middle of the morning, Joe showed up in my office unexpectedly and sat down. "Kid," he said, "as my old English teacher would say, you done good."

"Thanks, Joe," I said. "What was your take on the whole thing?"

"Great place, great food and drink, excellent award ceremony, and I think our vendors absolutely loved it. And one other thing," Joe said.

"Yes?" I responded.

"I'm sure glad we don't have to do that every night…I'd be in Bellevue in a month."

I smiled. It was fun to see Joe so animated and even trying to make a joke. "I was sweating a little, to tell you the truth, Joe."

"Why?"

"Well, it could have gone the other way and been a bomb, and I would have had a roommate in this office!"

"I suppose," Joe said. "But what the hell, for that kind of short money, it was worth a shot."

"That's not what you told me at the meeting about this subject," I said.

"Yeah, I know," Joe said. "But that's why we hired you. You got guts, kid, and you have the power of your own conviction. Don't let anyone take that away from you."

"Thanks, Joe," I said. "That means a lot coming from you."

"You're welcome," Joe said as he made ready to leave, then uttered, "Dom wanted me to tell you that there'll be an extra grand in your envelope this week. A little bonus, Dom says, to buy something for your mother."

"Wow," I said. "Thank you, Joe, and thank Dom for me, will you?"

"Will do," he said as he left the office.

A thousand dollars. These guys were crazy. Joe was such an enigma. He was an introvert, I was convinced of that. His happiest moments were when he was studying a balance sheet. But he could be gregarious when it was called for, and under that gruff, volatile exterior, I was convinced, beat a heart that cared for people. It was just hard for him to express those feelings. He was driven. A prototype of the workaholic type A personality but not as fearsome as he appeared at first glance.

I'd been on the job now for almost six months, but I hadn't cracked the mystery of the three stores that weren't living up to expectation. I was convinced we had very good people running those units, and the small-store culture that we engendered at our other stores was apparent in these stores as well. Unlike the big chains, we tried to learn who our consumers were...not just their demographic profiles, but, more importantly, their names and their likes and dislikes. But we should have been doing better; I couldn't figure out why we weren't up to our expectations.

One day I was in the "war room," staring at the map with competitors marked by different-colored tacks. *Sudbury, Concord, and Needham...*I kept saying those towns to myself as I stared at the map. All of a sudden something jumped out at me. These three stores had an inordinate number of A&P stores as competitors. Could this be a link to our problem? Was A&P doing something that was impeding our progress? The only way to find out was to visit those stores myself.

I left the building and went to store-check the A&Ps. At first, nothing seemed out of the ordinary. Pretty typical. Older stores, older employees, good shelf space, too much house-brand merchandising, and an excellent meat department. Slowly, though, it dawned on me that 10 or 12 very good selling items were selling at retails that were as much as 10 cents a unit below cost. How could they do that?

I wandered into the Needham A&P, grabbed a cart, and tried my best to look like a consumer. I wandered the aisles, putting a number of these items in the basket. As I was rolling down aisle five, I grabbed a 42-ounce size of Tide that was priced 12 cents per unit below cost, while, at the same time, spotting the grocery manager at the end of the aisle.

As casually as possible, I pulled up beside him and said, "How you doing today?"

"Fine, sir, how are you?" came the response from this man who had an A&P coat on, and, in his left hand, he held his order book for aisle five.

"Hey, these prices you have are great," I said with enthusiasm.

He turned toward me and said, "Yep, they are the lowest in the state." He seemed quite enthused about the subject.

"How can you do that?" I asked. "I don't know many prices, but I know the prices on this stuff, and they are way below Stop & Shop."

"Well, I don't know," he said truthfully, "but you know we're a national chain and none of our competitors are. So big may be helpful in this very discounted market. Places like Detroit and Chicago aren't as price competitive as this market."

"Never thought of that," I said sincerely. "Well, have a good day."

"You too," he said as he turned his attention to his order book.

I went through the register, bought all the items, and hurried out to my car. I was excited, even though I really didn't know why. Did I have something or not? If I did, could we do anything about it?

I drove back to my office, trying not to exceed the speed limit. I took my purchases to the conference room and put them on the table. Then I went to my office, took out the price book, and looked up the price of every item I had bought at A&P in our price book. Eleven items and they beat us on every one. *That's totally out of pattern*, I thought as I studied the prices. We should have been even or lower on half of the items, just on a law of averages basis. But we weren't.

I picked up the phone, dialed Dom, Joe, and Maria, and asked them to meet me in the conference room in 15 minutes, promising each of them that I wouldn't take more than 10 minutes of their time.

They all arrived in the prescribed time, and I tried to be brief. "Here are eleven items, all best sellers…Tide, Ivory soap, Cains Mayonnaise, and a quart of Hood's orange juice that I bought in the A&P in Needham today."

Dom got up from his chair and picked a couple of them up and said, "So?"

"Every one of these items is priced below the comparable item in our store."

"That is weird," Maria said.

"It can't be a coincidence," Joe said as he fingered a bottle of Heinz Ketchup. "They're not only priced below us, but way below us."

"Bingo," I said.

"So maybe they are just stupid," Dom said.

"Maybe," I said, "but how long could we afford to run those kinds of prices on these items in our eight stores?"

"We could do it for a while," Joe said, "but, long term, it would trim too much off the bottom line."

"You'd think that would be true for A&P as well," Dom said. "They have a tough union, their employees are older than ours and make more money per hour than ours, and they don't own the locations. Net, their bottom line has to be higher."

Maria said, "Maybe it's the old gag…they'll make it up in volume!"

We all smiled at that. It was the mantra of the supermarket industry. Sell items at a loss, but if you sell a lot of them, you'll make up the loss in volume. A very faulty economic theory indeed but right in line with the black humor of the industry.

Joe was the first to get it. "Holy shit, they don't have to make money here like we do."

"You put it right in the heart of the target, Joe," I said. "One of their divisions, like Chicago or Detroit, where pricing isn't an issue, is supporting these prices in Boston."

"Son of a bitch," Dom said.

"Yeah, but is it illegal?" asked Maria.

"That's the question that needs to be answered," I said.

Joe had his hands in his pockets and was looking out the window. He turned toward us and said, "Right now we got nothing but a theory. We don't even know if it's illegal, and if it is, it'll be tough to prove it. So let me handle this with our lawyers. In the meantime, we need a price analysis of A&P from top to bottom, and Dom, you and Russell need to build a plan for those three stores that gets the volume we need."

"You're right about that, Joe," Dom said, nodding his head in the affirmative.

"It's important…very important," Joe said, "and let me tell you why. If we can't build the volume to acceptable levels, we won't be able to expand without bringing the banks into play. The arrow will be stuck on eight stores, and all those site maps and locations you have in your office, Dom, won't be worth the powder to blow them up."

"Russell," Maria said, "this is an extraordinary find, regardless of how it turns out."

"Thank you, Maria," I said.

"I agree," Joe said, "and it gives me a hell of a good idea."

"Let's hear it, Joe," Dom said.

"How about three or four times a year, we stick Russell and Maria on a plane, and they fly out to different markets, like L.A., and steal the good ideas from chains out there, and then we run them back here. If A&P can beat us up from Chicago or Detroit, maybe we can return the favor."

"Joe, that's a really great idea," I said.

"Thanks, Russell," Joe said, "but I wouldn't have thought of it if you hadn't uncovered this A&P stunt."

"Let's go to work," Dom said as we exited the conference room.

Over the next five years, Maria and I traveled around the country, looking for good ideas that we could borrow and bring back to New England. We became very close. It's strange but when you travel together on business, there is a lot of one-on-one time. Delays at the airport, meals together, overnights in strange cities, and, pretty soon, you start to anticipate what the other will say before they actually do say it. There was never anything remotely sexual about our relationship, but I didn't think of her as my mother either. And neither did others in cities we visited. If I was a minute or two late in meeting Maria at the bar of our hotel before dinner, males would be buzzing around her like birds to a feeder in the middle of winter.

Maybe that's why I did feel as if I were a member of the family. The board of directors in that span of time were the brothers, Dom and Joe, whom I had grown up in front of, and Maria, whom I became very close to as a result of our business relationship. Eventually, I'd become the fourth member of that board.

Chapter 5: Dom Galetti

I couldn't help thinking that if Dom Galetti hadn't died unexpectedly, we wouldn't be in this pickle. It had been more than a decade ago that Joe's brother had passed away, but it was still very fresh in my memory.

Dom had been reading in his chair at home, and Maria found him slumped over, with his notebook upside down on the floor. She knew immediately that he was dead and not napping. She told me that she picked up the notebook, put it on the table by his chair, went to the phone, and called Joe. Dom was 47 years old, in the prime of his business life, and now he was gone. We were all in shock, but the person who took over completely was Joe. He made all the arrangements, and he stood by Maria's side throughout this tragic ordeal. She was a very strong woman, but it was all she could do to just get through the wake and the funeral. Alfie, Joe's wife, pitched in as well and helped Maria with the children. Trip was a senior in high school, and he spoke at the funeral. He was now the man of the family, but I worried about him. His personality was more like his uncle's than his dad's, and I was concerned that he was holding it all in without an outlet to release his pain.

Two days after the funeral, I made a point of picking up Trip at school just to see how he was doing. I started the conversation by saying, "How are you, Trip?"

"I'm mad," he said.

"Ohh."

"Yeah, I'm mad at God and anybody who had anything else to do with the death of my dad."

"I understand," I said.

"How could you?" he asked.

"I lost my dad when I was thirteen years old," I replied.

"I didn't know…" he said.

"Yeah, well that's not surprising. People don't like to talk about death," I said. "But I still think about him almost every day."

"I can't stop thinking about my dad," Trip said.

"Well, that's the good part," I said.

"How come?" Trip replied.

"You always want to remember your family after they have passed away. You keep them alive in spirit by recalling all the great memories you had with them," I said. "And over time the pain goes away…but you never entirely get over the loss of someone like your dad."

"He was a great man," Trip said.

"He was," I said. "He was a sharp guy, but what differentiated him from a lot of other people was his compassion. He cared."

"I didn't realize it until I was standing at the funeral," Trip said, "but he found a way to tell me he loved me every day."

"That's so neat," I said. "Think of all the people who never had a relationship like that with their dad. And, Trip…"

"Yes," he said.

"I was very proud of you at the funeral. You did a wonderful job portraying who your dad was…his warmth and his character."

I looked over at Trip, and he was wiping tears away from his face. We just rode in silence for a while as I handed my handkerchief to him. He wiped his face with it and blew his nose. As we pulled into his driveway, he said, "Sorry to have messed up your hankie," he said as he gave it back to me.

"That's okay. Plenty more where these came from," I said.

"Hey, Russ…" Trip said. "This little ride helped me a lot."

"Glad to hear it," I said. "Take care."

As I rode back to the office, my thoughts were filled with my relationship with Dom. In a number of ways, he was like my dad. I would miss his cheerful demeanor. I'm sure he had his dark moments, but he kept those slightly off-stage. He dealt with things with humor, and, frankly, he was a pure joy to be around.

With the exception of Maria, who had taken some time off to be with her children, most of us were back at work. Twice that first week I found myself wandering down to Dom's office, only to realize about halfway down the hallway that he wasn't there. Joe was keeping to himself while trying to deal with this tragedy in his own way. The brothers, and their families for that matter, were extremely close, so I was guessing that Joe felt as if he'd lost part of his own body. To say the brothers were joined at the hip, at least figuratively, was not hyperbole. There was plenty of work to be done, but for the first time in my business career, I was having trouble focusing on any one thing.

Finally, I went to Joe and said, "I'm going to take a vacation. You're paying me a lot of dough, and I'm not earning it right now with the effort I'm putting forth."

Joe looked up from his desk. "Go ahead if you want to, Russ. But don't worry about the paycheck thing; I haven't been worth a shit either since Dom passed away."

"I find myself walking down to his office only to remember that he isn't there," I said.

"I know. I know," Joe said. "I was in his office yesterday afternoon, remembering all the fun we had building this business. I think I may have taken him for granted. He was my business partner, but, more importantly, he was my older brother. When I was troubled or struggling with something, he always seemed to be able to get me back on track."

"How's Maria holding up?" I asked.

"She's doing okay," Joe said. "She told me, although I think she intends on calling you about this, that your talk with Trip was very helpful. Frankly, I worry about him; he keeps a lot inside."

"Reminds me of somebody I know," I said.

"Me?" Joe said.

"Yep," I responded.

"I haven't been able to cry yet over Dom's death, and, knowing him, if I did, he'd call me a jerk-off. I'll be able, at some point, to cry, but I've needed to keep my guard up for the family, especially the kids."

I was stunned by this admission and felt a good deal of empathy for Joe. I wasn't even a family member, and I'd been walking around in a fog for more than a week. I don't think I could relate to Joe's pain. Joe talked on, almost as if he were talking to himself. "I've got to become the surrogate father to Dom's children. So I'll be away from the office more than I have been in the past, Russ. I'm going to have to rely on you to make more of the decisions than you are now. I want to be at their sports events, dances, and graduations just like I would with my own."

"Well, you know Maria's daughters aren't that far off from dating. Are you going to give their boyfriends the third degree?"

"Damn right," Joe said with enthusiasm.

"Well, don't scare them off entirely," I said, "or you'll have Maria to deal with."

"Good thinking. Russ, I've got an idea; Dom and I have side-by-side condos in Bermuda. Why don't you use mine?"

"Thank you, Joe, that's very generous of you. I think I'll take you up on that."

"Get the keys from my secretary, and have her make a plane reservation for you, first class," he said.

"Oh, that's not necessary, Joe. I've never flown first class in my life."

"About time you learned," he said. "Now don't argue with me about it."

"Yes, sir," I said.

* * *

41

I didn't waste that much time following Joe's instructions. Two days later I was in Bermuda, sitting on the most beautiful beach I'd ever been on in my life. This island was a wonder. It just wasn't what I had pictured at all. I thought it would look like a sand trap with a coconut tree in it. But Bermuda was a lush island with beautiful vegetation, and the people seemed to move at a slower pace. It didn't take me long to adjust to this pace. As I looked at the women parading past me, I was stunned by the amount of skin that was revealed. I hadn't seen this much of a woman's anatomy since my sister and I were kids and my mother used to put us in the tub together.

Joe's condo was luxurious to say the least. It was just outside the main road to Hamilton, and it had a magnificent view of the water. As I arrived back at the condo after a day at the beach, I opened the door, and there was a note folded in half, laying on the floor. It said, "I'm next door; give me a holler when you get in—Maria."

I stepped next door and rang the bell. Maria opened it and was standing in her bare feet, with what I could only describe as an "all-world" yellow sundress on. It was such a contrast from what I'd seen her wearing at the funeral that it actually startled me a little. Maria must have noticed my surprise, because she said, "You look like you've seen a ghost, Russ."

"I guess I've never seen you without shoes on before...you look....ahhh...shorter."

Maria laughed out loud and said, "Well, I am five foot seven in bare feet, five foot ten in heels."

"That explains it, all right," I said.

"Joe told me you were down here and suggested I come down and take a break too."

"Great idea," I said. "I've just spent a day on the beach checking out the summer uniforms, and they were quite interesting."

"And how were they?" Maria asked.

"Brief," was my one-word answer.

"I think I'm going to look pretty old-fashioned in my one-piece suit," she observed.

"Maybe so," I said. "But you are prettier than anybody I saw today."

"Well, thank you, sir," Maria said. "That's nice to hear."

"I know. You're going through a rough time. But Joe is a wise man. If today was an indication for me...a few days in the sun will do you a world of good."

"I think you're right," she said. "I'm starved...want to get something to eat?"

"Let's do it," I said. "I'll see you in fifteen minutes."

"Give me thirty, Russ, I'm still unpacking."

"You got it," I said.

As I was showering, the thought crossed my mind that having dinner with the widow Galetti was somehow inappropriate. But we had traveled together on numerous occasions to a number of cities, trying to steal and implement good ideas for the chain, so this wasn't that different. I knocked on her door, and we walked into Hamilton and ate at a bistro on a second-floor deck overlooking the main street. We were very comfortable with each other, and we chatted about a number of subjects, but they all ended up in the same place: Dom Galetti. At one point in the conversation, she said, "I'm wondering if I should sell out to Joe. He's told me that he would buy me out if that's what I wanted."

"Well, it's none of my business, but that never stopped me before from offering advice," I said.

"I'd like to know what you think, Russ," she said, touching my hand with hers. I saw the guy at the next table looking at us with a strange look on his face. I could only imagine what he was thinking. Maybe he was saying to himself, *I wish that gorgeous woman were at my table, stroking my hand.* We were close enough in age that I was pretty sure he didn't think I was a gigolo. Besides, I didn't think I had the requisite good looks for that line of work. But Maria did look fabulous in a very simple A-line dress, cut just low enough for male watchers to knock over a glass of water trying to get a sneak peak. I could understand their quandary, as I tried very hard not to gawk myself. Maria left a lot to the imagination because she was a conservative dresser, but even the most obtuse observer would notice that God had taken his time forming this particular person.

Finally, before I could answer Maria's question, the man leaned over and said, "Aren't you folks connected to the Galetti chain?"

Maria answered immediately with a dazzling smile. "Why, yes, we are. I'm Maria Galetti and this is Russell Riley."

"I'm Ed Rollins from *Supermarket News*," he said. "I'm very sorry for your loss, Mrs. Galetti."

"Thank you, Ed," she said. "He was a great man, a wonderful husband, and a pretty terrific dad."

"I'm not surprised to hear that," Rollins replied. "He had a terrific reputation in the industry. Can I ask you guys a business question?"

"Sure," I said. "As long as you don't expect a direct answer."

Rollins laughed at that and said, "I wouldn't know a straight answer if it slapped me in the face. There's a rumor that your chain is on the block and that you are thinking of selling it."

"Am I on the record or off, Ed?" I asked.

"Strictly on the record," he said.

"No truth to it whatsoever," I responded.

"I thought that was the case," he replied. "But with the recent turn of events, I thought the rumors would surface all over again."

Maria responded by saying, "I'll give it to you straight, Mr. Rollins. I've got four kids to educate, and now, being a widow, selling out has no appeal to me."

"Got it. Thanks, folks…nice to have met you; enjoy your dinner," he said as he got up to leave.

"Nice to have met you, Mr. Rollins," Maria said as he began to stroll toward the exit.

"That just goes to show you," I said to Maria.

"Show me what?" Maria said.

"You're never off in this business even when you are on vacation."

"You're so right," she said. "Now where were we?" she said.

"Selling the chain," I said. We both laughed at that. "My advice now seems somewhat redundant, but what I was going to say was, don't do anything for six months to a year."

"You know, that makes sense," Maria said.

We finished dinner and headed back to the condos. Maria kissed me on the cheek and disappeared behind her door. I walked into my condo, hung up my clothes, put on some pj's, and started to write some postcards. I hadn't brought any work with me—just some books that I hadn't had a chance to read back in the States. About 30 minutes later I heard a knock on my door. It was so faint that I thought I might have just imagined it, but I went to the door anyway and opened it.

It was Maria and she was standing in the hallway in a white nightgown and slippers. I said, "Maria."

"I have a very strange request to make," she said as she stepped inside.

I said, "Okay..."

"Can I sleep in your bed tonight with you? No funny stuff...I'm just having trouble sleeping by myself."

"Sure," I said. "You must have a lot of faith in me, or you think I like guys."

"Why's that?" she asked.

"You're a beautiful woman but I kind of feel like that guy in the Bible who God told not to turn around or he'd turn into a pillar of salt."

Maria laughed and said, "I think that was Lot, and, for the record, I'm pretty sure you like girls."

"I'll give it my best shot, Maria," I said.

"That's all I can ask," she said.

Maria left me and went into the bedroom and got into bed. Ten minutes later I joined her, thinking I wouldn't sleep a wink. When I got into bed, Maria moved over and looped her arm over my chest, and the next thing I knew, it was eight o'clock in the morning.

I could smell bacon cooking, and Maria was up and dressed when I emerged from the bedroom. "How'd you sleep?" she asked.

"Like a rock," I said.

"Me too...it's the first night's sleep I've had in two weeks."

I sat at the table, and Maria served me scrambled eggs, bacon, and toast. "Hey, I could get used to this," I said.

"Don't count on it," Maria said. "It's only temporary."

"What do you think Mr. Rollins would say if he knew we slept together?" I asked.

Maria sat down, looked up at me, and said, "But it was perfectly innocent; nothing happened."

"That's what all my women say," I responded.

She burst out laughing and that may have been the exact moment that a special bond was created between us. At every turn we seemed to agree about just about everything. We were totally aligned on the business front, constantly pushing for change. We'd grown close as traveling mates, visiting a number of cities in the US and bringing good marketing ideas back to New England. I'd spent countless hours at her house with her husband and children. But this was definitely a new phase in our relationship. She was suffering the loss of her husband while trying to cope with now being the head of her family. But she had support. Alfie, Joe's wife, was almost as devoted to Maria's family as she was to her own, and I knew from my conversations with Joe that he would be there at every turn for his late brother's family. It didn't lessen the pain she was feeling now. I was sure of that. But to be suffering that loss by yourself and not having the family support she had would have made the situation almost untenable. "A dollar for your thoughts," she said as she poured us another cup of coffee.

"I thought it was a penny for your thoughts," I responded.

"A combination of inflation and the fact that you seemed so far away."

"It's a little embarrassing because I was thinking about you," I said.

"Oh," Maria said.

"I was thinking about how much I value your friendship and the fact that we seem so aligned on the way we see things."

"What a lovely sentiment," Maria said. "I hope I don't take you for granted, because you are one of the people I rely on as a matter of course."

"I sure don't feel I'm taken for granted. In fact, that's one of your many strengths. You make everyone you come in touch with feel special. I was also thinking that you're in a lot of pain, but you seem to be handling it as well as possible, and you have some wonderful family support during this time."

"Thank you, Russ," she said. "And you're right, I have some unbelievable support, and right now, in particular, it feels wonderful. It's the only thing that maintains my sanity. I don't think I could do it alone. For instance, before I could pack for this trip, Alfie was at my house telling me that she'd take care of the kids while I was gone. Joe handled everything. The funeral, the paperwork, meeting with the lawyers, and he's kept me in the loop on all these activities. This is a guy who has suffered a deep loss himself while taking on the burden of all the responsibilities of the chain by himself."

"Yeah, I know," I said. "But we're going to have to watch him a little. He and Trip are a little bit alike in this regard. They internalize everything and don't let it out. So we need to try and relieve that pressure a little when we get back."

"Good point, Russ," she said. "Well, I'm off to do a little shopping. Anything you need?"

"Nope. That's the advantage of not having a wardrobe…I never have to add anything to something that doesn't exist."

Maria laughed while getting up from the table and said, "Can a bachelor boy handle these dishes?"

"Hey," I said with a smile, "that's what I specialize in—nonskilled labor."

"Okay. See you later."

I went to work cleaning up the dishes, making the bed, and taking a long shower before shaving and dressing. Satisfied with my cleanup work, I was just thinking about where I was headed when I heard a rap on the door. I opened it and Maria was standing there looking as if she were ready for some serious shopping. She was dressed very simply: a sleeveless white blouse with button-down pockets, beige linen shorts, and black sandals. For some reason the simplicity of the outfit was alluring. She looked slender and her bare arms and legs looked like those of an athlete. She obviously wasn't a power lifter, but her arms had a pleasing symmetry and shape. The only jewelry she had on were small silver earrings. "I'm off to shop 'til I drop. Sure you don't need anything?"

"No, I'm fine, thanks," I said.

"Okay, see you. Where will you be in the afternoon?" she asked.

"Same old spot, checking out the summer uniforms between pages of Leon Uris," I said.

"Okay if I come join you?"

"I'd be delighted," I said.

I closed the door and tried to finish the postcards. This was becoming a three-day project. I always discovered something about vacations. The longer I stayed, the less I moved, so by the time it was time to fly back home, I could hardly muster the energy to get to the airport. I couldn't stop thinking about Maria. My emotions were high; our entire relationship was built on trust. I think I could tell Maria just about anything without sugarcoating it…and I think she felt the same way about me. And I didn't want to distort this trust. But, in my mind, she was so desirable as a woman, that for the first time, it was getting in the way of our relationship. As good as our ability to communicate was, I didn't think it was good enough to tell her that I had a craving to make love to her for a week straight. But a guy could only take so much, I rationalized, and having Maria lying next to me sound asleep, breathing on my neck, was enough to snap the rubber band of my resistance. My next thought was, one way to resolve this quandary was to cut my vacation short and head home.

Before I made any decision, I grabbed my book, a cooler of beer, and a towel and headed for Horseshoe Beach. It was tough duty but somebody had to do it…might as well be me. These beautiful, young things had spent a lot of money on their summer suits, and they needed someone to admire them. I was glad to comply. I drank a couple of beers, read my book, and fell fast asleep on the beach. The next thing I knew, Maria was gently shaking my shoulder. As I woke up I said, "Hi there…I must have dozed off."

Maria said, "It's three o'clock in the afternoon. When did you get here?"

"About noon," I said.

"Hungry?" she asked.

"Starved," I replied.

"Here's a chicken salad sandwich I bought in town. See how that tastes."

I sat up, opened us both a beer, and took a large bite from the sandwich. All I could mumble between bites was, "Yummy."

"I'm so glad you like it, but, Russ, you better put your shirt on; you're getting red."

"Good idea," I said as I slipped my shirt on and had a cold swig of beer. "How'd your shopping trip go?"

"Really well. I loaded up on some very nice sweaters that I'll use for Christmas gifts. What are you doing for dinner?"

"Nothing. Actually, I was thinking of packing up and heading back to Boston."

"Tonight?" Maria asked.

"Tonight or tomorrow morning," I replied.

"Why are you leaving early?" Maria asked.

"All good things have to end," I said.

"Did I drive you out early?" Maria asked.

"Oh, don't be silly, Maria. I love being with you, but I think I need to get back to the old grindstone."

"I feel terrible," Maria said. "I think you're afraid the widow Galetti will ravish you."

"I can think of a lot worse things than being ravished by you," I said.

"Are you afraid that if we begin a relationship, it will turn out poorly?"

"I don't know but I do know that neither of us is very subtle. Life could become very complex, the little white lies, trying to maintain a normal relationship at work. Sneaking around, and, of course, there is Trip and the other children…"

"You're right, Russ. I'm just not up to all that subterfuge either. Let's just cool it. We haven't done anything wrong at this point…maybe we ought to leave it that way."

"Agreed," I said.

"Russ…" Maria said.

"Yes."

"I want you to know that I think you'd make a great lover and that if both of us are unattached in a year or so, let's revisit this subject."

"Deal," I said with a smile.

"And, Russ," Maria said, "while I'm at it, I wanted to thank you for the talk you had with Trip the other day. It really helped him sort a few things out. I actually heard him laugh the other day, which is a really good sign."

"You're welcome. He's a good kid. I'm glad I could help."

We went back to the condos, dressed, ate dinner, and I caught the first flight back to Boston the next day. I was at least smart enough to know that

Maria was vulnerable, and I think we left it right where we should have, considering the circumstances. But the cynical side of me felt that if an opportunity rose again to make love to Maria, it would probably happen. I reported back to work at about noon, and Joe was standing in my doorway almost immediately. "Well," he said.

"I had a great time; feel totally refreshed and ready to go. Thank you for loaning me your place; it was fantastic," I said.

"And Maria?" Joe asked.

"Doing as well as can be expected," I said.

"Well, I thought you better see this before anybody called," Joe said as he opened up *Supermarket News* and laid it on my desk.

It was a small squib on page four, with a headline that said, "'Galetti Chain Not For Sale,' Hamilton, Bermuda, reported by Ed Rollins."

"This reporter, in an exclusive interview with Maria Galetti and executive vice president Russell Riley, learned that the Galetti chain, rumored to be for sale for months, will remain in the family. The for sale rumor gained momentum in recent weeks due to the untimely death of Dominic Galetti, 47, who owned the chain with his brother Joseph. Joseph Galetti also was contacted by this reporter and confirmed for *Supermarket News* that Galetti Supermarkets was not in negotiations with any firm to sell the supermarket chain nor was it actively seeking a buyer. Galetti Supermarkets operates sixteen supermarkets in Boston Metro, and they have the reputation of being one of the most innovative chains in that marketing area."

"I knew it," I said as I finished the article.

"What did you know?" Joe asked.

"You're never off in this business even when you're on vacation," I said. "And I don't like what the article doesn't say."

"And what's that?" Joe asked.

"What in the hell is Maria Galetti doing in Bermuda with another man so close to the death of her husband."

"Yeah, it crossed my mind too, Russ," Joe said. "But I'm the one that told her to go."

"It was a good call on your part, Joe," I said. "She's a strong lady but she's on the ragged edge right now."

"What about damage control?" Joe asked.

"Nothing to control," I assured him. "So let it ride."

"Okay," Joe said. "I need your help this afternoon. We really need to expand the board, and the sooner the better."

"I'll be there. Just buzz me," I said.

"Right," Joe said as he got up to leave.

"And, Joe…" I said.

"Yes," he replied.

"If I'm the executive vice president, shouldn't I be making a little more money?"

Joe laughed out loud and said, "Just because Rollins gave you a promotion doesn't mean it is so. And I don't know many people under thirty who are making what you're making."

"Neither do I," I said.

Surprisingly, my mail wasn't stacked up that badly, and I was able to get through it in about an hour. I returned a few calls and called down to the waiting room for Bill Hartman from Procter & Gamble to come to my office. Hartman entered my office, took off his coat, and threw it on a chair. His shirt was untucked, he had ink at the bottom of his shirt pocket, and it looked as if he had only shaved one side of his face. As he dropped his oversize body into a chair, I asked, "How's the Friar Tuck of manufacturing?"

Bill smiled and said, "Not as good as you, oh exalted one—thee of the executive vice president ranking."

I laughed at Hartman. He was giving me a hard time about the *Supermarket News* article. I knew as buyer and seller, we were supposed to be mortal enemies, but he was such a good guy, and he had more than his fair share of good ideas. On the other hand, he knew we would reward those ideas with strong support for his brands. So it was a two-way street. The other thing I liked about his company was I knew if he was giving us a dollar off a case on an item, then every competitor, big and small, was getting a dollar off a case. It didn't mean we saw eye-to-eye on all things, but integrity was never a question with this company. I asked my usual opening question: "What's new on the grapevine?"

"Pretty quiet, actually," Hartman said. "It's rumored that Galetti and Pantry Place are making beautiful music, and one freshly minted executive vice president at a prestigious food industry company is engaged after alluding the hangman's noose for many years."

"Bill, I've got to tip my hat to you," I said. "I don't know much about Pantry Place, but the engagement news is right on the button. How'd you find that out?"

"My wife was in Claire's shop the other day, and she spilled the beans," Hartman said.

"Loose lips sink ships," I said.

"No kidding. Congratulations. I'll tell you something else," Hartman said. "Claire really likes your intended, and I have a feeling she's a pretty tough grader."

"She is indeed," I replied, "What else have you got?"

"A half a presentation," Hartman replied.

"Where's the other half?" I asked.

"I was hoping you could supply it," Bill responded.

"There could be a charge for that service," I said.

"That's okay. That's what I love about the Northeast. People tell you exactly how they are thinking. You might not like what they tell you, but at least you know what they don't like, and, hopefully, you can fix it. I was down in Texas, and I presented a new line to the buyer. He didn't say anything at all during the presentation; told me to come back the next week. I did as I was instructed, and as I sat down, the buyer said in a Texas drawl, "I brung home the saddle, the hoss is dead."

I laughed out loud at Hartman's story and said, "I guess that didn't bode well for the new line."

"Nope, they didn't buy one size of it," Hartman said with a smile. "Anyway, here's my idea. I've got some large cube, fast-moving items such as Bounty and Charmin, in your warehouse. I went to the warehouse and basically followed a case of Bounty from the time it arrived to the time a consumer bought it from your shelf and walked out the door with it."

"With you so far," I said.

"How many days did it take?" Hartman said.

Having no idea, I said, "Eight days?"

"Three days," Hartman said.

"Wow. That means Bounty turns a hundred twenty times a year in our warehouse versus ten times a year for the average grocery item," I said.

"Right on," Hartman said. "Here's another way of looking at it. Our terms are two percent, fifteen days. That means you still have twelve days to pay the bill, collect the two percent discount, and the money is already in the register."

"As it should be," I said. "We're working on the manufacturer's money."

"I don't know if I agree with that," Hartman said, "but there's a story in here somewhere that has a nice ring to it, literally."

"Well, I can think of one thing that would warm the cockles of an accountant's heart," I said. "Interest avoidance. If we have the money in the bank twelve days before the bill is due, we don't have to borrow money to pay the bill."

"I like it," Hartman said. "And maybe Galetti looks at those items that turn fifty times or more a year with a favored nation status."

"Maybe," I said.

"Okay, let's leave it there for now," Hartman said. "Two other observations from the article. You want to hear them?"

"Sure. It's your nickel," I said.

"First, if you can't make it on your own, you can always marry the boss."

"That'll be tough to do seeing as I'm engaged to Holly," I said.

"Fair point," Hartman conceded. "The second point might actually have validity. That article gave an idea to several chains that weren't smart enough to think of it themselves."

"What do you mean?" I asked.

"I wouldn't be surprised if several chains put out feelers to see if you really might want to sell," Hartman said.

"Hartman, sometimes you amaze me," I said.

"Just your humble servant," he replied. "I really called you to thank you for your support for Pampers in the baby-food aisle. It's an initiative that's now working all around the country."

"Oh no," I said in mock horror. "Does this mean that I get you promoted again?"

"Could be," he said. "But I've got a long ways to go to get to executive vice president like someone I read about recently."

"Don't believe everything you read," I said, leaving Hartman to rifle through my stuff if he so desired. Joe buzzed me and I headed for his office. It seemed very weird to be meeting without Dom and Maria. Joe opened up by saying, "Russ, we need more on the board expansion, and here's who I'm recommending. He handed me a list of potential candidates:

Galettis Board Expansion

1) Norm and Al Parnelli, Parnelli Construction Co.
2) Lawrence Linehan, CPA
3) Harold Soloman, lawyer
4) Leonard Hirshberg, retired CEO, Shawmut Bank

I looked at the list and said to Joe, "Okay, why don't you take me down the list and tell me what you're thinking, then maybe we can kick it around."

"Okay. The Parnelli brothers have been with us from the start. They've built every store and shopping center that we've put up over the last thirteen years."

"Okay," I said. "Which one would make more sense for the board?"

"Both," Joe said resolutely.

"Joe, what's the purpose of this board?"

"To provide direction and sound decision-making for our business."

"What if the economy turns and we have to slow our expansion? Do you think the Parelli brothers will vote for that?"

Joe hesitated and said, "Probably not. But we have other connections with them. For instance, we have invested part of profit sharing trust in projects not related to building stores."

"Do you think they'll vote for removing money from those projects to more prudent investments?" I asked.

"Okay, okay...it'll be Norm. He's the CEO. How about Linehan and Soloman?" Joe asked.

"Don't know anything about them, but I had a chance to work with some of Linehan's associates during the A&P visit and really liked them."

"Hirshberg."

"I've met him and I like him and he has the time. Would he be your chief financial officer or would it be Soloman?" I asked.

"Hirshberg," Joe said.

"Good," I said. "Anybody else?"

"You and Maria—a total of seven. What do you think?" Joe said.

"You're setting me up, Joe!" I said.

"What do you mean?"

"Excluding Maria, who owns half the joint, you've got six white males, five of them over fifty."

"Yeah, but I've got Italians, Irish, and Jewish on this board."

"Joe, you need another woman and a minority board member—maybe the largest minority that our stores serve would be appropriate," I said.

"Let me meet you halfway...you and Maria find me a qualified woman, and we'll talk," Joe said.

"It's a start," I said. "Joe, I think you need a feisty board because you're at a real disadvantage from a publicly owned company."

"What disadvantage?"

"Well, your board can't fire you, where the board of a publicly owned company can fire the CEO. So, if you put all yes-men on the board, you won't get any resistance and you won't get any ideas. You've grown into a very influential businessman, and opposing you on an issue could jeopardize their income."

"Do I appear to be an ogre?"

"Not to me," I said.

"But to others?" Joe responded.

"Frankly, yes."

"So you're saying?" Joe asked.

"In the next round of appointees, one or two minorities and one or two people who are not dependent on you for a paycheck."

"It never stopped you from giving a contrary opinion," Joe said.

"Sure, but I learned from the master. And believe it or not, I've been around here a long time. I don't remember you in short pants but I'm close," I said.

For some reason that made Joe smile. "Well, I know I may seem like an ogre to some, but the reason I called you in this afternoon is I knew you'd give it to me straight," Joe said.

"Thanks, Joe. There are racehorses and plow horses; I may be a plow horse, but I'm an opinionated one, that's for sure. Anything else?"

"No. I called Maria about the article in *Supermarket News*," he said.

"And?" I asked.

"She just brushed it off," Joe said.

As I left Joe's office, I thought Maria had just the right attitude, but I also knew from Bill Hartman that tongues were wagging. The Army may travel on its stomach, but the food industry flourished on rumor and innuendo. I was waiting to see if Hartman's prediction came true. He had said some of the less creative chains might surface in the next few weeks to buy the chain.

My discussion with Joe had led me to another idea, but it had been such a long time since I'd been in the stores that I needed to do some research first to see if it had any merit. It was an idea I picked up from a chain on Long Island. During Passover on Long Island, which has a heavy Jewish population, the stores converted two or three 72-foot aisles to Passover foods. My talk with Joe today about the board led me in that direction. Should we have special ethnic sections in our stores where we knew we had a large influx of a certain minority?

Something else about the meeting today with Joe was bothering me, and I couldn't quite put my finger on it. Maybe it was the fact that Dom wasn't there to lighten it up a little. Maybe it was the fact that the Parnelli brothers were somehow involved in our profit sharing program. I'd done a lot of real estate work with Dom over the years and never heard anything about it. It didn't seem to be a very conservative place to put people's retirement money, but on the other hand, most things Joe did turned to gold. It was probably nothing.

Chapter 6: The Battle of the Booty

In the Galetti corporate building, Joe's office and my office were side by side. My office was large and well-appointed, but it was only about two-thirds the size of the one occupied by Joe Galetti. What set it apart was that Joe's walls were covered with framed pictures of himself with local politicians, sports stars, Hollywood luminaries, and other famous celebrities. Over the years Joe—through his participation in charitable events, chain promotions, and other social occasions—had rubbed shoulders with the elite establishment of New England on a regular basis. He knew it wasn't his sparkling personality that allowed him to travel in this circle, but rather it was his financial clout, which was considerable, that allowed him this access to critical decision-makers. On more than one occasion, I would come out of my office, often with my head down, reading a memo, and almost plow over the governor of the state or some well-known socialite who had just hit Joe up for her favorite charity. But Joe knew how to leverage these contacts. He knew whom to call to nudge a favorite nephew into an Ivy League school or to push a reluctant bureaucrat into granting a liquor license for a store in one of his shopping centers.

Joe's desk and credenza were covered with almost an equal number of framed pictures of his family, as was a long table directly in back of his desk that faced a large window. This table allowed Joe to work at it while stretching his long legs under it…something he couldn't do while sitting at his desk. One of the disadvantages of being this close to him was that he didn't even have to use the intercom to call me; he'd just holler through the wall, "Russell, do you have a minute?" It was a rhetorical question, really, because I can't ever remember saying, "No, I don't, Joe."

I was sitting in my office, visualizing those family pictures and wondering how I could head off this battle that was about to begin between the two sides of the Galetti family. In fact, I was almost sure I knew the exact moment that the seed was planted for this war. It was eight years ago. Maria was president of the company, and she had left me a message to call her at home regardless of the hour.

I dialed Maria's number, hoping that she really meant that I should dial her at this hour. She answered on the first ring, and I said, "Hi, Maria, sorry to call you so late, but your message sounded somewhat urgent."

"I'm glad you called, Russ. I wanted to let you know about something before you get to work tomorrow," she said.

"Okay," I said.

"Joe has removed me as president of the company today."

"That's preposterous," I said. "What in the world is going on?"

"He found out I was having an affair and removed me from the board."

"Can he do that? You own half the company."

"He can and he did. He is the CEO and he has the votes on the board if I choose to fight it," she said.

"But why? A friend of mine told me the other day that the majority of the boardrooms would be disguised as empty seats if everyone who had an affair was forced to resign."

"Well, he's serious and he has affidavits from my lover and his wife that, in fact, we were having an affair."

"I'm shocked and I'm pissed off about it. I will resign tomorrow in protest. This just isn't how you treat people who have made the kind of contribution you've made over the years. To say nothing of the fact that you are family."

"More an outlaw than an in-law, I'm afraid. Joe is deeply offended that his dead brother's wife would have an affair," she said.

"It's none of his goddamn business," I said.

"Look, Russ, that's why I called. I knew you might do something you'd regret later. Now hear me out. You know Joe asked me to marry him before Dom did, and I turned him down. So I was never the favorite in-law. Secondly, he and I have agreed to keep this between us and tell everyone I just want to be with my kids for a while. Thirdly, Trip is just starting out, and if he knew about this, it would certainly make our relationship pretty shaky, and it would split the family right down the middle. For reasons I don't think I have to explain, having you and Trip still working at the company is a good thing. Basically, Joe is an honest man, but I'm beginning to think he thinks this company now belongs to him. So I have a vested interest in having friends in high places."

"Where is Alfie in all of this?"

"Well, she's in a tough spot. Her first loyalty is to her husband, but we are very, very close. So we're going to have to work it out over time."

"Who knows the real story?" I asked.

"Joe, me, Alfie, someone in the legal department, my playmate and his wife…and you."

"Am I supposed to know?"

"You'll find that out tomorrow. We'll see what story Joe wants to tell you."

"Maria, I'm saddened beyond belief. I need to ask you one other question," I said.

"Okay," Maria said.

"Do I have permission to resign if I think the situation is untenable?" I asked.

"Certainly," Maria said. "I just didn't want you to be blindsided by all of this. It's not pretty, but I wanted you to know the truth. Also, I was afraid you'd get to work and think that you somehow were implicated. You're not...in any way."

"What kind of guy signs an affidavit saying he is having an affair?"

"A worm," Maria responded. "A very bad judgment on my part all around. Live and learn."

"How are you holding up?" I asked.

"Truthfully, I'm devastated by it, but I'm a big girl, and I need to live with a mess that I created...and I will. You know Joe has been like a father to my kids. He's put out a very sincere effort, and I can see how he feels that I have betrayed a family trust," Maria said.

"Well, you hang in there," I said. "I know you are a very strong person. But I must tell you, I'm not sure I can go to work now knowing what I know. I've kind of lost faith in Joe. No matter what...you don't draw up affidavits injurious to your own family."

"Listen, Russ, don't draw any conclusions right now. Sleep on it, hear Joe out, and then decide."

"Okay," I said.

"Promise me," she said.

"I promise," I said.

Maria hung up and I went for a walk. My thoughts drifted back to Dominic, when I was a boy working in the store. Life was so simple then. Nobody locked their cars, Ike's photo ops were mostly on the golf course, the only computers we had were too big to fit into a garage, and trying to hit a curve ball was my biggest challenge. Now we'd had three assassinations, the riots of the Democratic convention in Chicago, Kent State, and a drug culture that seemed to be becoming worse with every passing day. Galetti Markets had seemed to follow this trail of complexity. We had 24 stores with more on the board, accounting firms, a legal staff, and 1500 employees. And now we had an internal mess that had the potential to take the whole business down. Maria was telling me in her own way that she thought Joe was moving to take the chain over and make it his own personal domain. Firing Maria from the corporation certainly made it seem as if he had some designs that had not surfaced yet. Changing the name of the stores and questionable dealings with the profit sharing plan, to me, were starting what I believed was a very unhealthy pattern. Maria still owned half of the company, so maybe I was making more out of this than really existed.

What would my role be? Joe had a board of directors, but they could only suggest changes. This was not a public company, and he could literally fire the board at any time. I didn't want to take a side. Even though I owned stock, I wasn't a family member, and I felt I shouldn't have a voice in these matters. I made my way back to my front door and went to bed, but I didn't sleep well.

The next day Joe called me into his office in the middle of the morning. He didn't look well. He was pale and he had large bags under his eyes. He asked me to sit down and I did. Joe opened up by saying, "I've got a management change to tell you about, and you're not going to like it."

"Ohh," I said.

"Maria has resigned from the company," he said.

"How could that be?" I asked. "She loves working here."

"She just decided she wanted to be a full-time mom," Joe said without blinking.

At least I knew how Joe was going to play this one. Not straight up. It saddened me, really, because, to my knowledge, this was the first time anybody had lied to me at this company since I was 13 years old. My response to Joe was pretty direct. "Tell it to the Indians, Joe, I'm not buying it," I said.

"Who says you got to buy it? You're an employee of this chain, and, as CEO, I'm telling you something as a courtesy in advance of the public being notified."

"Joe, I've been working here for nineteen years, and ten of those have been with Maria. Now, I don't know if you think I fell on my head recently and will believe any bullshit that comes my way, but Maria would never opt to become a full-time mom. Period."

With that, Joe stood up and shouted, "I don't give a fuck what you think. If you don't like what I'm telling you, find another line of work."

Now I was standing up. "Are you firing me, Joe?"

"You can take it any goddamn way you like. Who the hell are you to question my authority or my decisions?" Joe asked at the top of his lungs.

"Nobody apparently. I'll be out of the building in thirty minutes," I said as I turned and left this office.

I was so irritated that, on my return to my office, I turned the corner in the hallway and flattened a young secretary who was carrying a stack of documents. After apologizing profusely and picking her and her papers off the floor, I gathered my things from the office and left the building. It was kind of sad. I had to carry my stuff out of this office in a box. I didn't even own a business bag. They were all issued by the company. Also, I had to call a cab to take me home because my car belonged to the company. It happened so quickly. A three-minute conversation and 19 years were down the drain. I really hadn't known how my conversation with Joe would turn out, but I knew when he lied to me that I didn't want to be a part of the operation any longer. That's something I treasured the most about the Galettis—no subterfuge, no bullshit…they gave it to you straight from the hip. You might not like it, but you knew you weren't getting it from the public relations department. Until today I always thought of that as Galetti's competitive advantage…the truth.

* * *

As I returned from that event eight years ago, I remembered that Maria's loss to me was very impactful, but I'd forgotten that Joe had fired me as well. He had hired me back a week or so later. I never was sure why he did, but by that time I'd cooled down enough that I accepted his offer. We went back a long way, and I think over time the scars healed between Joe and me. After all, we'd been yelling at each other since I was a junior or senior in high school. In fact, as I thought about our relationship, I thought back to how I became involved in the company stock situation.

I was in my early 20s at the time, and Dom and Joe invited me to a family ceremony that touched me deeply. The two families, including the children, met at Dom's house for dinner. It was a pretty typical gathering—boisterous, warm stories of the old days and Dom and Joe singing a duet with Alfie at the piano. The kids were in various parts of the house, but Trip, who was 13, stuck with the adults.

Before dinner Dom and Joe gathered everyone in the living room for an announcement. As we all congregated, finding chairs or comfortable places to sit on the floor, Dom stood with a piece of paper in his hand and said, "We gathered you here tonight for a little ceremony, and while I'm talking, Joe will fill champagne glasses for the adults and ginger ale for the kids."

"Can I have champagne like the grown-ups, Dad?" asked Trip. In truth, Trip had such a serious demeanor that I thought of him as an adult. He was already taller than his dad. He was the same age I was when I started working at Galetti.

Dom glanced at Maria quickly and said, "Okay…this time…but don't get used to it!" He waited until Joe made sure everyone had a glass and continued. "This is a family gathering, but we've added Russell to it because we think of him as family. Joe and I went to the lawyer's this week and drew up an agreement that produced these two documents. These are share certificates and each of them is for five hundred shares. Galetti is a private company, so these aren't publicly traded shares, but rather represent the total assets of the company.

"We realize, particularly in this family, that blood is thicker than water, and that, to some, this may seem like an unnecessary step. But as Joe and I talked about it, we wanted to have something on paper that says we each own fifty percent of this enterprise, in case something happens to either Joe or myself. We both hope to live as long as Poppa, but we're no longer a one-store operation. We now have eight stores, with four more on the board, so this is fast becoming a multimillion-dollar business, and we just felt better issuing this class A stock with each family receiving five hundred shares. Joe, did I miss anything?"

Joe stepped forward and said, "Not really, Dom. I'd just add that this is a symbolic gesture, but it's real as well. Dom and I have talked about this extensively, and what we want you children to know is that if one of us is not around, the other will be like a dad to you."

It was a very somber moment. I couldn't tell what the children were thinking, but they were uncharacteristically quiet. Joe had a way of delivering a message that nobody could misunderstand. Maria broke the ice by saying, "A toast to the Galetti brothers…and our families."

We all drank from our glasses and proceeded to the dinner table. I was walking with Trip when he looked at me and said, "I'm going to own this company someday."

"That's right, Trip. You, your brother, sisters, and your four cousins," I said.

"Does that mean you'll be working for me someday?" he asked with a smile.

"Could be," I said.

"Why wouldn't it happen?" he asked.

"Well, you never know. I might be working for someone else by then."

"Oh," he said, "well, I certainly hope not. I think my dad and my uncle wouldn't want that to happen."

"Me either…but there's always that chance."

"Do you like working here?" he asked.

"You're a very inquisitive fellow, aren't you?" I said.

"Yeah, I guess. But I know my mom thinks you are really good, so my guess is that they'd want to make sure you were happy here."

"Trip, I'll tell you the truth," I said. "I love working here, so unless Uncle Sam drags me off, I think I'll still be here when you get into the business."

"That's good," he said as he sat at the table.

I remember thinking that this kid was mature for his age. Maybe it was because I lost my dad at about his age, but I think if I were Trip, I would have been thinking more of my father's mortality during this dinner than of assuming the reins of a very large enterprise.

During the dinner, Maria was my other seatmate at the table, and I asked her what she thought the effect of this meeting was on the children. She responded by saying, "I think most of it went over their heads, but the two oldest understand. I think I'll be fielding some questions from them in the next few days and weeks."

Later that evening, when the kids were in bed, Dominic and Joe invited me out to the porch, handed me a cigar and a glass of red wine, and Dom said, "I hope you don't choke to death on this cigar…like you did on that red wine when we offered to pay your way through college."

"You know, you two guys are leading me down the steps to fire and brimstone with these bad habits. First, serving me wine as an underage teenager and now, handing me a big cigar."

"See, Russell, that's what you don't understand about the Italian culture," Joe said. "There's no such thing as underage for Italians when it comes to red wine."

"How about champagne?" I asked, referring to Trip's drink earlier in the evening.

Dom laughed and said, "I checked it with the real boss, and she thought it was okay."

"I can tell you this," I said, "it didn't stop him from giving me the third degree."

"What did he ask you?" Dom asked with genuine interest.

"He wanted to know my intentions long-term. Trip asked me if I'd still be on board when he would be running the company."

"What did you tell him?" Joe asked.

"I told him that I loved working here for you guys and that it was possible that I could be working for a third generation of Galettis…but that it wasn't probable."

"What does that mean?" Dom asked.

"Well, I think I was just being philosophical. He's thirteen and a lot of water will run under the bridge before he's ready to become CEO. I could end up running my own shop, getting hit by a car, be killed in a war…who knows. Ever since Kennedy's assassination, I've got a new perspective on how fragile life can be."

"That's a little heavy for a twenty-two year old, but I hear what you're saying," Joe said. "It's funny that you'd talk this subject with Trip because that's what Dom and I wanted to talk to you about."

"Really," I said. "You want to talk to me about the future?"

"We sure do," Dom said. "We had a reason—believe it or not—for inviting you to this dinner, that deals with our company stock, but before we tell you about it, we want you to know that Dominic approved this plan. He may be retired but we still sit by his knee when we are making important business decisions."

"To tell the truth, I was honored to be asked to the dinner," I said.

"Good. Let me see if I can explain," Joe said, folding his hands while looking directly at me. "We now have eight stores that average forty thousand dollars a week in volume, so the chain is doing sixteen million a year, and we have a one share of market. Over the next twenty years or so, we want to grow to fifty to sixty stores with a seven share of market. But we're not going to be able to do it unless we have good management. That's defined in our minds, Russ, as much better than the competition."

"Wow. That makes sense but the goal seems so far away," I remarked.

"You're right," Dom said. "At our current rate of expansion, we'd have about half that number of stores. But that's the beauty of it; as we continue to build and open stores, cash flow grows almost exponentially. It's a lot easier to provide cash to open one store when you have twenty stores than it is to open one store when you only have five stores. Get it?"

"Yes," I said.

"But here's the fly in the ointment," Joe said. "If these twenty stores aren't running at their full potential, expansion slows dramatically."

"That makes sense too," I said. "This is the one time you don't need an anchor to windward."

"Absolutely right," Dom said with enthusiasm.

"But how do I figure in all of this?" I asked.

"We thought you'd never ask," Joe said with a smile. "When we did the stock deal this week, we made a provision for you to have twenty-five shares. You are the only nonfamily member to be included."

I just sat staring at the Galetti brothers. When I finally spoke I said, "That's so very generous of you…that's really not necessary. But wait…the last time we had a conversation like this was when you told me you would send me through school."

"And…" Joe said.

"And there was a hook, as Dominic would say," I said.

"You're getting better at this," Dom said with a hearty laugh. He was puffing on his cigar so hard that he seemed to disappear behind a cloud of smoke. "In the agreement we have offered you twenty-five shares or two and a half percent of the business."

"If we sold the business today, you'd walk away with a cool four hundred thousand dollars," Joe said.

"Oh my God," was all I could utter. "But why would you do that?"

"Because we can't get to our goal without people at the top who are committed for the long run. We think you are one of those that will help us win in a very competitive industry. You've already shown us on several occasions— the sales banquet and your work discovering what A&P was up to—that you have a creative side and the energy to be a factor in our accelerating growth," Dominic said.

I was flustered but not so much so that I didn't understand the ramifications of this offer. If we grew seven or eight times the size we were now, my shares would be worth over three million dollars…not adjusting for inflation.

"I just saw the light go on," Dom said, "and you're right. If we are successful, you'll be a millionaire several times over by the time you are forty."

"Just what I was thinking," I said honestly. "What's the hook?"

"You'd be under contract to us exclusively for twenty years. We can fire you but you can't quit. But if we do fire you, we have to buy you out. You have twelve and a half shares each from the two family holdings of five hundred shares."

"Where do I sign?" I asked without a moment's hesitation.

"The paperwork is in your office right now," Dom said as he stood up and shook my hand. Joe did the same and, for a while, we just stared out at the front lawn puffing on cigars and drinking red wine.

I found it very hard to sleep that night. The generosity shown by the Galettis was overwhelming. I loved my job and I thought to myself that it was a good bet I would work for them for 20 years without the stock incentive. Perhaps I should tell them that before I sign the papers. This truly was icing on the cake. I hoped I didn't fold under the pressure. The stock incentive was wonderful, but now I had to produce. The Galettis always had a hook, but it seemed almost inconsequential to the benefit derived from what they were offering.

The next day I signed the papers and returned them to Joe Galetti before he had a chance to change his mind. When he saw me in his outer office handing the file to his secretary, he waved me into his office. I entered the office and said, "Good morning, Joe, I wanted to return these documents all signed before you guys decided to change your mind."

"Have a seat, J. Beresford Tipton," he said, referring to a TV show where a million dollars is given to somebody for some worthy cause. Of course, the show's million was fiction; mine wasn't.

"I just wanted to take this opportunity to thank you again for that very generous incentive we talked about last night..."

As my thoughts returned to the current situation, I suddenly realized that I wasn't exactly a neutral party. My 25 shares could be a deal breaker. Each side actually had 487.5 shares of stock, and I had the remaining shares that added to a total of a thousand shares. I was starting to realize that I was more integral to this case when I caught a glimpse of Maria entering Joe's office. She never came to the building anymore, so I was guessing whatever she came to say was pretty important. Maybe they had come to an accommodation. Wouldn't that be a positive turn of events?

Joe had closed his door, so all I could hear at first were voices, but I couldn't make out the words. But the voices became clearer as they grew louder.

"Joe, our relationship is about to change and not for the better," Maria said. "But I wanted to tell you what's about to happen myself instead of leaving it to the lawyers."

"Lawyers," Joe said as he started to fidget but smiled at Maria nevertheless. "Why would you need a lawyer?"

"Because I received a tax form that says I've sold three million dollars' worth of stock," Maria said.

"What?" Joe said. "I'm sure that's just CPA mumbo jumbo to get us a better tax rate," Joe said.

"You'll have a chance to explain all of that in court," Maria said as she laid the court documents on Joe's desk facing him.

"What's this?"

"It's a court order. You have thirty days before the court is requesting that you explain to them where the shares are now and who owns them."

"You're kidding, right?" Joe asked.

"I've never been more serious in my life," Maria said.

Joe lost it completely when he said, "I've taken care of your family all these years, and this is how you pay me back. You fucking bitch. I told Dom not to marry you but he wouldn't listen."

"You better not use that as a defense, Joe, because if memory serves me, I couldn't have been all that bad because you asked me to marry you," Maria said.

"Get out of my sight, you cunt," Joe screamed. "If I did ask to marry you, I'd claim temporary insanity. And let me tell you something else. I'm going to put a team of lawyers together that will bury you once and for all," Joe raged on, very nearly out of control.

I looked up from my desk just in time to see Maria leaving Joe's office and heading for the exit.

Chapter 7: Game Plan

It had been two days since Helen Cortez had had the abortive interview with what turned out to be part of Joe Galetti's defense team posing as an international law firm. She had reported it immediately to Judge Matthews, fearing that he would terminate her employment for cause. She should have known better. He simply did what he always did when they were together and told her to research the incident for legal precedent and to get back to him. He admonished her for speaking on his behalf about how he felt personally about the litigants but then told her something she thought she would never forget.

"Listen, Helen, this may seem like the biggest debacle in your life right now, and if it turns out that way, consider yourself lucky. These shysters may be doing something legal, but, believe me, my judgment is that it's on the ragged edge. If it's legally permissible, it's a low blow morally, at a minimum.

"Let me tell you where my disappointment lies. You are a trained lawyer. Are you going to take this lying down, or are you going to use that three years of legal training to fight back?"

"What do you mean?" Helen Cortez asked.

"That's all I'm going to say. We shouldn't say anything more on this subject. There's always the chance that they will call you as a witness for the defense, and, at that time, I'd have no choice but to put you on temporary leave," Matthews said.

"I understand, Judge," Helen said. "Thanks for your time, understanding, and counsel."

Helen kept thinking about her conversation with her boss. A day later that thought process led her to Professor Harry Ulmer at the Boston College Law School. Ulmer had been her mentor while she was in law school, and Helen had excelled in his classes. They had stayed in touch since her graduation, and, on two occasions, she had come back to school at his request to talk to his students basically about life after law school. She liked Ulmer immensely.

He had been a very successful corporate lawyer, was a graduate of the law school, and had come back to the campus as a visiting professor. Ulmer was over 60, she felt certain. He had salt-and-pepper hair and was a handsome man with the biggest, bushiest eyebrows she'd ever seen. They looked like dark-black caterpillars placed above his eyes. His most wondrous attribute was his laugh— deep, loud, mirthful. She thought of him, in spite of his personal success, as a real man of the street. He loved big, black terrible-smelling cigars, the racetrack, and The Capital Grill in that order. He'd been known to have a drink now and then, but Helen thought she'd finally figured out why he was such an articulate teacher. He loved his work. It was fun and the interaction with the students kept him stimulated and able to stay up with the modern world.

Harry stood up as Helen entered his office and said, "What's up, Trixie?"

"Do I look like a Trixie to you?" Helen asked.

"Not really. But Trixie is my favorite name. She was Ed Norton's wife on *The Honeymooners*, with Ralph Kramden and his three-propeller boat," Harry Ulmer said.

"*The Honeymooners?*" Helen asked.

"Never mind. BMT," Ulmer said.

"Before my time," Helen responded.

"Right," Harry said. "But, anyway, it's a compliment. If somebody hasn't told you yet today, you look absolutely tremendous," Harry said.

"Thank you, Professor, I needed that," Helen said.

"How can I help?" Harry asked.

Helen took a deep breath, crossed her legs while sitting in a chair in front of Ulmer's desk, and launched into an explanation of what she had thought was an interview with the firm of McAlister, Dodd, Eden, and Lancaster. She concluded her story by saying, "So, the two interviewers, Mark Graceson and Harry Tremble, turned out to be Nicholas Blaine, a lawyer for Joe Galetti, and Arthur Modello, a private detective. It was a ruse. There was no position with a law firm. They threatened extortion if I didn't appear for them as a defense witness stating that Judge Matthews was prejudiced and favored Maria Galetti."

Ulmer took out a cigar, rolled it around between his fingers, and stuck it in his mouth. He didn't say anything for 30 seconds and then looked up at Helen Cortez and said, "That's one hell of a story."

"Yeah, I just wish it were someone else's," Helen said.

"What did the judge say?" Harry asked.

"He didn't say a lot. He didn't admonish me much for getting into this pickle, but he told me that he was disappointed that I wasn't using my head to try and resolve it," Helen responded.

"He makes a solid point," Harry said. "Want to know what I think?"

"That's why I'm here," Helen said.

"Okay. When there's a billion dollars at stake, the price of poker goes way up. Coming in second place is not an option. Next, I know Nicholas Blaine.

He has a solid reputation, going back to the days when he worked for the Kennedys. If he's involved, what they did may seem like dirty tricks, but I think it's legal. They'll be hiding behind some kind of disclosure precedent or ruling. Lastly, but importantly, what they did is ethically borderline, particularly threatening to expose you to the media. At the very least we could raise enough of a dust storm to bring an ethics panel together or file a civil suit. There's only one problem with all of that," Harry said as he munched on his cigar.

"And that is?" Helen asked.

"I'm presuming they didn't record the third session, so it's your word against theirs," Harry said.

"I think you're right. There was a recorder on the table in the conference room, but I don't believe it was turned on," Helen said.

"Okay. I need to make a few calls. Why don't you scoot on out of here, have lunch, and be back in an hour. Can you do that?"

"I can. See you in an hour. And Harry..." Helen said as she stood up to leave.

"Yes," he responded.

"Thanks for your help. I really appreciate it. I can't believe how naive I've been. I was sure my career was over before it began, but now I'm feeling a little more positive," she said.

"You're welcome. I see this as fighting fire with fire. See you in an hour," Harry said.

Helen wandered around the campus, sat on a bench in the sun, but she had no appetite. At the appointed time she stood in Harry's doorway, and he waved her to a seat. A man was sitting in a chair, and he stood as she entered the room. "Helen, this is Agent Larry Nelson; he's with the FBI," Harry said.

She felt her face flush as she said, "Nice to meet you, Mr. Nelson."

Nelson responded by saying, "Don't worry, Ms. Cortez, I'm on your side."

Somehow Larry Nelson knew that Helen had some trepidation meeting an FBI agent. She thought he had a very gentle, soothing voice for a man who towered over both Harry and herself. Nelson, she was guessing, was at least 6'4", solid, with large hands and a crew cut. But his most arresting feature was his eyes. They were cobalt blue and they hardly ever blinked. She felt as if Nelson were looking right through her.

Harry sat down behind his desk, and Helen and Nelson followed his lead. He opened the discussion by saying, "Helen, Larry and I have worked together on a number of cases. Additionally, he's a lawyer, having obtained a law degree from the University of Virginia. Not a bad school of higher education, if I say so myself. I've had a chance to fill Larry in on our little predicament, and he has a course of action to recommend to you. Strictly voluntary...but I thought you'd want to hear it."

"Okay. Fire away," Helen said.

"Well, Ms. Cortez, basically, I'd like you to make an appointment with Mr. Blaine for a fourth sit-down," Nelson said.

"That's the last thing I'd want to do," Helen said.

"We know," Harry Ulmer said. "But we're going to try and turn the table on these folks."

"That's right," Nelson said. "This time we want to have you wear a wire. And we need to do it fairly quickly."

"Why?" Helen asked.

"Because they haven't made a move yet to call you as a witness. What we really need is a record from them of what the consequences will be if you don't play their game," Larry Nelson said.

"But I don't even know how to contact them," Helen said.

"I know how," Harry said. "What do you say?"

"What have I got to lose? I'll give it a shot," Helen said.

For almost two hours the three participants were hunched over Harry's desk, working on questions that Helen would ask while in Nicholas Blaine's office in a face-to-face situation. Additionally, Harry Ulmer turned around, put a piece of paper in a very ancient Royal typewriter, and started to peck away with surprising speed with only the forefinger of each hand. When he was finished he extracted it from the typewriter and handed it to Helen. She began to read it and quickly realized it was a conversation she was to have on the telephone to set up this meeting. Harry looked at her and said, "Feel free to adjust it any way so that they seem more like your words."

"Actually, it looks pretty good as it is," Helen said. "When do we do this?"

"No time like the present," Harry said, handing her a slip of paper with a telephone number on it.

"Okay," Helen said. "But can I ask you two guys to leave while I do this? I'll be more nervous with an audience."

"Certainly," Harry said as he rose to leave. "Here, come around and take my chair. When you're ready hit nine, one, area code, and number."

Ulmer and Nelson left the room together as Helen moved around to Harry's desk chair. "Break a leg," Nelson said as he smiled at Helen Cortez and closed the door to the office.

Helen almost absentmindedly pulled the phone toward her without looking at it because she was studying the script that Harry had given her. She took a deep breath, picked up the phone, and dialed the number. On the second ring a very pleasant female voice said, "Mr. Blaine's office; how may I help you?"

"I'd like to speak to Mr. Nicholas Blaine, please," Helen said.

"Yes, ma'am. Whom may I say is calling?"

"Helen Cortez," Helen responded.

"He's in conference, Ms. Cortez. May I take a number where you can be reached later?"

"I wonder if you could do me a big favor and interrupt him to let him know I'm on the line. I'm in court, so I really can't leave a number," Helen said.

"Hold on, Ms. Cortez," the voice said. This was followed by an excruciating silence that was beginning to unnerve Helen.

"Ms. Cortez, what a pleasant surprise," said the deep baritone of Nicholas Blaine. "What can I do for you?"

Helen heard Blaine's voice and it reminded her that she had really liked him until the third interview. Looking at her script, she said, "I think we need to talk, but my suggestion would be in person, not on the phone."

"What is it that you'd like to talk about, Ms. Cortez?" Nicholas Blaine asked.

"Without going into too much detail, I'd like to talk about the specifics of your proposal to me earlier this week," she said. She felt as if she was beginning to lose Blaine's interest but she pushed forward. "I need to hear for myself those recordings you mentioned."

"Ahh, yes," Blaine responded. "I see. Would they have a material effect on your decision?"

"They would," Helen said.

"It'll take me some time to pull those excerpts together. How about tomorrow, say about ten?" Blaine said.

"I'll be there," Helen said as she hung up. She walked out of the office, into the hallway, and immediately saw the two expectant faces of Nelson and Ulmer. "He didn't go for it."

Both of their faces showed visible disappointment at this news. "Just kidding," Helen said with a smile. "He wants me in his office at ten tomorrow morning." Helen realized that it was the first time she had smiled all day.

Nelson spoke first. "I guess the next step is for you to meet me tomorrow at my office, and we will fit you with a wire."

"I love it when you talk dirty," Harry said.

"Truthfully, he didn't seem that interested until I mentioned the tape recorder. I think he thinks that I don't believe that the two interviews were recorded, and tomorrow I believe he'll try to convince me beyond the shadow of a doubt that he has me right where he wants me."

"I hope you're right. Good things will happen if you can steer him to those recordings and let him talk. He's going to want to tell you how smart he is," Harry said.

"One other thing, Helen," Larry Nelson said. "In the interest of full disclosure, we recorded the conversation you just had with Mr. Blaine."

"You won't get much from it," Helen said.

"Maybe, maybe not," Nelson said. "It could provide valuable context later."

"Just make sure you get that bug off my phone posthaste," Ulmer said to Larry Nelson.

"Something to hide?" Larry asked, looking at Harry Ulmer in a quizzical way.

"Not right now but you never know," Harry responded.

* * *

Helen Cortez passed through the metal detector at the FBI office 15 minutes before her scheduled appointment with Agent Larry Nelson. In circumstances such as these, she usually would have been anxious about the events that were about to transpire, but she wasn't the least bit nervous. Determined would better describe her state of mind. A receptionist greeted her in the lobby, and she was directed to Nelson's office on the fourth floor.

Larry Nelson was standing by the elevator on the fourth floor when she stepped out of it. "Good morning, Ms. Cortez," Nelson said.

"Good morning to you, Larry," Cortez responded. "Why don't you call me Helen, okay?" she said.

"Absolutely. Helen it is. First thing's first. I'll be taking you to our lab, where we will fit you with a recording device. I think you'll be surprised how easy and compact it is. You won't have to tell Blaine to talk into your necklace or anything like that. Also, unlike the movies, we won't be listening in on the street in a panel truck that says, 'Luigi's Pizza and Subs.'"

Helen smiled at Larry Nelson and said, "Too bad. I was hoping that just when the bad guys were about to whisk me away to the Chelsea dump, you'd arrive in the nick of time to save me."

"Oh, I kind of like that scenario myself," Nelson said. "Believe me, Helen, you'd be the most beautiful damsel in distress this office ever rescued!"

"I can't believe that," Helen said.

"Believe it. I've sworn to tell the truth, the whole truth, and nothing but the truth," Nelson said. By this time they had reached the lab, and Agent Nelson introduced Helen to Brandy Williams, who would fit Helen with a recording device. As he left he instructed Brandy to bring Helen back to his office. Less than 15 minutes later, Helen was back in Nelson's office, sitting in front of him. He looked up at her and asked, "Comfortable?"

"Very," Helen replied. "I'm afraid it's in a place where I can't show it to you."

Helen noticed that this big, rugged FBI type actually blushed at her last comment. "Uh, yes…I know where it is," was all Nelson said. "Questions?"

"Any last-minute advice?" Helen asked.

"Not really. Just be yourself. You're a very bright person, obviously, but so are the people you will be talking to. I think your story is simple: you're from Missouri and, before you make any decisions about testifying for the defense, you want to be shown what they have," Nelson said.

"Yep. Doesn't seem that difficult on the surface. Hope it stays that way in actual practice," Helen said.

"You'll be fine. Good luck," Larry Nelson said. "When your appointment is over, don't pass go, don't collect two hundred dollars…come right back here, okay?"

"Will do," Helen said. As she stood to leave Nelson's office, she walked around to his side of the desk and gave him a peck on the cheek and said,

"Thanks again, Agent Nelson, for all your support." For the second time that morning, she saw the big man blush. It made her smile to herself as she left his office and headed for the elevator.

She entered Nicholas Blaine's office at nine forty-five, taking long, purposeful strides toward a receptionist, who, at the time, had her back turned toward Helen Cortez. She was so focused on her mission that she didn't notice the beauty and opulence of the reception area. After a very brief period of waiting for the receptionist, Helen said, "Excuse me, could you help me, please?"

The woman turned slowly toward Helen and said, "Sorry, I was a little wrapped up in the task at hand and didn't hear you. How can I help you?"

"My name is Helen Cortez, and I have an appointment with Mr. Blaine at ten o'clock," Helen said. The woman checked an appointment calendar, looked up at Helen, and said, "I see it here. Let me ring Mr. Blaine's office and announce that you are here." She turned toward the phone, dialed a number, mumbled something Helen did not hear, hung up, looked at Helen, and said, "Ms. Cortez, if you would, walk by the elevators, take the hallway to your left, and Mr. Blaine's suite is at the end of the corridor."

"Thank you," Helen said as she moved toward the elevators. When she turned the corner, the doorway at the end of the hallway was open, and Nicholas Blaine stood in it, waiting for her. He greeted her when she was within 10 feet of him by saying, "Good morning, Ms. Cortez. How are you?"

"I'm fine, thank you. How are you?" she said as she entered his office. They walked by his personal assistant without a word, into his office, and he waved her to a seat. A steaming cup of tea was sitting next to her on a very elegant antique end table. Nicholas Blaine went around to his side of the desk, sat down, and opened the conversation by saying, "Helen—may I call you Helen?"

"Certainly," Helen said.

"First, I want to apologize for what may seem like very rough and unfeeling tactics by my office. I refer specifically to our last three meetings, where you felt you were interviewing for a job with a prestigious international law firm."

"I felt that way because you and Mr. Modello told me that was the purpose of those interviews," Helen said.

"Yes, yes, it may seem as if we misled you, but we had researched our precedents very carefully to make sure we were doing nothing illegal. In fact, that's why we held the first two meetings in Montreal and New York, because that is where these precedents occurred," Blaine said.

Helen didn't want to lead Blaine off the track they were on, but a strange saying passed through her mind from her childhood: "Liar, liar, your pants are on fire." But Blaine's pants weren't on fire; he was in his usual impeccable pinstripe suit, high-gloss shoes, looking and acting the part of a successful and confident lawyer. "I don't mean to split hairs with you, counselor, as I have no doubt that you are well-fortified with legal precedent. But I'd have to contest the word 'seem' in the sentence 'It may seem as if we misled you.' You did mislead me to the point that you used assumed names in my first two interviews."

Blaine chuckled slightly and said, "Okay, okay, it's a fair point. But I must say I did like the name Mark Graceson. But, honestly, Helen, I just want you to know that if I were, in fact, interviewing you for McAlister, Dodd, Eden, and Lancaster, I would have hired you."

"Let's not go there, shall we?" Helen said. "As you may have guessed, I've had a chance to check you out since our last meeting."

"And what did your research tell you?" Blaine wanted to know.

"Just what I thought when you were interviewing me. An experienced lawyer with an excellent reputation stretching over more than thirty years. The odd part is that, legal or not, you'd be involved in a scheme like this one," Helen said.

"I guess we all have our price," Blaine offered. "When this trial is all over, Helen, I'm guessing the fees will be somewhere around a hundred million dollars."

"That is impressive," Helen said as her mind was trying to figure out how to move Blaine to the subject of the tapes. But Blaine, sensing that the small talk was at an end, helped her in this cause by saying, "What is it that I can do for you this morning?"

"In a nutshell I'd like to hear what I said in those interviews before I come to a decision to testify," Helen responded.

"Fair enough," Blaine said as he set a device on the desk. "There were several other comments you made both about the trial and Judge Matthews, but what I'm about to play is central to our case."

Blaine turned on the cassette, and they both heard Blaine's baritone coming from the machine.

Blaine: Tell me, Ms. Cortez...unofficially, of course...a little bit about how Judge Matthews views the case.

Cortez: Well, the judge is a very bright man, but he feels this is a complex case. A lot of these cases are complicated, but the event that caused this disagreement— the death of the younger Galetti brother—happened almost fifteen years ago.

Blaine: How does he size up the two sides?

Cortez: I think he has some sentiment for Maria Galetti. He feels she was a major contributor to the business and that she may have not been treated fairly by Joe Galetti. It's an interesting insight, really. Judges are supposed to be impartial, but they are human too.

Blaine: So the judge isn't that fond of Joe Galetti.

Cortez: It's nothing personal. He told me that people like Joe Galetti don't get where they are going without strewing a few bodies on the highway. It's not that Maria Galetti is a penniless widow, but think about it. She's not being accused of anything: the person's character that is being questioned is Joe Galetti, and the judge doesn't think he's as pure as the driven snow.

Nicholas Blaine turned off the recorder and said, "Heard enough?"

"Unless there's more," Helen responded.

"Not really. One other piece where you allow that the judge turns to you sometimes when a case is particularly sticky."

Helen could feel her face heat up with that comment. She remembered it quite precisely. She looked up at Blaine and said, "It's pretty thin gruel, Nick," Helen said.

"Maybe. But the slightest indicator of a judge showing any partiality could turn this case over for us," Blaine said.

"Well, let me sleep on it," Helen said. "I'll be back to you in the next couple of days."

"I'll look forward to that," Blaine said as he led Helen Cortez from his office to the lobby without another word.

Helen practically ran out of the lobby onto the sidewalk, looking, at the same time, for a cab. A car door swung open close to her on the sidewalk, and she saw Agent Larry Nelson behind the wheel. He said, "Hop in; I'll give you a lift."

"What are you doing in here? I thought you said you wouldn't be outside the building in a panel truck," Helen said as she sat in the front seat and closed the door.

Nelson sped away from the sidewalk and said, "Hey, I was in the neighborhood."

Helen laughed out loud and said, "Good for you. It's great to see you!"

"Thanks. How'd it go?" Nelson asked.

"Okay, I think. He apologized for what might seem like dirty tricks, mentioned he was interviewing me under another name, and played the tape for me," Helen said.

"Sounds good," Agent Nelson said. "Let's get you back to the lab and turn the tape over to our legal folks."

As she rode in the car with Larry Nelson, Helen suddenly realized that she was very tired. After leaving the tape with Nelson, Helen went home, ate a peach, curled up in a chair with a magazine, and slept for four hours. A ringing phone awoke her, or she might have slept until morning. "Hello," she said, picking up the phone.

On the other end Professor Harry Ulmer said, "Hey, it's me, Harry. I've got some news."

"Fire away, Professor," Helen said, now fully awake.

"I've heard the tape and so has the FBI legal team. We both agree that if it isn't illegal— and it probably isn't—then it's at least an ethics violation," Harry said.

"Tell me what that means," Helen said.

"Well, in this state it means that short of a civil suit, which you could bring if you so choose, that Nicholas Blaine would be brought up to a board of his peers to see if he committed an ethics violation," Professor Ulmer said.

"Could he be disbarred?" Helen asked.

"Probably not. But he could be censured and possibly have his license suspended for a period of time," Harry said.

"What do we do next?" Helen asked.

"Nothing. Leave it to the experts. Agent Nelson and other FBI folks will visit Nicholas Blaine in the next day or so, and we'll see how he likes being on tape," Harry said.

"I don't know how to thank you, Professor, really. My career may not be over after all," Helen said.

"Not by a longshot," Professor Ulmer said, "and remember the key element..."

"The key element?" Helen asked.

"Fight fire with fire," Ulmer said as he hung up the phone.

Chapter 8: Warner, Scott, and Dunbar

When she came out of her office to the reception room where I was sitting, I was struck by her beauty and the fact that she looked exactly as her mother did 25 years ago. She was tall, with dark black hair and the darkest blue eyes I'd ever seen. Diane Dunbar had a beautiful smile, one that had captivated me for years. I knew she was 38, had gone through a not-very-friendly divorce with a fellow barrister, and subsequently done well enough to have her name on the door of one of the most prestigious law firms in the city. But that was only part of the story; very importantly, she was my first love. First kiss—first everything else, come to think of it. We went together through high school and college, but she went to London for an advanced degree, while I started as a management trainee for the Galetti brothers. It was just one of those things; it never worked out in the long run, and it took me a long time to get over it.

As she walked toward me in the reception room, I had a weird thought: if she bestowed that same smile on opposing counsel in a courtroom, he might just throw his hands in the air and say, "Let's settle this thing your way." Probably not. As I stood to greet her, she threw her arms around me, brushed my lips with a kiss, and hugged me so hard that we almost fell back in my chair. I was betting the other two people in the waiting room would be sorely disappointed at the reception they received from their respective lawyers after the greeting I had just received. As if she were reading my mind, she turned to the other two people in the waiting room and said, "It's okay, we were an item in high school and college."

One of the two people turned and looked at us and said, "I'd have given a pretty penny to be one of your items in high school," which made everyone in the room laugh.

Diane had her arm wrapped around me as she ushered me back to her office. It was enormous. The room had to be 400 square feet. It had a working area with a beautiful mahogany desk and a matching credenza with three elegant chairs in front of the desk. The other half of the room was similar to a living room, with a loveseat, an antique coffee table, and two wingback chairs that were not only pleasing to the eye, but were built for comfort. Along the far wall was a library of important-looking law books, with a sliding ladder built in so one could reach a volume on the very top shelf. Diane sat me down in a wingback and said, "Watch this." She walked over to the far corner of the bookcase, touched something that I couldn't see, and the bookcase started to move. I said, "Holy mackerel, it's the monster that ate Chicago." About 25 percent of the wall started to rotate, and, as the books disappeared, a wet bar appeared in its place.

"How's that?" Diane asked.

"Pretty darn spectacular," I replied. "But I've got a feeling I'm going to be paying for this kind of extravagant overhead."

"No, no, Russ," Diane said. "You get the clergy discount, and that takes you right down to cost."

I laughed very hard. "Diane, I forgot what a sports fan you are. Not to be chauvinistic, but not many women would quote Al McGuire's clergy discount."

"Hey, I don't read *Time*. I read *SI*," she said. "Some things never change."

"C'mon, catch me up. What are you doing? How's your family?" I asked.

"Let's see, Mom and Dad are well. They both still talk about you. No kidding, you've got some real fans there. I've been single now for six years and very busy and happy. I think my parents worry about me and wish I were happily married, but I think overall they're glad that I'm no longer in a bad marriage. How about you? I know you're married to Holly and that you have two children."

"That's as good a summary as I can think of," I said. "My mother is still going strong. She's sold her business to attend to the eight grandchildren she has. She's very close to Holly, which is another way of saying that, when they get their heads together, I don't have a chance."

Diane smiled and said, "I'm so happy for you, Russ. Really. It proves to me that nice guys don't have to finish last."

"Leo Durocher," I said.

"Yep," she responded. "Want some coffee?"

"Love some," I said. "By the way, I wanted to share something with you. When I first saw you today, I couldn't help remembering back to the first time I saw you with your mom when you were sixteen years old."

"I remember it as if it were yesterday," Diane responded.

"What I thought when I saw you today is that you have turned into your mother. I was so mesmerized by you that I had forgotten until today how beautiful your mom was that day."

"That's so nice of you to say. My dad is always telling me that we are dead ringers for each other," Diane said. "I just wish I had her grace and manners."

"Oh, please," I said. "There's no one from our generation who is as gracious and well-mannered as you are."

"Holly?" Diane asked.

"Okay. But after you two I don't know anyone that comes close. So find something else to beat yourself up over, okay?" I said.

I was really starting to settle in when Diane looked at me and said, "I presume you had a reason for contacting me this afternoon. What can I do for you?"

"I think I've forgotten," I said.

Diane laughed and said, "Yeah, I've got a lot of clients like that. They get very forgetful, especially when they are on the stand."

"What I'm about to tell you hasn't surfaced yet, and I, for one, am not supposed to know about it," I said.

"Sounds mysterious," Diane responded.

"There's about to be a war between the Galetti families over ownership of this chain. All I really know at this point is that Dom's widow, Maria, is bringing suit against her brother-in-law, Joe. Joe is Dom's brother and I'm guessing the battle is over the private stock that was issued to each family."

"Do you know anything more about it?" Diane asked.

"Well, I attended the ceremony many years ago, where the brothers became executors of each other's wills and pledged to take care of each other's families if one should die. Included in that agreement was that they each owned fifty percent of the food chain."

"Okay. I got it. But how do you fit into the picture?"

"Going back to even before I knew you, I worked in the original store for Dom and Joe's dad, Dominic," I said.

"Oh, I remember him. He was a lovely man," Diane remarked.

"He was, indeed. At this ceremony, which was family only, I was invited to attend. Remember, they put me through college, and this became kind of a follow-up deal to that?" I said.

"How so?" Diane asked.

"Well, the original deal was that if they put me through school, I was to work for them for three years after graduation."

"I remember that now that you mention it," Diane said.

"Well, after the ceremony the brothers gave me twenty-five shares of stock out of the original one thousand shares."

"So you, in effect, own two and a half percent of the Galettis' business," Diane said.

"Yes," I said.

"Do you have anything on paper that backs that up?" Diane asked.

"I do," I said as I pulled out the copy of the paperwork that I had received the day after the ceremony.

"Can I make a copy of this?" Diane asked.

"Sure, but make it yourself, will you? I may be a little paranoid, but I want as few people as possible to see it."

"Okay," Diane said. She stood up from the couch and said, "I'll be right back."

Diane walked toward the door, took off her jacket, and hung it on a chair and headed out of the office with my stock certificate. While Diane was out of the room, I drifted back to the day of her wedding to Randy Plummer. Up until that day I always thought there was an outside chance that we would somehow get together. My mother, Claire, and I were heading for the church, and I said, "Ma, you look wonderful. I'm telling you, you've got the body of a thirty-year-old."

"Oh, now hush, Russell. You're embarrassing me," she said.

Secretly, I think she was pleased at my comment. Truthfully, she was in her mid-50s, but she still had a great figure, and she did look like a schoolgirl to me. "I'm not kidding you, Ma, you're going to have to beat the boys off the running board with a stick," I said.

"Where have you been? We haven't had running boards for forty years," she said, laughing.

"It's an image of sorts, Ma," I said. "You know, a metaphor."

"Oh, okay," she said softly. "How are you going to be today?"

"What do you mean?" I asked.

"Well, emotionally, I think this is going to be a little rough. You and Diane were an item for quite a number of years."

I usually shot straight with my mother. "You know I handled it by not handling it all these years. I just tucked it away somewhere and didn't deal with it. But the wedding invitation made me deal with it. Up until that point I thought there was that one chance in two hundred that we would be together at some point. But that one chance disappears today. So I've been dealing with it, and I'll get on with my life."

"Funny," my mother said. "But I think I knew that before you told me. I think it's time to move on, and today marks the day, if you ask me. And, Russell…"

"Yes, Claire?"

"Mother, if you please," she said with a smile.

"Yes, Mother?"

"Don't fall in the punch bowl or make a spectacle of yourself. Hear?"

"I hear," I said solemnly.

We were all in pews at Trinity Church. The mother of the bride had been seated, and the music had started. We all stood, turned to the rear, and there she was—all in white, with her dad beside her. I was on the aisle, so I had an unobstructed view. In a word Diane Dunbar was at her most spectacular. Tall, slim, in a very elegant but not ornate wedding dress, walking down the aisle. When she passed me she was looking straight ahead. I wasn't sure if she even saw me. But her dad saw me, winked at me, and said, "Long time, no see, Bubba." I smiled at him as they passed my aisle, and I imagined I saw a tear in her eye. Tears of happiness, no doubt.

She joined her husband-to-be, Randy Plummer, at the altar. Diane Plummer, Diane Riley, Diane Riley…oh, what might have been. Randy was tall, dark, and, yes, I had to admit, he was handsome. I was looking for a potbelly, maybe balding just slightly, or someone three inches shorter than Diane. Not a chance. He looked great, so I did the next best thing. I rationalized; of course he was drop-dead good-looking, Diane always had good taste in men. The service ended but we made little progress getting out of our aisle. The bride and groom and the remainder of the wedding party had a receiving line going just outside the church. I said to my mother, "Let's sneak out the side door and be first in line at the bar at the reception."

"Don't be a coward," she said, chastising me only slightly. "Stand up and do it right."

"Okay," I laughed. "You're right."

"But, to tell the truth, I could use a drink," my mother said.

It was finally our time. My mother preceeded me and she was wonderful. She schmoozed with the groom's parents, gave Diane a hug and told her that she was the most gorgeous bride she'd ever seen, and then moved on to Diane's parents. I was standing directly in front of Diane Dunbar and said what first came to mind. "Diane, I've never seen a more beautiful bride, and it was a beautiful ceremony."

"Thank you, Russell. Nice of you to come. This is my husband, Randy Plummer."

"Hello, Randy...congratulations on your big day."

"Thanks," he said, not unpleasantly, and I moved to the Dunbars, who gave me a hug.

"I expected I'd see you with the BoSox by now," Mr. Dunbar said.

"You know I could never hit the curve ball," I said.

"Maybe so," he said. "But, man, when you hit it you gave it a ride. See you at the reception?"

"You bet," I said.

The reception was being held in an exclusive club in Waban, so we had a little time to ride together. "How'd that go?" my mother asked.

"Great," I said. "Thanks to you. You were really schmoozing."

"Was it tough being that close to her?" she asked.

"Not really; I just said what I was thinking and moved on," I said. "I had this feeling she was straining to remember my name."

"Oh, nonsense," she said immediately. "Women remember everything a lot better and a lot longer than men; believe me."

The reception was really fun. They had a great band, fabulous food, and the champagne flowed like water. I had a chance to see some people I hadn't seen in years, and they told me some stories from my youth that made me howl with laughter. I think my recall was blunted: I'd started to work at an early age, and, over the years, I mistakenly felt I didn't have a normal, carefree youth. But these people and their stories made me think I was wrong. I may have been working, but they reminded me that it wasn't all work and no play.

I danced with my mother, and I could tell she was having a pretty good time herself. She said to me, "Russell, you're a pretty good dancer. And all these years I thought you had two left feet!"

"How could I have two left feet?" I responded. "You sent me to three years of dancing school. I had to have picked up something."

"I know, I know," she said, laughing. "I always marveled at what a good athlete you were. Fast, light on your feet…but somehow I had this vision that it didn't translate to the dance floor."

Just at that moment the bride and groom tapped us on the shoulder, and I found myself holding Diane as Randy danced off with my mother. I'd had a few glasses of champagne. I wasn't drunk, but uninhibited might have fit how I was feeling. I looked into Diane's eyes and said, "It's been a long time since I've been this close to you. I think I might get a case of the flop sweats."

"You mean like a comedian who is telling jokes and nobody is laughing," she said, smiling that all-world smile.

"Exactly," I said.

"I've thought about you a lot, Russell," she said as she buried her face in my shoulder. "Have you thought about me?"

"Not really," I responded, "up until I got the notice of this shindig. It was just too painful."

"Oh, Russell, that's terrible. I'm sorry," she said.

"Hey, it's okay. Storybook endings are mostly fiction."

"You don't know how many times I wanted to call you. That breakup was my doing. I just wanted to be with other men."

"How did that turn out?" I asked.

"Not great," she replied. "You were my first love, but by then you were gone with your own agenda, and the bond was broken. For the record, I never got over you, but, to this day, I didn't think you had the ambition to take me where I wanted to go. You were the hometown honey, the convenient local yokel that I took for granted."

Diane's words stung me deeply, but I tried to stay calm and unruffled. "Thank you for your honesty; that was always a strength of yours. It may have taken you a while, but I think you've found a terrific guy in Randy Plummer."

"I hope so. It's always a crapshoot, but Randy is kind, caring, and totally devoted," she said.

I wanted to say that Randy sounded more like man's best friend, but I bit my tongue. "Well, I wish you the best, Diane," I said.

Diane kissed me on the cheek and walked off the dance floor. My last thought as she walked away was, *You poor bastard, Plummer.* I thought my first love walked on water, but it turns out she was in the water all the time with the other barracudas.

So strange. In business I was always thinking, taking action, anticipating how a certain scenario would play out, and stirring the pot. In my love life I didn't even know when or where Diane started to slip away from me. Completely clueless.

We rode home after the reception, and I think my mother knew that her middle child was reflecting on what might have been. I think she was surprised when I told her that human interaction sometimes takes funny bounces. In the end I think she was just glad that I hadn't fallen in the punch bowl...

Diane returned with a copy of the stock certificate and gave me back the original. I snapped back to the present.

"A couple of more questions," Diane said.

"Okay," I responded.

"Do you have an idea what this is worth?" she asked.

"Not really. But we do well over a billion dollars a year in volume."

"Holy shit...pardon my French, Russ, but this piece of paper could be worth twenty-five million dollars," Diane said.

"I don't think I can count that high, but yeah, something like that, and I'm qualified to collect it."

"Why don't you know about this officially?"

"Joe Galetti, the CEO, hasn't told me. I'm the president and COO, but almost a week has gone by, and he hasn't said a word to me."

"How did you find out about it?"

"Trip told me about it, and I overheard Maria and Joe talking about it in his office."

"Okay. I wouldn't be that surprised at Joe's behavior at this point. My guess is that he is lining up his legal defense before he tells anyone anything. Secondly, he really can't call a board of directors meeting to hash out strategy since his nephew is on the board. Here's something else you may not have thought of that could be critical down the road," Diane said as she got up and started to pace. "You could be holding the swing vote on these shares. If Joe has, indeed, usurped shares illegally and a jury orders them returned to the plaintiff, you could be in a shootout, in which your shares become pivotal."

It was my turn to say, "Holy shit. I don't want to have to play Solomon's sword with a billion dollars riding on the line. You're liable to find my remains in a New Jersey landfill next to Jimmy Hoffa."

"Are you telling me this family is connected to the mafia?" Diane asked.

"Absolutely not. But do you know how much juice Joe Galetti has in Massachusetts and Rhode Island?" I asked.

"No, but it doesn't matter if a jury convicts him," Diane said matter-of-factly. "Anything else I should know?" she asked.

"Uh-uh, I'm just a working stiff with a twenty-five-million-dollar profit sharing program," I said.

Diane laughed out loud. "You're such an idiot. Did you have any idea fifteen or twenty years ago that you would be this successful? I mean, I know you loved your work, but did you even have a clue?"

"Absolutely clueless," I admitted. "And I'll tell you something else for your information only. If the whole twenty-five million goes up in smoke, we'll still be in pretty darn good shape. Holly has invested wisely—not only for us, but the kids too. So, it's not a case of me looking for my next square meal. What really worries me is where the chain will end up after this is all over. I've been working for them for the better part of twenty-five years, and I feel privileged to have known the founder personally."

Diane hesitated before she spoke and then she said, "You're right. These kinds of things can tear the heart out of a business, Russ. And what's worse is there's nothing like a family fight. I swore I would never take divorce cases after what I went through personally. But these kinds of scraps have the same vicious acrimony as a divorce. In fact, it is a divorce of sorts—a family divorce."

"Okay, counselor. What do I do next?"

"Nothing. Stick to your knitting and play Mickey the Dunce," Diane said.

"I was tailor-made for that role," I said with a smile. "That reminds me, Diane, how did I do for a hometown honey, the convenient local yokel?"

Diane's face colored crimson and I knew she understood the reference from her reception on the dance floor. She hesitated before answering. "Well, you're no dunce, that's for sure. And, through hard work and determination, you've risen quickly in the Galetti Supermarket chain, but…"

"No time to be pulling punches now, Diane," I said.

"Well, the question becomes, what would have become of you if you'd chosen this same career with a market leader, a real chain?" Diane asked.

"One billion dollars doesn't meet the requirement of a real chain?" I asked.

"You know what I mean," Diane said. "I'm not denigrating your accomplishments, but Galetti doesn't have the corporate presence of, say, a Stop & Shop."

"I see your point. Galetti is the local yokel," I said. "After this conversation I'm glad to have such a tough-minded person as my lawyer."

"Think of it this way, Russ; if you and I had married, you might never have met Holly. What do you think about that?"

"I'll take the fifth, counselor."

"Okay. Get the hell out of here, will you? I've got paying customers to attend to," Diane said.

As I started to drive back to the office, I decided to change my destination. Time to go home. My thoughts drifted back to Diane and the session that just concluded. I was comfortable with her, and I felt she would do a good job of representing me. It made me realize, at the same time, that I was so fortunate to have found Holly, the love of my life. Holly would not be happy with my choice of lawyers, but somehow I needed to convince her that it was strictly business… not monkey business.

Chapter 9: Holly Lansing

I knew seeking legal counsel was a good idea, but it wasn't until after my chat with Diane Dunbar that I started to ponder what was at stake. I'd been connected to the Galetti family most of my life. They paid my way through college, offered me an opportunity to work full-time, and had given me ownership in a corporation that had grown from one store to 58 stores. I had started working for them at the outrageous wage of $6850 a year and had a six-cylinder Comet with no radio and no air-conditioner as a company car. In a relatively short period of time, I'd risen to president of the company, made $250,000 a year, and drove a Mercedes. And in my heart of hearts, I knew it paid off for me in a way that wouldn't have been possible in a big company such as Stop & Shop. I was appointed to the board of directors at a very early age, dealt directly with ownership every day, and prospered in direct proportion to the growth of our organization.

I'd seen enough of the other side of the mountain to know that I would never have moved up the ladder or been given the opportunity to succeed or fall on my face as I had with the Galetti Corporation. My mind drifted back to a situation that transpired between A&P and Galetti, where Joe and Dom sent me to A&P to meet their vice president of merchandising, Arnold Cable, at their very imposing New York headquarters. I was one year removed from Boston University at the time.

Joe Galetti had called me into his office, pulling his glasses down over his nose while looking at some very official papers. "I need you to go to New York City tomorrow, the Graybar Building, to call on A&P headquarters for me."

"Okay. What are we selling?" I said with a smile on my face.

"Peace of mind," he said. "You'll be accompanied by two of our lawyers."

"Glad to, but if this is about what I think it's about, shouldn't you or Dom be there?"

"Ordinarily, yes…but there's some gamesmanship going on, and we need to play the game. We have contacted them about possible restraint of trade. They have chosen to answer us by having their legal staff and a fairly low-ranking executive meet with us."

"Ahh, I get it. You're going to match their low-ranking official with a low-ranking official of your own…me."

Joe actually laughed and said, "See, kid, that's why you own stock in this company. We give it to you with the bark off around here because we know you're too bright to go for a BS story."

"Thank you, Joe. That's frankly what I've always liked about you guys. Being subtle just isn't our strength, and I'm happy about that. How should I be thinking about this call?"

"Let the lawyers do all the talking," Joe advised me. "All I want you to take with you is that price comparison of the top items that shows A&P selling those best sellers ten to fifteen cents below cost. If the opportunity arises, you may want to leave it with your counterpart."

"Got it," I said. "Otherwise, I play the young hick from a small chain who doesn't really know a lot."

"Yeah," Joe said. "And I'll tell you something else."

"What?" I asked.

"You won't have to stretch to play that role," he said with an ear-to-ear grin.

"Thanks for the confidence in me, Joe," I said sarcastically. "And I'll tell you something else."

"What?" he asked.

"You're smiling too much. I'm worried that you're losing your edge!"

"Don't worry…it's only a facade," Joe said. "Good luck tomorrow."

"Thanks," I said as I got up to leave the office.

I went back to the office and pulled together my pricing comparisons for the next day. As I was driving home that night, my mind was racing, trying to figure out how the next day would develop at A&P headquarters. When I arrived home I told my mother about my call on A&P in the big city the next day. The first thing she said was, "Get that shoe brush out, and shine those shoes while I iron up your best shirt." We had everything laid out the night before, and, by 5:45 a.m., I was on my way to Logan to take the Eastern Air Shuttle to Manhattan. At the airport I met the lawyers for our side—both in their early 40s and very conservatively dressed. One of them— Harry Doyle— came right out and said what the other—Dick Piper—was thinking. "You're Russell Riley?"

"I am," I said. "You were expecting someone a little older?"

"Well…yeah, to be honest," Dick Piper said.

"I'm your ace in the hole, actually."

"How's that?" Harry asked somewhat dubiously.

"My understanding is that they are sending a junior executive to this meeting that will signal their lack of concern over this whole matter."

"So," Dick said.

"So we trump them. I'm not only junior, but it appears that I don't shave yet."

Both lawyers laughed at that, and Harry said, as we were climbing the stairs to the plane, "You just might have something there, Russell."

The two lawyers huddled all the way to LaGuardia, while I looked out the window. I'd been on a plane once before, but it was a thrill for me. The pilot told us we were going to West Point and hang a left—and that's just about what we did. Coming in and seeing the skyline of Manhattan and flying low over a bay to land on a dock that extended out into the water was a thrill of a lifetime for me. People kid about the "blackboard jungle" that is Manhattan, but the beauty of the skyscrapers and the fact that eight million people were scrambling around on this tiny island was mind-boggling. As we exited the plane, Dick Piper said to me, "Now, Russ, our job is to do the talking, so if you could, please don't feel free to join in."

"Is this how you treat all your customers?" I asked.

"Only the ones we like," Dick said.

"Okay, I'll be quiet as a mouse."

The cab from the airport took about 40 minutes in traffic, and I swear that my fanny left the backseat four times as the cab, traveling at a very brisk speed, hit the most formidable potholes I'd ever seen. One thing was consistent, though. Every time we hit one, the cabbie would yell, "Fuck." Seven "fucks" later we were standing in front of A&P headquarters, glad to still be in one piece.

We made our way through security and to the seventh floor, where Dick Piper gave the receptionist his card and told her that we had an appointment with Arnold Cable at nine o'clock. We were ushered into Mr. Cable's office, where he made the introduction of but one lawyer, Harold Cranston, for A&P.

"I'm sorry to have made you wait, but we had a little emergency up here," offered Arnold Cable.

"Oh, that's quite all right; we understand completely," said Harry Doyle.

Cable then looked at me and said, "Russ, you look like you're fresh out of school."

"Yes, sir, I just graduated from Boston University last year, and, as a matter of fact, I'm thinking about going back to graduate school."

"Oh, to study what?" Arnold Cable asked.

"Price fixing," I said, looking directly at Arnold Cable. I could see Dick Piper, sitting to my left, turn white as a ghost as a silence dominated the room.

Cable looked at me, threw his hands up in the air, and burst out laughing. "Touché, Mr. Riley. I usually never underestimate an adversary, but I might have this time...I apologize very sincerely. How about coffee before we get started?"

"Sounds great to me," I said.

The lawyers went back and forth for about an hour, talking about FTC compliance, the Robinson-Patman Act, and restraint of trade. Both Cable and

I were trying to look interested, but when lawyers lock horns with lawyers, they seem to have a language all their own, and, frankly, to the layman, it's almost incomprehensible. At one point during the proceedings, Dick Piper looked at me and said, "Russ has an exhibit that he'd like to share with you."

I opened my briefcase and handed Arnold Cable and the A&P lawyer, Harold Cranston, a single piece of paper. I also gave a copy to Dick and Harry. I gave them a second to glance at it and then said, "This is a retail price comparison of fifteen items at A&P and at our chain. I also included a chain B and a chain C, who also compete in this marketing area. For your personal information, chain B is Stop & Shop, and chain C is First National Stores. Simply put, A&P is ten to fifteen cents below cost on each of these items and, subsequently, anywhere from fifteen to thirty-five cents below the three other competing chains on every item."

"So what?" Arnold said.

"That's what I said too, Arnold, until I talked with one of your store managers in this area." I saw Harold Cranston move in his chair when I mentioned this.

"And?" Arnold asked.

"He told me that New England was a very competitive area to sell groceries, and because you were a national chain, you could borrow money from less competitive areas—he mentioned Detroit and Chicago specifically—to subsidize retails in New England."

"Preposterous," barked Arnold Cable. "We've got five thousand stores across the country, and you think we're trying to run an eight-store chain out of business?"

"It does have a David and Goliath look to it, doesn't it, Arnold?" Dick Piper asked.

"Well, chains B and C have about five hundred stores combined, so that evens the odds a little...about ten to one if I did the math right," Harry Doyle added.

"What do you propose to do with this circumstantial evidence?" Harry Cranston asked in a very offhand way.

"We really don't know," said Dick Piper. "But we thought we'd come to you first. We were not anxious to spend a lot of time and money with the FTC and the courts...but I want to make one thing very clear: we will if we believe the playing field is not level."

Arnold looked at the three of us, stood, extended his hand, and said, "Thank you for coming down, gentlemen. We'll be back to you in a timely manner with this issue."

We were exiting the office when Arnold called me back inside. He walked from behind his desk and said to me, "Tell the Galetti brothers to expect some price changes in your marketing area shortly."

"Will do, thanks for your time, Arnold," I said.

"And Russ..." he said.

"Yes, sir," I said.

"If you're ever in New York City, give me a call, and I'll buy you lunch."

"Thank you again. I'll look forward to it," I said as I left his office.

As we stepped out on the sidewalk in Manhattan, Dick waved down a cab, and we all piled into it. "What was all that about?" Harry asked me.

I said, "You guys must have been pretty effective, because Arnold told me to tell Dom and Joe to expect some price changes in our marketing area shortly."

"Are you kidding?" Dick Piper asked.

"I kid you not...that's almost exactly what he said," I replied.

"Holy mackerel...that's great," inserted Harry. "You know, I expected this to be just a preliminary dance of the whooping cranes. A feeling-out process if you will."

"Something got to them," Dick said. "A vicelike grip on Arnold's balls if you ask me."

We all laughed at Dick's remark as he continued. "Russ, you could do me one favor in the future if you would."

"Okay, if I can," I said.

"Lob up a softball when you initiate a conversation with a chain that could squash us like a bug next time."

"Whatever do you mean?" I asked, smiling at Dick.

"Well, I almost had a heart attack when you told Arnold Cable you were going to get your graduate degree in price fixing."

Both Harry and I laughed hard at Dick's comment, and I said, "I promise I'll do that, Dick. I just wanted to see if Arnold was really listening."

"And...?" Harry asked, looking at me.

"I'd say he was," I said.

We grabbed a hot dog at the airport, and before we knew it, we were back in Boston and headed for the parking lot. As we were parting Dick looked at me and said, "Thanks for coming. I really enjoyed meeting you."

"Same here," I said as we all headed for the Sumner Tunnel.

As I rode home that night, I thought about the A&P call in New York City. I wasn't a lawyer, but I thought our case was pretty thin. But I was beginning to see what Arnold Cable and A&P might be thinking. Even the hint of impropriety could turn the FTC loose, sorting through the A&P financial records, and that was something I was guessing that this national chain would like to avoid. And if we didn't have substance to our case, we would curry favorable public opinion, as we were a little eight-store chain being mauled by one that had five thousand stores across the country.

Sure enough, as Arnold had told me at the A&P headquarters, the giant chain moved its prices up on those key items that previously were 10 to 15 cents below cost. As this happened I reported it back to the Galetti brothers, and, within 60 days, our sagging volume in those three stores started to improve. We took the liberty—because the supermarket industry is perverse by nature—to take our prices down on those items to about where A&P had them before we made our call in New York City. We were swimming in a sea of red ink on those items, but overall store volume was improving, and the Galetti brothers felt that once they had a customer in their store, they would come back because of superior produce and meat departments. But it made me laugh to myself. We were adhering to the old supermarket mantra of selling items below cost and telling ourselves that we'd make it up in volume! In an industry that averages a net profit of one penny for every dollar that goes through the register, this could be a suicidal strategy.

I would have never had that opportunity to jaw with Arnold Cable representing another large chain, but at the time we had four people on the board of directors of the Galetti Corporation, and I was one of the four. As it turned out, some years later, Arnold Cable wanted to come back to his roots in Rhode Island, and so he was currently working for me as our operation manager. He was a great hire. I only had two people I trusted outside the family that I'd talk to before making a decision. If it had to do with suppliers, I'd call in Bill Hartman from Procter & Gamble, and if it had to do with our side of the business, the first person I hunted down was Arnold Cable.

But my talk with Diane Dunbar had made me realize that this impending court fight could pretty quickly escalate to the point where one side or the other would determine that my services were no longer needed. The safest bet was to stick with Joe Galetti, because, on the surface, he would seem to be holding most of the face cards. But on the other hand, I had a strong allegiance to Maria, Trip, and her deceased husband, Dom. It was weird in a perverse way. I was pretty sure that Trip wanted to ask if there was ever anything going on between his mother and me, but he never quite got up the nerve to come out with it.

If that was all there was to this puzzle, I'd be fairly overwhelmed, but there was one other very formidable obstacle. Holly Lansing. She'd be extremely unhappy with my choice of lawyers, and with her penetrating mind, I knew she'd ask a lot of questions, all of them difficult to answer.

I had met Holly Lansing at a trade function, and for the first time since Diane Dunbar, I found myself thinking about her when my mind wandered to no particular subject. She worked in Boston at a large mutual fund company, and her area of expertise was the supermarket industry. She had brown hair cut short, with red highlights, and she was tall and thin and quite beautiful. But that wasn't what drew me to her. It was her manner; she had her own beat, slower than most of us in the Northeast. When I asked her a question, she considered it, turned it over in her mind, and often gave very thoughtful responses. She had her own tempo, cruising through life, unlike the frantic "pedal to the metal" people in my part of the United States. I asked her if I could call her when we first met, and she considered it for a moment and said no. I was too shocked to mumble anything except "okay" and we parted company.

It really wasn't ego, because I had been turned down before, but more a case of persistence. We in the grocery trade are nothing if not tenacious.

I called Holly at work, and she picked up her own phone and said, "Holly Lansing, how can I help you?"

I said, "I'd like to place an order for anything you are unable to peddle today."

"Oh, I'm sorry," she replied. "You want…who is this?" she said, suspecting a prank.

"It's Russell Riley, the guy you unceremoniously kissed off the other night at the Massachusetts Food Association dinner."

She laughed and said, "I didn't mean to hurt your feelings. Did I bruise your ego?"

"Right on target—I have terminal hurt feelings and a wounded ego," I said. "But you know, I thought you were worth the potential of a second turn-down. I've geared myself for rejection."

"What did you have in mind?" she asked.

"Dinner by candlelight," I said.

"Okay," she said.

"How about Saturday night at 7 p.m.," I said.

"It's a deal. Let me give you directions."

See, that wasn't so tough, I told myself.

Saturday night arrived and I hated to admit it, but I was nervous about this date with Holly Lansing.

I arrived at her apartment in the Back Bay right on time, and she greeted me at the door with a peck on the cheek and a big smile. She looked so elegant in a short-sleeved white tunic and a very simple light-blue skirt that ended just below her knees. She was thin but not angular, soft, and she was totally at ease with the way she appeared. She was really quite exquisite, but I guessed that she didn't spend hours making herself beautiful. My thought was that she'd look pretty good in just about anything, including a barrel going over Niagara Falls.

When she opened the door to her apartment, she said, "Hi. You are a very persistent man, Russell Riley, and I'm very glad you are the tenacious type."

That comment just made me feel so good. I said, "Some things are just worth pursuing, and, as one of my sales friends says, 'No is just a request for more information.'"

She laughed at that and said, "I was very flattered, actually, that you tried to pick me up at an industry function, but I needed to know if you had any 'stick-to-iveness' to your line of blarney. How about a glass of wine?"

"That would be fine unless you have a beer," I said.

"I've got one with your name on it," she replied. I sat down in her living room, while she went to the kitchen. I almost never notice what's in a room, but this room was so elegant, it was hard not to notice. It was done in a light, almost powder blue wallpaper, and she had some truly beautiful antiques, including the most beautiful blanket chest I'd ever seen. Fortunately, though, the couch was not one of those hardscrabble turn-of-the-century models that is too low to the ground, with seating that makes me think I am really sitting on plywood instead of a cushion. This couch I was sitting on was elegant but very comfortable. There was a huge oil painting of an ancestor on the wall and it fascinated me. As I moved around the living room, the eyes of the man in the portrait seemed to follow me.

Holly came in with her wine and my beer and said, "What are you doing?"

"I was fascinated by your portrait...wherever I move, his eyes seem to follow me," I said.

"That's my great-grandfather, Ethan, and he had the reputation of being a pretty tough bird."

Holly handed me my beer, and we clinked glasses as she sat down next to me. "I wonder if Ethan thought he could produce such a beautiful great-granddaughter," I said.

"Thank you, but looks can be deceiving," she said.

"What do you mean?" I asked.

"I'm in a pretty tough business, where you can't afford to have a thin skin and not many women compete."

"Same problem in our industry," I said. "Are you difficult to deal with at work?"

Holly smiled and said, "No, but I'm quietly tough, have a lot of confidence, and I've had some success to date."

"What do you do?"

"I'm an analyst for a large mutual fund company. One of my areas of expertise is the food industry."

"Do you like it?" I asked.

"Love it," she said.

"That's all I need to know," I said. "You're already ahead of about ninety percent of workers who trudge off to work every day but really don't like what they are doing."

"Totally agree," she said, "but it hasn't been great for my personal life particularly."

"Why's that?" I asked.

"Well, I think I scare people off a little," she said, sipping from her wineglass. "I think men think women should be teachers, nurses, or stay at home. Anything else seems threatening to them."

"We're about to have our first disagreement, I think," I said. I told Holly about my mother and also about Maria's contribution to our business. I was amazed that I was even on this subject. I was talking to Holly as if I'd known her all my life. She was a wonderful listener—probably a trait that helped her in her job—but at the same time, I was hoping I wasn't boring her with my views on the working world.

I thought her next comment was not only insightful, but it proved that she was indeed a good listener. She said, "But, Russell, you have to remember that you've achieved a position in the world where you can be a little more generous with your views of women at work. Some people work all their lives and don't reach the stage of management that you've reached already."

"I suppose," I said slowly, "but, you know, one of my two bosses is a woman, and my other role model is my mother, who became the breadwinner when my dad died at an early age."

"Touché," she said. "I didn't mean to disparage your point of view. Frankly, I haven't even met your mother, and she's become one of my heroes too."

"No offense taken. We've had our first scrap, and we're both still standing!" I said.

She laughed heartily and said, "Hey, let's talk about something really important; where are we going to eat?"

"Aha…so this is how I make points with you. Finding a good place to eat is critical, is it?"

"Absolutely," she replied.

"I was thinking about Anthony's Pier 4. It's a tourist trap but I think the food is excellent."

We stood up, took our glasses to the kitchen, and we were on our way to dinner.

Dinner was not disappointing. We had a table for two by the water, and there never was an uncomfortable silence. In fact, we were a little perturbed that the waiter interrupted us three times to ask how our meal was. I wanted to tell him, "It was great but now go away, will you? Can't you see I'm busy?"

She asked me at one point, "Russell, I hope you don't think of me as too nosy, but why aren't you married by now?"

"Not at all…you've got a beautiful nose," I replied.

"Is that some kind of line?" she asked.

"Probably, but a pretty poor one, I think," I said.

"Pathetic would be a more apt description," she said.

"Go ahead. C'mon, don't hold back; tell me what you really think," I said.

We both laughed. "Sorry, I could have been kinder upon reflection," she said.

I told her about Diane Dunbar from beginning to end to include the wedding.

She really seemed to enjoy the story. When I was finished she said, "What a wonderful, poignant story. A lot of guys wouldn't tell that story because they came in second in a two-horse race. Diane sounds lovely but the woman has no J."

"J?" I asked.

"Judgment," Holly said.

"Well, thank you, ma'am. I very much appreciate that comment."

"You're welcome," she said. "Geez, I feel badly that I don't have a similar tale to tell you."

"Believe me, you didn't miss anything. It took me a long time to get over it," I said.

"Let's see," Holly said, smiling, "you could always marry the boss."

I was shocked at this comment. "It's crossed my mind," I said.

"I know," she said.

"How? I'm beginning to believe in your powers as an analyst...over and above the equity market."

"If I told you that, you'd know all my secrets," she said.

"Would that be so bad?" I asked.

"Sure. Don't you want your women to be somewhat mysterious?"

"Are you one of my women?" I asked.

"I hope so," she said.

"Has a nice ring to it," I said.

Before I knew it we were walking down the sidewalk back to her apartment. At the door she turned and kissed me. This was no peck on the cheek. This was a long, wonderful kiss, and, as we parted, I said, "Holly Lansing, you are a wonderful kisser."

"You're not so bad yourself," she said as she waved and slid behind her door and disappeared. I walked down the steps and back to my car, not really knowing how I got there. I was too heavy to float, but my step was definitely lighter.

I arrived at my apartment about a half an hour later, and, as I walked into the front hall, my phone was ringing. I picked it up, thinking, *Who would be calling me at this hour?* and a voice said, "I wish you had huffed and puffed and blown my door down."

I laughed and said, "I wasn't up to the task. I was so weak, I don't think I could have climbed a flight of stairs."

"Have you recovered enough to climb some stairs now?" she asked. "Be here in thirty minutes, and, Russ..."

"Yes?" I asked.

"Bring your toothbrush."

"Yes, ma'am."

* * *

The next day at work, I couldn't do anything. I was daydreaming like a kid in school staring out a window. Fortunately for me, I was sitting in with the buying department as they heard new item presentations from the sales representatives. I was trying to listen to the presentations, but my mind kept drifting to Holly Lansing. She was different. Aggressive, successful in a man's world, articulate, and beautiful. But last night at her apartment, she wasn't wildly passionate—she was warm, sensitive, loving, not in a hurry. She didn't want to lead; she wanted me to feel pleasure, she was unselfish, and we just surrendered to each other in a warm embrace at the end and fell asleep.

Holly was bright, beautiful, perceptive, and very successful in a business that sounded as rough as the food industry. But she didn't have a rough edge to her. She was gentle, thoughtful, slow to react to a question. But her answer usually reflected her considerable mental acumen. What I am trying to say is that she was a lady in a very unladylike industry. In one date she had learned about Diane, Maria, and Claire Riley. On our third date I asked Holly to marry me. My heart was in my throat—perhaps I was rushing her, but she made me feel a whole lot better by saying she almost asked me to marry her on our second date.

We spent that night wrapped in each other's arms, and I was hoping the sun would forget to rise. It was time. I was 32 years old, and maybe I was a little slower than the rest, but the wait had been worth it. Holly Lansing had brought joy and peace to my world. I just felt as if the last piece of the puzzle had fallen into the proper slot. I called Claire from work the next day and said, "Ma, I'm going to finally do it."

"You are not," she said.

"I am," I replied.

"Holly said yes?" Claire asked.

"She did," I said.

"Well, I have something for you to celebrate this most grand occasion."

"What is it?" I asked.

"Your grandmother's engagement ring," she said. "I'd kind of given up hope, but it's in my jewelry box, waiting for you to claim it."

"That's super. It happens I have a need for just such a bauble."

"How did I know?" she asked, laughing.

"Yeah, how did you know?" I asked.

"Lucky guess," my mother said.

"I'll be over," I said.

"Anytime," my mother said as she hung up.

The next day I took off for my mother's house to collect the ring. She had it ready for me, and I said, "I hate to grab the ring and run, Claire, but I need to make a delivery."

"Come see your old mother when you have more time, Russell," Claire said.

"Will do," I said, feeling a slight twinge of guilt.

I picked up Holly at work and took her to the place of our first date, Pier 4. We covered the events of the day, but the focus turned to our parents pretty quickly.

"What did Claire say?" Holly asked brightly.

"'Thank God, it's about time, what will I wear, and Holly is a lovely girl,'" I responded.

"In that order?" Holly asked, smiling.

"Yep," I said. "But that's pretty good billing, actually…right behind 'What will I wear.'

"How about your parents?" I asked.

"Let's see, I haven't talked to Dad directly, but Mom said, 'What do we know about him, do you love him, oh dear, isn't Riley a Catholic name, what will I wear, and I'm very happy for you, dear.'"

"And do you?" I asked.

"Do I what?" she asked.

"Love him," I said.

"With all my heart," she said.

"The nicest thing I've ever heard. And here's something to seal the deal," I said as I put the ring on the table.

"Oh, it's beautiful, Russell," Holly said.

"Well, it was my grandmother's, and Claire was pretty sure it would never be used," I said.

Holly slipped it on her finger and it fit perfectly. "I love it, Russ," she said.

"I'm glad because I love you," I responded. "If it isn't what you want and you change your mind, we'll get something else."

"I won't change my mind," she said.

We finished dinner and I drove Holly home. We talked about the wedding. When we had kicked it around for a while, we knew we had a difficult sale to make. We were going to have a small family wedding, and we knew that would not be a popular decision.

* * *

That had been six years ago. Since that time, we'd had two children and moved to a comfortable four-bedroom house in Sudbury. We missed our apartment in the Back Bay, but when Holly became pregnant with our first child, I suspect we did what a lot of folks do—moved to the suburbs. Sudbury was a wonderful old New England town. Twenty miles to the west of the big city, 5000 population, and it still had a general store and an old-fashioned post office that hadn't changed a lick since the turn of the century. A feeling of calm tranquility fell over me whenever I turned into the driveway of our house after a busy day at work. And it was no different today in spite of all the things that were on my mind. The house was white, with dark-green shutters, and it was situated on a hill about a hundred yards from the road. It had the look of a colonial, but it was a little lower and a little longer than a typical colonial. There was a two-car garage to the left and off of that was a stable that I had converted into a workshop. The house came with seven and a half acres. I was sure in the almost five years that we'd been there that we had not walked all of the acreage. It was a great comfort to me that a housing development was not going to spring up anywhere near the house.

Holly adjusted to the suburbs immediately, but I was a little slower in making the transition. She had given up her job with the idea that, when our youngest reached first grade, she might want to work again, at least until the kids came home from school. She was a full-time mom and a part-time financial advisor to our family. She had immediately opened four Merrill Lynch CMA accounts, and she had purchased shares of Microsoft for us, which was then a small software company on the West Coast. In addition, she took over Claire's portfolio, and she must have done a pretty good job with that as well, because Claire couldn't stop talking about it and "what a woman of means" she'd become since hooking up with Holly. She had also become portfolio manager for a local bank, and while Savings and Loans were declaring bankruptcy all around us, her bank was in the pink—not to be confused with the red! It was comical because Holly's rank among the local banks was near the bottom because her dividend return was low. What the other banks couldn't see was that Holly's stocks were appreciating at an astronomical rate. The president of the bank told me one day that Holly had 6 percent of the bank's assets, but she produced 39 percent of their profit. I knew Bill Hartman would love that story because that was almost the exact story in terms of percentages that he revealed to me, way back when, about the contribution of health and beauty aids to total store volume and profit. As a result, Holly was placed on the board of directors at the local bank, and they paid her 25 dollars a meeting. In the pay-for-service-rendered category this had to be one of the best deals since the Indians sold us Manhattan. I marveled at her capacity. She could play with her friends, take care of the children, fix a gutter, keep a bank solvent, and provide financial expertise to my mother while reading two books a week and attending to me. For some reason I always remember what Claire told me just before the wedding about treating Holly right or else. I wasn't sure what the "else" was, but I tried to tell her as frequently as I could how much she meant to me and how much I loved her.

I pulled into the garage, burst in the front door, and gave Holly an extra strong hug and kiss and said, "You'll never guess who I saw today."

"Animal, mineral, living, or dead?" Holly asked.

"Babe," was my one-word answer.

"Diane Dunbar," Holly responded.

"Give that woman a chocolate-covered cigar," I said.

"Ugh, give me the second prize, whatever it is," Holly said. "Ran into her how and how hard?"

"Let's not go there," I said with a smile, "business, strictly business. Hey, where are the kids?"

"Claire has them for a sleepover, and they are being spoiled rotten."

"No doubt," I said. "Big doings at work, which, by the way, I don't officially know about yet, so if anybody should call you about it, you know nuttin', okay?"

"Okay. While you're unraveling this soap opera, go get out of that suit and get into something more comfortable that I can get off you very quickly if the need arises," Holly said.

I spun around and faced Holly, taking her in from head to toe, and totally lost my train of thought. She was in a very flimsy, transparent dress that showed off every wonderful curve, and she was laughing because she knew that I had been in the house for five minutes and didn't realize my wife was as close as you could be to being naked while still having a piece of apparel clinging to her body. I said, "Holly, you are the most amazing woman on this

Earth. God, you are so gorgeous and such a great person. I can't believe you married me. After all these years I'm more in love with you than ever."

"I know," she said as she moved into my arms and kissed me. It was a long, passionate kiss, and my clothes were being discarded as fast as two sets of hands could remove them. We were headed for the bedroom, but we never made it. We made love on the floor in the den, with the windows and the curtains wide open, hoping that no neighbors were crossing the back lawn, looking for the ubiquitous cup of sugar. When we were totally spent, Holly rolled off me and said, "I hope the adoption agency doesn't call."

"Our kids aren't adopted."

"Ohh, that's a relief," she said. "Well, I suppose we ought to get cleaned up in case Claire stops by with the kids after making an ice cream run."

"Good idea," I said. "How about a glass of wine?"

"Good idea," Holly said, "but first get some clothes on."

"I thought you liked this outfit," I said.

"I do. But I don't want to share it with the neighbors," Holly responded.

Later, when we were sitting at the dinner table, Holly said, "Ahh, yes, where were we when we were so delightfully interrupted with sex in the den?"

"Diane Dunbar," I replied.

"Right, now the rest of the story…" she said.

"Well, there's about to be a fight for control between Maria and Joe Galetti," I said.

"If you're not supposed to know about it, how did you find out about it?" she asked.

"Trip told me but Joe hasn't said a word to me about it," I explained.

"Man, this could get nasty before it's over. Maria strikes me as someone I wouldn't want to tangle with, and, frankly, I think Joe is the ultimate barracuda."

"Good summary…and I've got a twenty-five-million-dollar stake in this, so I think you could describe me as a more than uninterested spectator," I said.

"So you went to see Ms. Dunbar," Holly said.

"Yeah, I'm pretty naive about these things, but I figured I'd better be represented by legal counsel," I said.

"Sure," Holly said. "But here's the important question."

"Yes," I said.

"How did she look?" Holly asked as her eyebrows raised to their uppermost limits.

"Old, fat, bags under eyes, bags in her hands, bags all around her. In other words, like a bag lady," I said.

"Russ…" Holly said.

"Okay. Gorgeous…but, for the record, she can't hold a candle to you," I said.

"Right answer," Holly said with a smile. "Are you worried?" she asked.

"Not really, at least officially, since I'm not supposed to know anything. But there's no good time for this kind of a mess. The company is gushing money. I'm not kidding, we're a geyser of profit, but this could freeze us in our tracks."

"I think I'm following your oil and frozen tundra metaphors, but what about your employment?" Holly asked.

"Nothing to worry about in the short term. I've had several good job offers, but I can't exactly say to my new employer, 'Listen, that's a great offer, but it's about twenty-five million dollars short.'"

"That would be a little awkward," Holly said.

"Holly, are you really okay with Diane Dunbar as my lawyer?"

"I'd be lying if I said I was totally all right with it," Holly said. "But I love you, I know she's good, and the stakes are pretty high. But she's divorced, attractive, high-profile, and I'm guessing she still has a thing for you. But in life you have to take some risks, and I'm betting you'll keep things on the up-and-up. Plus, you know what Claire will do to you if you go astray, and, believe me, that'll be nothing compared to what I'm going to do to you in that case."

"Thanks for the vote of confidence…I think. Rest assured your faith in me will be rewarded," I said.

Chapter 10: Let the Games Begin

The next morning I was in my office when Joe walked in without a word and closed my door. Among my unreturned phone messages was one from Maria, so I knew things were about to heat up. He didn't take long in getting to the point. "Listen, Russ, this place is about to be turned upside down internally, and I want you to know about it before you hear about it from someone else. Maria is suing the company, specifically me, in an attempt to gain majority ownership."

"Jesus, Joe, I can't believe you guys would go to court against each other," I said, trying my best to be surprised by the news. "I know you two have had your share of disagreements, but going to court with what is potentially a lot of money at stake is going to turn this place into a three-ring circus."

"I know but this is a fight to the death," Joe said.

I think I surprised Joe with the next question. "What's Alfie think of all this?"

Joe hesitated and said, "She's really pissed off at me. In fact, she's been pissed at me ever since I had Maria removed from the board of directors."

"Is there any way you can settle this out of court?" I asked. "This case could have a negative effect on the business."

"It's too late for that. The attorneys are exchanging papers, and the battle lines are drawn," he said.

I didn't say anything. Joe stood up and walked over to my window and said, "Where do you line up in this thing, Russ?"

"Well, I'm certainly more than an interested spectator. I figure my shares are worth about twenty-five million bucks, and until you tell me otherwise, I'm the president of the company. But relatively speaking, I'm small potatoes, because I'm guessing that you and Maria will be arm wrestling over a billion dollars or more," I said.

"You're right. But that's not what I asked you. Whose side do you line up with?" Joe asked.

"I line up with the corporation. And I have a feeling, if you are in court, that my responsibilities will be even greater than they are now. I line up with your dad. Twelve and a half shares for each side. And, frankly, if I'm going to be running the business in the near term, I'd think you'd want someone running it that didn't have a political ax to grind," I said.

"That's what my dad would want...but I'm looking for an edge. I want you in my pocket so I can spring you on the other side at the appropriate time," he said.

"Sorry, Joe. I couldn't do that and look myself in the mirror every day," I said.

Joe stood up and left the office without another word. I knew he wasn't pleased with what I told him, but I'm not sure that he was surprised. Over the years we'd had our battles, and we'd go days without speaking to each other. But we usually got over it in time. But I wasn't sure about the current circumstance. My stuff could be in a box on the sidewalk by tomorrow, and even though I had a dog in this fight, I wasn't going to take a side.

I swiveled in my chair and dialed Maria, figuring I might as well piss off the other side too. Maria picked up on the first ring, and I said, "Hiya, Maria, it's Russ."

She said, "How are you? How's the family?"

"Doing great. Thanks for asking," I replied.

"You know what's going on, right?" Maria asked.

"Joe just left my office," I said. "So, officially, I know a Galetti family storm is brewing."

Maria didn't take long getting to the heart of the matter. "Okay, where are you in this thing?"

"I'll tell you what I told Joe. I work for this corporation, and I'm going to do my best to see it doesn't go down the drain while you guys are battling in court. I line up with Dominic Galetti, Senior, fifty-fifty. I'm not taking a side," I said.

"Fair enough," Maria said. "But, Russ, you may be called as a witness for my side."

"And that's okay. We've been through a lot with each other, and, as you know, I work with Trip every day. I'll just tell it the way it is," I said.

"Okay, Russ, I understand," Maria said.

"Maria, I wish this was just a bad dream but it isn't. Anyway, good luck."

"Thanks, Russ," said Maria as she hung up.

The next day the story broke in the paper. Some very astute local newspaper guy had been thumbing through the upcoming cases at the Second District Court of Plymouth and saw "Galetti v. Galetti" on the upcoming docket. It was headline news: "GALETTI VERSUS GALETTI: AND IT AIN'T CHICKENFEED" screamed the headlines of a major Boston newspaper. "GALETTI FAMILY SQUABBLE: LET'S GET IT ON." This article's lead sentence was, "Where is Mills Lane when you really need him?"

I had anticipated that this case would be high-profile once it was made public, but I didn't get a real feel for it until I arrived at work the next day. News trucks and reporters had staked out the front of the building. I was about to go around to the side door when I spotted Natalie Jacobson, one of the really high-profile TV newspeople in Boston. I and several hundred thousand other males in the metropolitan area had been in love with her, it seemed, for decades. I couldn't resist. I had to get a closer look. I was almost standing next to her when she turned quickly and was looking right at me. I wasn't disappointed; she was more gorgeous in person than she was on the tube. As I was about to enter the building, I should have been thinking about business or this three-ring circus, but the only thought that was going through my mind was that Chet Curtis (Natalie's husband) was a very fortunate fellow indeed. But, on the other hand, so was I.

As I passed through security, the receptionist told me that Joe Galetti wanted to see me. I went straight to Joe's office, and he was pacing in front of the window, watching the mass of humanity below. "Jesus, there must not be much news out there if all the newspeople in Boston are here," Joe said.

"Money and lots of it is big news, I guess," I said. "Anytime there's a shit fight, you're going to draw a crowd. Hey, but I got to see my idol, Natalie J., up close and personal, so at least the day isn't a complete loss."

"I guess you're right. Chet Curtis gets my vote as luckiest stiff on the planet," Joe said.

"My thoughts exactly. Have you got public relations grinding something out?" I asked. "Not really," he responded.

"Okay, I'll take care of it. I'll tell them to issue a statement telling the reporters that we will not be commenting on the issues before the case is heard in court et cetera, et cetera..." I said.

"Good," Joe said.

I left Joe's office and walked down to mine only to find Bill Hartman from P&G sitting in my office doing his paperwork. As I walked in he said, "For Christ's sake, Russ, you didn't have to call the press out on me just because I was a little late with my billbacks!"

I laughed so hard that I had to sit down and find a Kleenex to wipe my eyes. "Hartman, you are such a buttwipe."

"I know. But did you see Jacobson? Christ, she's old enough to be my mother, and I'd run away with her to anywhere she wanted to go!" Hartman said.

"Amen, brother," I said. "What can I do for you?"

"Nothing. I just stopped by to tell you that if it gets too intense in the next few weeks, you and Holly and the kids could hide out at our place down at the Cape," Hartman said.

"That's mighty nice of you, partner," I said as I was interrupted by my phone buzzing. "Hello?"

"Russ, it's Diane," she said.

"How are you?" I asked.

"Good. Now that the cat's out of the bag, I'm assuming it's okay if people know that we are representing you."

I thought about that for a moment and said, "Why don't you delay it for a few more days so it doesn't look like I knew about something before it happened," I said.

"Okay. Will do. Bye."

"So long, Diane," I said.

I should have known. Hartman was on me in a flash. "That wouldn't be the very circumspect and revered attorney, would it, by chance?" Hartman said.

"It would be indeed," I said.

"Geez, Jacobson and Dunbar; you're traveling in style, my friend," Hartman concluded.

"Strictly business," I said.

"I knew that," Hartman said. "Don't forget my place if you need to get away and stick your feet in the sand."

"Many thanks, Bill," I said as Hartman unfolded his huge frame and headed for the door.

* * *

Claire came to the house for dinner that night and wanted to know all about the upcoming court case. I said, "I don't know about the court case, Ma, but I do know this—you're a darn sight more attractive than Natalie Jacobson."

"Oh, go on," Claire said. "She's the poster girl for all of us over fifty."

Holly jumped in and said, "I agree with Russ. She's very attractive but you've got her by a mile."

"Okay, okay, I get it," Claire said. "I smell a babysitting assignment in the very near future."

"Well, now that you mention it, we'd like to take off to the Cape for a couple of days and visit the Hartmans," I said.

"Consider it done," she said. "Another chance for Grandma to spoil these two youngsters."

We took off the next day for the Hartmans' place on Cape Cod, after delivering our kids to Claire. It was great when they went to Grandma's because we didn't have to lug a lot of stuff. Claire's place looked like a mini day care center, and the kids loved to visit their Grandma, so it worked out pretty well.

What a pleasure it was to sit on Craigville Beach with the Hartmans and watch the world go by. Jenny Hartman was as small as Bill Hartman was big. Tiny. Beautiful. Funnier than Hartman, which I thought impossible. No pretense, just people you want to be around. Bill had a cooker on the beach that looked like a wastebasket, but it had a curious design that allowed Hartman to turn out wonderful burgers and dogs no matter how hard the wind was blowing. So we spent most of two days sitting on the beach, drinking beer, and stuffing our faces with food. At one point Holly and Bill were engrossed in a conversation about the stock market, while Jenny was telling me a story about her crazy Aunt Helga. "You see, Helga was a woman of means who felt she could make her own rules," Jenny said. "One day she was speeding down one of these old Cape roads when she turned a blind corner, and there was a cop on the side of the road, having already pulled over two other speeders. Helga decided to play the law of averages, waved to the guy as he was signaling for her to pull into line behind the other two offenders, and kept on motoring."

"That takes nerve," I said.

"Yeah, but the cop was so pissed that he left his two birds in the hand and chased Aunt Helga down. Helga pulled to the side of the road, and now the cop was burning. You could see the smoke coming out of his ears as he marched up to her car and said, 'Where did you get your fucking license, lady?' Helga, without missing a beat, said, 'I didn't know you needed a license for that endeavor.'"

I dropped my beer in the sand and howled with laughter. "I've got to meet Aunt Helga," I said. "Did she end up getting a ticket?"

"No," Jenny said. "The cop had the same reaction you did. In fact, today Helga and the cop are the best of friends."

The giant shadow of the trial was only two weeks away, but that weekend with the Hartmans reduced it to a minor irritation. The other benefit was that, with the kids in the very competent hands of Claire Riley, Holly and I had a chance to make love without fear of interruption, and we took advantage of their absence. Sunday, after breakfast, we packed up and headed home, after saying good-bye to the Hartmans. I don't think we said anything for the first 15 minutes of the drive, but it was a very comfortable silence. Finally, Holly said, "You know, maybe someday we ought to get a little hideaway on the Cape."

"Great idea. We're going to have to steal Hartman's wastebasket cooker if we do," I said.

"They are a great couple. I feel so at home with those guys, and I don't really know them all that well," Holly said.

"Yep. Hartman has been a friend and a great business guy as well," I said.

"Have you been thinking about the trial?" Holly asked.

"Hardly thought about it this weekend. I'm starting to get philosophical about it, you know. What will happen will happen. I just don't want to get run over by it and become a casualty."

"Well, just remember one thing. You have a very supportive family, including Claire, and whatever you decide to do, we'll back you up all the way," Holly said.

"Thanks, sweetheart, that means a lot to me. I don't know if I tell you and the kids that I love you all very much enough, but I do. Especially you.

You may be slim and gorgeous to the unsuspecting eye, but you're as tough as a dollar ninety-nine steak. So, if I have to go to war over this family fight, I'm sure glad you're on my side."

"Thanks, Russell. I just want to be clear about one thing. If you want to walk away because it just becomes too mean-spirited, don't say to yourself, 'I can't do this because I have a family to support.' I know you don't have much of an ego, but I've talked to Cable and Hartman, and they both say you can write your own ticket in this business. But know this, even if it weren't so, financially, we are in very good shape. You wouldn't have to do a thing for five years, and we'd still be okay. Furthermore, I can always go back to work. My old boss keeps calling, so that's a good sign."

"Sure, you say okay…as long as it's work-related!" I said.

Holly laughed at that and said, "I've only got one man who turns me on, and he's sitting right next to me."

She started undoing my belt as I was driving up Route 3, and all I could say was, "I'll give you twenty minutes to cut that out. Thanks for that summary. It certainly puts me at ease to know that I can walk if I have to and not worry about us."

"Part of you isn't at ease," she said as she rubbed my thighs.

"Cut that out, Holly, will you? I'm going to run us off the road. What if one of those big trucks passes us and sees what you're up to?"

"It's no nevermind; his friends will never believe him. Now pull over," Holly said. I pulled over and Holly straddled me in the front seat, and we made love as cars ripped by us, doing 70 miles per hour. By the time they figured out what was going on, it was too late to slow down and take another look. I was just hoping Claire didn't ride by with the kids. When we were done we just sat in the front seat and laughed until our sides hurt. I was also glad Aunt Helga and her friend, the cop, didn't come by, because I was pretty sure we didn't have a license for this type of endeavor.

* * *

The next day, when I arrived at work, I was still smiling, thinking about Holly making me pull over on one of the busiest highways in Massachusetts. Unfortunately, the return to business was abrupt and unyielding. Trip was in my office when I arrived, and I could tell by the look on his face that something was wrong. I greeted Trip with a pat on the back and a smile and said, "How are you, buddy?"

"Not so good. When I arrived this morning, my stuff was outside the office door, and the locks had been changed," he said.

"What?" I asked.

"Joe has a court order that asks me to be off the premises by ten this morning," Trip said.

"Can he do that? You're an owner and you're on the board of directors."

"Apparently, he thinks he can. My lawyer is on the way over to get the court order. But, for now, I'm out," Trip said.

I could see that Trip was near tears. I'd promised myself I'd stay out of this, but I felt very badly for him. His mother had warned him that it was going to be nasty, but I don't think he thought he'd ever be locked out of his office. Frankly, I wasn't prepared for it either. "I don't know what to tell you, Trip, but I think you did the right thing calling your lawyer. Don't make it any worse by confronting Joe. Handle it through the system. You've done the right thing. In fact, let's go get your stuff and get you out of here before the deadline. Have you called your mother yet?" I asked.

"No, I haven't," Trip said.

"Okay, I'm going to step outside my office and close the door. Call her and come get me when you're done."

After Trip had called his mother to tell her he was being locked out of the building, we picked up his stuff and took it to his car. As we stood in the parking lot, I put my arm around Trip and said, "I had to do this once when Joe and I were going at each other, so I'll give you some advice. Give the paperwork to your lawyer, pack up Melissa and the baby, and go to the Cape and enjoy yourself."

"You're kidding," Trip said.

"Never more serious in my life," I said. "I went over to Holly's apartment and just took a couple of days off. It was fun, a change of pace, and, eventually, Joe and I kissed and made up."

"Why did you quit?" Trip asked.

"Because I didn't like the way Joe handled the situation with your mother," I said. "I knew the real story because your mother had told me. Joe didn't lie outright; he just omitted certain details and we ended up yelling at each other and I quit or was fired—I'm not sure which it was."

"Russell Riley, you've got balls," Trip said.

"You do too, my friend. I just wish we could get this thing settled, but I have a feeling it will be a long time before it's over. This thing has the potential to do something no competitor could ever do to us, and that deeply saddens me," I said.

Trip opened the door to his car and got in. "I'll be seeing you," he said.

"Not if I see..." I said. Trip started to smile at my inane retort, and I said to him, "Let that be a lesson to you. Keep your head while all about you are losing theirs."

I turned and walked back into the building. For the first time since I found out that the Galetti family was going to court, I had a glimmer of how intense this battle was going to be. The gloves were already off. The once-beloved uncle barring his own nephew from the building. This wasn't just any relative. Trip was the executive vice president, and he earned the job on merit. He was bright, committed, and he'd made real contributions to the bottom line of this organization. In a way I felt as if he were my kid or younger brother. I'd trained him just the way I knew Dominic would have wanted me to. I pointed him in the right direction, but I never gave him the answers. He had to find those for himself. I'd stuck his nose in it by making him an aisle clerk and having him do other intensive labor activities so he knew what his employees were going through every day. And you know what? He had passed every test with flying colors. For God's sake, I even introduced him to his wife, Melissa, and now they were growing a family of their own. From a purely selfish point of view, having Trip on the sidelines wasn't a good thing for the chain.

I returned to my office, and Joe Galetti was standing there looking out the window. I said, "This must be the day for the Galettis to visit my office."

"How'd he take it?" Joe asked.

"Like the man he is," I responded.

"It's sad but I can't have a member of the family from the enemy camp in my tepee."

I didn't say anything. Joe and I just stared at each other. Finally, he said, "You don't approve, do you?"

"Joe, don't use me for your sounding board. This is family stuff and I'm doing my best to stay out of it. I will say this from a nonfamily perspective: locking a man of Trip's ability out could be detrimental to our long-term business. Regardless of what's going on now, he's a Galetti; in fact, he's a Dominic Galetti. And as much as you and I thought of his two predecessors, he's their equal in every way. So, from a business standpoint, we're at a competitive disadvantage with Trip on the sideline."

"I hear you," Joe said as he slowly left.

Trip never had the chance to take that vacation I had recommended. Ned Gerrity, Maria's chief counsel, obtained a court order prohibiting Joe Galetti or any family member from barring any other family member from the business until the case was resolved. For me, a working atmosphere that had been open and pleasant had turned into an armed camp. Joe's thought process basically dissolved the board of directors because Trip was on the board, and he withdrew to the point that I saw him very infrequently. It was tough walking a tightrope at work, but it was amazing to me how quickly the human condition can adjust to just about any situation. Both Arnold Cable and Trip reported to me; we had solid management, extraordinary store managers, and one of the best buying staffs in the Northeast. So, in spite of internal turmoil, we were turning an excellent profit, and our sales objectives were being met or exceeded.

Meanwhile, the court case was dragging on. First, it was weeks, then months, caused by the long, drawn-out and contentious discovery process, but at the same time, it helped bring down the profile of the event in the media dramatically. As a rule the media wasn't a patient lot, and they became distracted by other newsworthy events that seemed to pop up daily. It was almost nine months before the lawyers approved a jury, completed the discovery process, and called the first witness. I missed seeing Natalie Jacobson, but, believe me, I got over it as our story was shoved aside for more current happenings. The press's prediction that our business would decline because of the court squabble and we'd be prime candidates for a takeover turned out to be erroneous. Our business was excellent and reputation with our competitors was intact. Although I'm sure there was hyperbole involved, our vendors—people such as Bill Hartman— told us that our competitors would "rather take on a twenty-foot saltwater crocodile with a paring knife, then run against us head to head."

Knowing Hartman to be a colorful person with the gift of gab, I added a grain of salt or two, but he wasn't far off the mark. The one thing about the food industry that you could absolutely rely on was that if a competitor smelled a weakness, he'd be on it faster than a shark to blood. Apparently, the competition was content to see if we would drown in our own internal spittle.

In spite of the looming legal fiasco, life went on. Trip and his wife Melissa had a second child—a fourth generation of Dominic Galetti—and we bought a house on the Cape on the same beach as the Hartmans.

The long-anticipated trial finally began. The jurors had been selected—16 in all—but the original 12 consisted of eight women and four men. I didn't know much about courts and trials; in fact, I'd only been in a court once and that was for jury duty, but we never were called. That didn't stop me from forming an opinion, however, and my thinking was that a predominantly female jury favored Maria. But Joe's people had had as many peremptory challenges as Maria's lawyer did, so they must have felt comfortable with the final selection. The judge in the case was a fairly young minority. He was a 42-year-old African-American named Cleon A. Matthews. From the very beginning it was clear that he would tolerate no funny business in his courtroom but that he had a sense of humor. In his opening statement Ned Gerrity immediately went on the offensive by, in effect, calling the rival's law firms from Washington and New York "carpetbaggers." Joe's lawyer, Jerry Saxe, from a Boston firm, jumped up to object to this "heinous reference," and before the trial was two minutes old, Gerrity and Saxe were staring each other down.

Having watched these antics from the bench, Judge Matthews gave his gavel a good wrap and said, "Gentlemen, gentlemen, sticks and stones...the court will give you ten minutes to go out and arm-wrestle or whatever you need to do, but when you come back, I expect you to act like officers of the court for the remainder of the trial. If you cannot comply with this request to behave with decorum rather than like juveniles, I will ask the second chair to take over for each side. Do I make myself clear?"

"Yes, Your Honor," the two lawyers said at the same time.

"Do you want the ten minutes?" Matthews asked.

"No, Your Honor," the two lawyers said again at the same time.

"Proceed, Mr. Gerrity. Keep it to the facts," Judge Matthews said.

And although the trial would last for 70 days, the outward acrimony, at least by the lawyers, was minimal. Ned Gerrity had tested the judge with his "carpetbaggers" comment, and, truthfully, he was pleased with the judge's reaction. This trial would be arduous, but it would be all business. Saxe had quite the opposite reaction. His case was built on finesse, on the quirks of human behavior, on odd angles, and on complexity. He needed to muddy the water, and he wasn't sure Matthews would allow it.

Gerrity proceeded with his opening statement. "This is a simple case, really. It's about trust and, specifically, family trust. Joe Galetti was given this sacred family trust, and only two months after his dead brother Dominic was in the ground, he was scheming to break it. Here are the facts. Joe and his late brother Dominic, in a family ceremony, became executors of each other's wills with the proviso that they would be equal partners in the business. At this same family gathering, each family received five hundred shares of privately held stock, signifying this equal partnership.

"What we intend to prove beyond a shadow of a doubt is that Joe Galetti, over the course of the last twenty years, systematically bilked his dead brother's family of their rightful share of the Galetti Supermarket business. We contend that, through a series of real estate moves and other questionable tactics, he now has control of seven hundred fifty shares of the business, and, in fact, he also pocketed the great majority of profit that is generated by the two hundred fifty shares that remain with my client's family.

"It is fraud, ladies and gentlemen...plain and simple. My worthy adversary will, no doubt, try and blur the issue by way of character assassination and by running you down a number of blind alleys. While you are still fresh and your minds are nimble, I want you to keep saying to yourselves, 'One thousand shares; where are they now?' It'll be a tough process because Joe Galetti is a giant in New England business lore. He is an icon, a man who has given generously to the community and who has provided employment for twenty-five hundred people here and in the state of Rhode Island. He walks among the political and business elite, and his public persona is to be admired. He is an entrepreneur extraordinaire, with a business that ranks in the Fortune One Hundred for private businesses in the United States.

"This is a business that's worth over one billion dollars. Think of it this way, folks; each of the thousand shares is worth a million dollars, so we're not talking pocket change in this case. But at the same time, I'd ask you to try and differentiate between the public persona of a business magnate and what he has done in private over the last fifteen years to my client, the widow, Maria Galetti. Sure, it's a case of Goliath versus David...the resources of a billion-dollar empire against a widow and her family, who had no reason to even suspect her brother-in-law, and the godfather of her children, of nearly two decades of financial manipulation and chicanery. When all else fails I'd ask you to keep your eyes glued to the thousand shares. Where are they now and how did they get there? Thank you."

I was blown away by the opening statement of Ned Gerrity. He didn't rant and rave or show any other signs of theatrics, but his words were powerful. Short, concise, and he went to the heart of the matter and found two or three different ways to show it to the jury. One thousand shares. That was it.

Where were they today? End of story. Case closed. This thing will be over in a week.

Then Jerry Saxe stood up to give his opening statement for the defense. He was a marked contrast to Ned Gerrity. Gerrity's suit looked as if it came from Goodwill, and his hair looked like it had been brushed by the leg of a chair. Saxe was smooth, he was silk, Gucci, two-seater Mercedes, and fine wine. His suit cost at least $2000, he had a Vacheron Constantin watch, and his hair was immaculate. But when he spoke that image was quickly blurred because his voice was shrill, and the words flowed out of his mouth faster than an M-60 machine gun can fire rounds out of the chamber. That's what he was, actually—a human projectile—and if you were unlucky enough to get in his way, somehow you knew it wasn't going to be pleasant. He was standing next to the defendant, Joe Galetti, with his hand on Joe's shoulder, when he said, "You *wish* you had an uncle or brother-in-law such as Joe Galetti. Only in your dreams. Here sits a man who, when he wasn't at work, was attending to the wife and children of his late brother. A man who, when one of the boys couldn't get into the college of his choice, made a few discreet phone calls that magically opened its doors. An uncle who, as we speak, underwrites financially one of his nephews, who has been perusing the fine museums of Europe for the last seven years. A brother-in-law who has provided the widow Galetti—and I use that word advisedly—with a two-million-dollar home in Dover free and clear, as well as luxurious condominiums in Bermuda and West Palm Beach. In addition, she has seven cars at the three residences, and her daughters are in the finest private college in the United States, and Uncle Joe has picked up all the bills for what my learned adversary would have you believe is a woman and her family who are five minutes from the repo man."

Saxe had moved away from Joe Galetti now and was standing at the rail of the jury box, looking right at them. My eyes were still fixed on Joe. To the average person who didn't know him, he did look like the kindly, benevolent uncle. He continued. "Ladies and gentlemen of the jury, I beg you not to be drawn into the big versus little, David and Goliath, and the poor widow in the alley with a shopping cart for a suitcase scenario. This whole case is about money and lots of it…nobody at either table is looking for a handout or has to work for food."

Jerry Saxe then did what I thought was an odd thing. He broke off his statement and slowly moved over to the defense table and picked up a leather-bound notebook. Strategically, I thought it was an error, because it was obvious to this point that the courtroom participants, with the notable exception of Judge Cleon A. Matthews, were clearly enthralled with what he had to say. It was as if he had broken the trance with his silence. He said, "This isn't all about financials. This is Maria Galetti's oldest boy's diploma from high school. Maria's son, Trip, gave it to his Uncle Joe when he graduated from high school as a token of his love and appreciation for all he had done for him. Attending his athletic events, concerts, and supplying him with those things he needed to graduate from high school with honors. By the way, that young man is executive vice president of Galetti-Pantry Place at twenty-eight years of age and made two hundred fifty thousand dollars last year. And Uncle Joe attended the high school graduations and college graduations of each of the children, as well as being the uncle that they could go to with questions that they couldn't determine the answers to because of a lack of experience.

"Is this an uncle that you would turn your back on and sue without ever talking to him first as family? His niece will tell you that he even played in the father-daughter sports events at school, and they laughed because their uncle wasn't much of an athlete, but he was out there, giving it his all. He attended dozens of teacher conferences for these four children. They will tell you that it was a little embarrassing because, the next day, some of the teachers would tell the children that their Uncle Joe was always pressing to have Italian taught in high school."

I don't think Saxe meant for that to be funny, but, for some reason, the court had a good laugh. The audience just seemed to relate to a parent having an agenda when they went to these conferences.

Saxe adjusted, though, as he continued. "He might not have sold Italian as a language option, but you can see he had plenty of opportunities to try and sell it with the number of trips he made to their schools. I wanted you to get a glimpse of the private Joe Galetti, the one the public never sees, and how he spends his time. I think you've all read about what he has done for the community, and if you haven't, you may want to look it up. But this is clearly a devoted family man who was there for every communion, graduation, teacher-parent conference, and who was readily accessible twenty-four hours a day. In fact, he was a devoted two-family man because he also was doing the same thing at the same time for his own children. So, if my worthy adversary is going to pick on character, he'd be well served to pick on me, because Joe Galetti is well above any standard that I am aware of as a family man who takes his family obligations seriously.

"My last point has to do with the thousand shares that counsel for the plaintiff has beaten with a fairly hefty shillelagh."

I looked at Ned Gerrity, and he broke into a wide grin. The fact that this immaculate Jewish person used an Irish term to denote Gerrity's repeated reference to the Galetti shares truly amused the opposing lawyer. It was clear to me that the Galettis—both families—had chosen their representatives in this case well.

Saxe continued by saying, "Let's look at the facts. When Dominic Galetti died more than fifteen years ago, the chain had sixteen stores, or they were twenty-five percent of the size they are today. I don't think anyone would argue about who was responsible for the growth of this food chain since that time. Two words…Joseph Galetti. So if it is true that Maria Galetti has two hundred fifty shares today, she, in effect, would own one hundred percent of the chain as it was when her husband passed away. Does a quarter of a billion dollars in stock seem reasonable to you, ladies and gentlemen of the jury, for a part of the family that doesn't participate in the business? And there are other issues:

statute of limitations as an example. We're talking about a case that is more than fifteen years old and very complex. I've been an attorney for thirty years, and I've never been involved in a case where discovery proceedings took nine months. It will be a complex case, but make no mistake about it, a lot of elements that are prevalent in many court cases are rearing their ugly heads here as well. Greed, power, pride, and, yes, money are all key elements of this case.

"But none of those is critical to Joe Galetti. He has power, pride, and money. But no one in business or in his philanthropic work would accuse him of greed. It's important to remember that Joe Galetti is the defendant in this case. He doesn't want to be in court. There's nothing more heinous to him than having to testify against a family that he has helped raise for fifteen years. His life's work has been building a business that he can be proud of because it was successful; built on character, his word being his bond, and, of course, leaving a legacy that people in the business world and the community will look upon with pride. But even more important to him than these lifetime achievements is the fact that he stood where his dead brother would have stood if he were alive, to finish the job his brother was unable to do because of his premature and untimely death. Thank you."

Oops. Maybe this wouldn't be over in a week. Saxe had been brilliant and I thought I saw on the face of one of the jurors the same feeling I had. After listening to Gerrity, they thought it was an open-and-shut case, but Saxe had now convinced them that nothing about this case was going to be simple. This case was about human beings; emotions flowed heavily for a widow who had been taken and for an uncle who seemingly did everything imaginable to support his dead brother's family. My thoughts centered around how this family disagreement—and I didn't mean to minimize its impact—ended up in court. It was clear that both sides were going to march out all the dirty linen they could muster, and the public would be picking through every delicious detail before it was deposited in the washing machine. No matter what the jury decided, the privacy and, yes, the decency that was once the hallmark of the Galetti family would be totally destroyed.

I walked out of court with Arnold Cable about noon. The judge had closed down early—it was a Friday—and they would resume again on Monday morning. Both sides of the Galetti family filed out of the courtroom without looking directly at each other. I said to Arnold, "Want to get some lunch?"

"Sure, I know a spot down the road that has cold beer and great pastrami sandwiches," Arnold said.

"Sold. Let's do it," I responded.

As we slid into a booth, Arnold surprised me by saying, "This is going to be more than one trial."

"You mean appeals?" I asked.

"That too, but the judge has already indicated that this trial is about fiduciary duty, fraud, and or wrongful conversion of the stock in question."

"Okay, but how do you know all of this stuff, Arnold?" I asked.

"Well, I went to NYU law school and graduated. I just never took the boards. The job at Pantry Place came along and then A&P, and before I knew it, I was in the twilight of a so-so career."

I laughed at Arnold as we ordered two pastrami sandwiches and two beers. "I wonder why I didn't pick that up on your résumé. So you're a real student of the courts," I said.

"Worse than that," Arnold responded. "I subscribe to *Lawyers Weekly*, and, for fun, I read Supreme Court opinions from the Social Law Library. It's a hobby of mine. I might even try the law boards after I retire to see if I can pass them."

"The things you never know about your friends," I said. "Well, what did you see so far, Perry?"

"I'm no Perry Mason, but here are the issues. Did Joe use good fiduciary judgement over the last fifteen years in fairly apportioning the stock and dividends to the two families? If he didn't and favored his own family, Joe is on the way down a slippery slope. If the jury is convinced that he was playing games, then the fraud and wrongful conversion of stock becomes a no-brainer," Arnold said as he took a bite out of the man-size sandwich.

"Okay, I got that," I said. "But if that should happen, what's left?"

"Plenty," Arnold said. "The jury can award damages in dollars, but a second trial is necessary to figure out the worth of the stock as it exists today."

"I thought the stock would be worth whatever the gross assets of the chain are valued at today," I said.

"Maybe," Arnold said. "But what if the thousand shares are only for the Galetti stores and don't include the addition of Pantry Place?" Arnold must have seen my face turn ashen because he said, "Are you all right?"

"Not really. If that's true and the jury agrees with Joe, my twenty-five shares just became so much kindling for a fire in my living room."

"You have stock?" Arnold asked.

"I do," I responded.

"Well, you know what Sam Walton said in 1987 when he lost six billion dollars in that downturn in two days?"

"No, what?" I asked.

"Oh well, it's only paper," Arnold responded with a grin.

"I don't know if I can be that cavalier," I responded.

"Well, just for the record...Sam's shareholders agreed with you. He had to recant that statement and tell them he was only being flippant."

"Any other gems in that kit bag of yours, Mrs. Lincoln?" I asked.

"Well, one other that apparently isn't public knowledge and somehow the newspeople haven't got a hold of it," Arnold said, almost in a whisper.

"Oh," I responded.

"Yeah, a lawyer buddy of mine told me that, in a separate court, the plaintiffs' lawyers have filed RICO charges against Joe for playing fast and loose with the profit sharing program."

"What is a RICO charge?" I asked.

"It stands for Racketeer Influenced and Corrupt Organizations Act. Formerly, it was only used against organized crime by federal prosecutors, but it can be now used in civil cases. In a nutshell, Maria's side is saying that Joe invested in questionable investments in real estate to help the Parelli brothers, who were having cash flow problems," Arnold stated.

I was stunned at this disclosure by Arnold because I knew about the transactions, and, at the time, I had thought they were a little shady. I ordered coffee for both of us to delay lunch a little and then said to Arnold, "So what are we looking at here when the smoke clears?"

"I can guess but it would only be an educated guess," Arnold said.

"Fire away, Perry," I responded.

"Okay. It's really pretty well outlined by the opening statements today. First, both lawyers I heard this morning are first-rate, and they have a definite strategy. Tell me what you think they are up to," Arnold asked.

"Let's see," I responded. "Ned Gerrity wants the jury to never let the thousand shares out of their sight. He wants them to decide whether a sacred trust was broken or not. Saxe, on the other hand, is saying that Maria's side of the family is a bunch of wastrels who spent their birthright on fast cars and fast women, while Joe, a pillar of the community, built a billion-dollar business with sweat and dedication."

"Bingo," Arnold said. "So it's a classic strategy, but there are too many zeroes attached for the jury to have much empathy for either side."

"What do you mean?" I asked.

"Look," Arnold said, "how much empathy are you going to have for a widow who is worth between two hundred fifty million and seven hundred fifty million dollars? She isn't exactly grubbing around for a square meal in a homeless shelter. Frankly, that strategy could backfire in favor of Joe. They already know he's one of the richest men in Massachusetts, but they are going to like the fact that he's a stand-up guy who was always there for his brother's children."

"So, you see Joe with a little edge in the proceedings after the first day," I said.

"Not really. Maria is odds-on to win this thing, but Saxe closed the gap a little today on Ned Gerrity."

"The least I can do is pay for lunch after that eye-opening assessment," I said.

"That and you're also the boss," Arnold retorted.

I paid the bill, wished Arnold a good weekend, and headed for the office. For some reason I was thinking of Joe Galetti and the biblical story of Joseph with the coat of many colors. This modern-day Joseph had a court with many issues, but my mind started to move to his life after the court battles. He would probably have to resign as CEO, and he would be shoved to the sidelines of a business that he had spent his life building. And Maria. She had never found anyone to share her life with after Dom died. Sitting home with wheelbarrows of money and no life to spend it on. It actually brought me to a peaceful and tranquil place. I didn't mean to ride on the shoulders of other people's misery, but I couldn't help thinking about my own life. Imagine suing Claire Riley for any reason. Preposterous! Not for love or money. I always thought I was the luckiest stiff in the world when Holly agreed to marry me, but this debacle that was now unfolding in front of me really brought my situation into perspective. Any accomplishments that I could ever bring to fruition would pale in comparison to having Holly choose me for her husband. And I'd leave no legacy behind more thrilling to me than my children. One could only hope that others would look at this case and say no matter how onerous a situation seemed, it wouldn't be worth taking it to court. After all, look what the Galettis are doing to each other. No disagreement is worth this kind of public airing.

As I entered headquarters and moved to my office in the executive wing, I was surprised to see it was almost empty. This was the first visual sign to me that things were going to be different. Usually, on Fridays this hallway was filled with people, and getting any work done during this time was almost accidental. Last-minute decisions on the newspaper advertising for the next week were still being made, volume and share for that week were coming across the computers, and people were wrapping up those last-minute things that always seemed to pop up on a Friday. Today it was eerily quiet. I marched into my office and asked Mary, "Where is everybody?"

Mary looked up at me and said, "I don't know. They all went to court this morning, and I guess they all decided to go home."

I took off my coat, hung it on the back of my door, and said, "You might as well join the gang, Mary; go home, get a jump on the weekend."

"Really?" she asked.

"Yeah," I responded. "Give me my messages and hit the road."

"Okay, thanks," she said. "Your messages are on your desk. Have a good weekend."

"You too, Mary," I responded. "See you on Monday."

I sat down and looked through my messages but nothing looked urgent. As I reached for my stuff in the inbox, Trip came through the door and closed it. He said, "Got a minute to talk?"

"Absolutely," I said.

"I'm the first witness on Monday," he said.

"How are you feeling about that?" I asked.

"Nervous," he replied.

"I would be too," I responded. "There's something about a courtroom that makes it very customer unfriendly."

"I agree," Trip said. "Any hints?"

"Yeah, just one. Tell the truth and be concise."

"I'll do that and I'll try not to faint on the way to the witness box," Trip said with a smile.

"You'll be just fine," I said.

"What do you think so far?" he asked.

"It's a battle of the Titans, but it's already having an effect on us," I responded.

"How so?" Trip asked.

"Have you ever seen the place as quiet as this on a Friday?" I asked.

"Never," Trip responded. "Now that you mention it, I wonder if our business will survive?"

"I think it will, Trip, but you should be ready for the consequences," I warned.

"What consequences?" he asked.

"Do you remember when you were walking to the table with me after your dad and uncle had the ceremony with the stock? You were thirteen at the time."

"No, I don't," he answered.

"You asked me if I would be working for you someday," I said.

"Oh yeah," Trip said. "Jesus, that was a stupid thing to ask you," he said, somewhat chagrined.

"Well, if your mom wins this case, my bet is that you'll become CEO," I said.

"You know, you're right. I'm kind of wondering why I didn't think of that yet," Trip said.

"Because you're too close to the flame. You're worried about testifying against a guy who helped to bring you up," I responded.

"Strange as it seems, I'd love to be CEO someday but not this way," Trip said.

"I think I knew that before you said it, and I don't want to make your load any heavier than it is, but sometime soon you're going to have to start thinking beyond the end of your nose," I said.

"Russ, you're a pain in my ass," Trip said with a smile.

"At least I'm consistent," I said.

"How so?" Trip said.

"Your uncle has been telling me that for twenty-five years," I said.

Trip actually laughed, got up to leave, and said, "Have a good weekend, and, Russ…"

"Yes," I said.

"You're still an asshole."

"And proud of it," I responded.

Chapter 11: Fish Fry in the Parking Lot

Although the trial had now officially started and I was dreading the outcome—no matter how it turned out—the weekends served as a marvelous distraction to the upside-down world at work. I loved rolling in the leaves with the kids and listening to their happy, carefree laughter. Holly knew that there was more strain at work for me; but once I was home with her, it was as if I were in an impenetrable fortress far from the distraction of lawyers, courtrooms, and a fight over control of the Galetti empire. They say blood is thicker than water. I suppose that is so, but the corollary must be true as well when parts of the same family turn on each other. I had a ringside seat. I was the highest-ranking nonfamily member of this billion-dollar-plus food business that would witness a family devastate each other both in and out of court. I was pretty sure that, in the end, there would be no winners, as the usual suspects—greed, power, pride, and money—might prove to be fatal to both sides.

But I was more than a spectator; I was a participant. My 25 shares could be the margin of victory. Whenever my mind wandered I thought about the possibility of casting my shares for one side or the other. At one point I was sure I'd side with Joe Galetti. Certainly, we had our differences over the years, but I felt a special loyalty to him and his father. But at other times I'd make the case for the team of Maria and Trip. Would I be extending an injustice by voting with Joe? It wasn't making me lose sleep—yet—but, clearly, I couldn't make up my mind.

Monday at nine o'clock Trip was on the stand, having been sworn in, and articulated his name and current address. Ned Gerrity's first question was, "How would you characterize your relationship with Joe Galetti?"

"Very close. He's my uncle and I love him. He's been there for every important event in my life, and I report to him as executive vice president of the business," Trip said.

"How would you characterize your contribution to Galetti-Pantry Place's business?" Gerrity asked.

"Well, in tandem with the president, Russell Riley, I'd say I was a major contributor. For instance, during our expansion years, I found a way to deliver a new store from foundation to opening in seven months," Trip said.

"Why is that important?" Gerrity asked.

"Well, the industry average is ten months, so, in effect, I had a store up and running for three months, returning a profit, while our competitors were still struggling to get their store open," Trip said.

"I see," Gerrity said. "How would you characterize your mother's contribution?"

"Objection," Jerry Saxe said. "This response calls for speculation. Speculation from a son. It's biased and could be characterized as hearsay."

Judge Matthews looked at Ned Gerrity and said, "I'd have a tendency to agree with Mr. Saxe unless you can convince me otherwise, Mr. Gerrity."

"Your Honor," Gerrity responded, "I'm trying to lay the groundwork that, in fact, this side of the Galetti family made major contributions to the business. In my worthy adversary's opening statement, I received the inference that Joe Galetti built the business all by himself, while the other side of the family ate bonbons and entertained their friends."

"Okay. The witness will answer the question. I'll allow it," Judge Matthews responded.

I thought, although I was a neophyte at these types of proceedings, that Gerrity was hoping Saxe would object so he could tell the jury exactly what he was trying to do. Trip continued by saying, "I think she was a major contributor, and, before her resignation, I believe she was the only female in the United States who was the president of a major food chain. Among other things, she brought a flower department to the supermarket aisle, as well as gourmet foods and a café where people could sit and relax before or after they shopped. My grandfather, Dominic, and Uncle Joe's wife, Alfie, were her biggest supporters, and I think the record will show that they knew what they were talking about. It was my Aunt Alfie who said that ninety percent of our customers are women, so, therefore, we should have a woman in a responsible position in our organization."

There were another 45 minutes of questions that I thought did a good job of establishing Trip's credibility as a businessman who had earned his position on merit and not nepotism. Then Ned Gerrity said, "Given all you've said about your uncle from both your personal and professional relationships with him, why in the world would you and he be intense rivals in a courtroom?"

Trip didn't answer immediately. It was clear that he was trying to formulate an answer. Finally, he said in almost a low whisper, "It's a principle that both my dad and Uncle Joe harped on. It's about integrity. This case is about trust, a bond that two brothers struck many years ago. It was a promise he made to my dad. We trusted our uncle and he didn't keep his word to my dad. Our side of the family needs to stand up and be counted. As a youth my dad and my uncle were my heroes; but as I grew up, my mom joined that group as well. As heartwrenching as the trial is going to be, I want to tell my mother that I'm proud of her for standing on principle and trying to claim what is rightfully hers."

Ned Gerrity just stood in front of Trip for about 20 seconds. The court was totally silent, nobody was coughing or blowing their noses…totally silent. I felt a tear running down my face. Trip's pain and anguished face had an emotional effect on me. The last place he wanted to be was in a courtroom, but he was proud that his mother was standing up for what she thought was right.

Ned Gerrity walked slowly over to his side of the courtroom, sat down, looked at Jerry Saxe, and said, "Your witness."

Before Jerry could start his cross examination, Judge Matthews called a recess, and we all filed out of the courtroom. As I walked outside I was greeted by Diane Dunbar. "Hey, this is better than prime-time TV," she said.

"How are you, counselor?" I asked. "What do you think so far?"

"Too early to tell but I thought Gerrity asked good questions and then got out of the way. It's like a boxing referee; if you are not aware of him, then he's doing a good job," Diane said.

"You always were a sports fan," I remarked.

"But in this case, it's a good analogy," she said.

"Hey, am I on the clock?" I suddenly asked, thinking that Dunbar was representing me after all.

"God, you're a cheap Scotsman," she said. "I won't bill you until we're actually working together."

"Whew," I said with a smile. "Nice seeing you, Diane."

As we trooped back into the courtroom, she said, "Nice to be seen."

As I took my seat, I was thinking how glad I was that I was communicating with Diane again. It was mostly because I was her client, but it struck me as strange that I had been so close to one person during a time in my life and then had no contact at all. That just may be how it should have been given the circumstances that had transpired after college, but I was glad to see her, talk to her, even laugh with her. I'm sure Claire and Holly wouldn't be pleased with my thinking, and, in truth, if some old flame of Holly's was hanging around on the periphery, I'm sure I wouldn't be too open-minded myself.

After the recess concluded Jerry Saxe was up and walking toward Trip when he asked, "Where's your high school diploma?"

"It's hanging on a wall in my uncle's office," Trip responded.

"That's a strange place for it to be, isn't it?" Saxe asked.

"I suppose," Trip said, "but, you know, Uncle Joe was like a father to me. He attended every sports event, teacher's conference, and ceremony I was ever involved in. I gave it to him because I wanted him to know how much I appreciated his support."

"What college did you attend?" Saxe asked.

"Dartmouth," Trip responded.

"Was it your first choice?" Saxe queried.

"Yes, it was," Trip responded.

"Did you receive an acceptance letter from this school?"

"No, I didn't. In fact, I was on the waiting list," Trip said.

"How did you end up going there?" Saxe asked.

"My uncle pulled some strings," Trip said matter-of-factly.

"How did you ascend to executive vice president of a corporation before your thirtieth birthday?"

"Well, I started working at the chain when I was thirteen years old, and I was trained by the best people in the world."

"And who might they be?"

"My uncle and Russell Riley, our current president."

"What was your salary this past year?"

"Two hundred fifty thousand dollars," Trip responded.

"Did you make a bonus?" Saxe asked.

"Yes, I did," Trip said.

"How much?" Saxe asked.

"Five hundred thousand dollars," Trip responded.

"Are you telling me, at twenty-eight years old, you made three-quarters of a million dollars?"

"Yes," Trip responded.

"I wish I had an evil uncle like yours," Saxe said.

"Objection," Gerrity responded.

"Sustained," Judge Matthews said.

"What's in this case for you?" Saxe asked.

"My family's fair share of the business," Trip responded.

"Oh, c'mon, Mr. Galetti, get off it. If your family wins this case, you stand to gain the most. If Joe Galetti is replaced as CEO by the court, you become CEO. This isn't about integrity; it's about your quest for greed and power. Isn't it, Mr. Galetti?"

"No, it's not," Trip responded. "Let me tell you something, Mr. Saxe, that probably won't surprise industry insiders. If everything you say comes true, I'm sure, with my mother's approval, we would appoint an outsider as CEO."

"Oh, bull," Saxe said. "Who would have the credentials to become CEO who isn't a family member?"

"My vote would be for our current president, Russell Riley."

The courtroom as a whole shifted on its seat. Saxe's attempt to paint Trip into a corner as the greedy nephew had fallen flat. Before Saxe could continue Judge Matthews called a lunch break.

As I left the courtroom, I saw Diane Dunbar climbing into a two-seat Mercedes and back out of her spot. I waved but she didn't see me as she exited the parking lot. I was aware of someone directly to my left. It was Maria Galetti, who now was standing right next to me. I said, "Hi, babe, how you doing?"

"I love it when you call me babe," she said.

"Well, I'm glad you like it because, in spite of this current distraction, you'll always be a babe to me," I said.

"Are you flirting with me?" she asked.

"Of course I am. You're very high on my list of the sexiest women in the world. Just don't tell Trip I said that."

"Well, thanks for that pick-me-up," she said. "How do you think we're doing so far?"

"I thought Trip was great. First of all, he told the truth, and he was very concise."

"I don't know. That Saxe guy scares me to death," Maria said.

"He's just another guy in an expensive suit trying to make a buck," I responded.

"I suppose," she said as she got into her car. "Take care, Russ."

I missed the afternoon session because I was at work. Apparently, it was more of the same. Saxe trying to chip away at the credibility of Trip and his side of the family. He scored some points by asking about Trip's brother, Arthur, who, at 26 years of age, hadn't worked a day in his life. He spent the great majority of his time in Europe, living on a trust fund that Saxe proved fairly conclusively was supplied and replenished by Joe Galetti. But, overall, Saxe's assault could not diminish the fact that Dominic "Trip" Galetti wasn't just a relative taking up space in the business. In fact, at least in my mind, Ned Gerrity had done a good job of showing that Trip was a vital cog in a family business and that he made meaningful contributions to that business. I guess the only disappointed person would be a headhunter who saw a great young executive whom he couldn't peddle to a competitor because he was making three-quarters of a million dollars. From a pride standpoint I guess I'd be the other person who was somewhat disappointed that someone who reported to me was making more money than I was! That was really a point in Saxe's favor as well. The jury now knew, well before Maria ever took the stand, that this wasn't a story about a widow who was left to beg for a meal on the street.

I knew where I was in the pecking order of the trial. Maria was next, I followed Maria, and then came Joe Galetti. I really wasn't concerned about testifying, but I wanted to hear what Maria had to say so that I could get a feel for the rhythm of the trial. On Tuesday the judge was in chambers with both attorneys in discussions that I was not privy to. Wednesday morning Ned Gerrity had Maria on the stand, and, truthfully, she looked nervous but she also looked the part. She was in a beautiful, conservative beige dress, with no jewelry except for silver earrings. I knew she was past 50, but to me she looked exquisite. Her hair was dark with some gray in it, and her face featured high cheekbones, dark-blue eyes, and very little makeup. She wore two-inch beige heels that showed off her best asset in my mind—her legs—and she had an air of self-confidence. She didn't appear to be cocky, but rather confident in her abilities and in herself.

Gerrity didn't waste a lot of time. His first question for Maria was, "What is your relationship to Joe Galetti?"

"He's my brother-in-law," she said.

"How long have you known him?" Gerrity asked.

"Since childhood," Maria responded.

"How would you characterize your relationship with Mr. Galetti?" the lawyer asked.

"The two families were very close. Joe and my husband, Dom, were inseparable. Joe's wife, Alfie, is my best friend, but Joe and I weren't close—cordial but not close."

"Why not?" he asked.

"I'm not sure, really. As I said I've known him since childhood, so we have a history," she said.

"What kind of history?" Gerrity asked.

"Joe asked me to marry him many years ago," Maria said.

For some reason that caused a stir in the courtroom. Perhaps they were anticipating a juicy follow-up question, but it didn't happen as Gerrity asked his next question. "What was your working relationship with Mr. Galetti?"

"Cordial. He was my boss and he ran a tight ship. Joe Galetti epitomized the hardworking executive who was a little smarter and a little quicker than his competitors."

"Does that mean you never had disagreements at work with Mr. Galetti?"

"Heavens no! We fought like cats and dogs over issues. But when the day was done, we left all that stuff in the conference room. Joe was the bottom-line guy, our financial wizard, and so, in the end, he made the final decisions based on cost and return on investment," Maria said.

"Why did you leave the company?" Gerrity asked.

"Do you want the real answer or the public relations release we put out?" she asked.

"The truth," Gerrity replied.

"I was fired by Joe Galetti. Fired as president and removed from the board of directors."

"Why?" Ned Gerrity asked.

"For having an affair with a married man," Maria said as she looked straight at Ned Gerrity.

This caused more than a stir in the courtroom. Several reporters actually left their seats, and Judge Matthews asked the room to settle down. Gerrity then said, "Were you married at the time?"

"No, my husband had been gone for two years. And I know this sounds naive, but the man I was having this affair with told me he was separated from his wife."

"Were you upset by this decision?"

"Very," Maria responded.

"Is that why you are now taking Mr. Galetti to court?"

"Certainly not," Maria responded. "I didn't agree with his decision, but he had the votes to remove me from the board. I'm taking him to court because I believe he's sold stock that belongs to me."

"But why wouldn't you have gone to Mr. Galetti first to get his side?" Gerrity asked.

"Because I didn't trust him. I inadvertently received a tax form that said I sold three million dollars' worth of stock, and I know I didn't do that," she said.

Gerrity entered the tax form in question into evidence and continued his questioning. "Mrs. Galetti, why did you have Joe Galetti continue to handle your financial dealings after you were fired?"

"Because he's a business genius. He and my late husband built this business from one store in Newton Center to a billion-dollar business. I thought I was in very good hands. I had no reason to suspect Joe Galetti of anything. He'd been like a father to my kids for sixteen years. He's family. He's my dead husband's brother; why would I suspect him of anything?"

"I understand, Mrs. Galetti, but won't people think you're just getting even for being fired by Mr. Galetti?"

"People are going to think what they want. But let me ask you this. I haven't worked at the company for eight years. Does it make any sense that I would wait eight years to seek revenge?" Maria asked.

"Not to me, it doesn't," Gerrity said. "Your witness," he said to Jerry Saxe.

Judge Matthews called for a recess, but I just sat in my seat. I was trying to figure out Gerrity's strategy. It certainly wasn't the poor misunderstood widow dabbing her eyes with a handkerchief. Maria's answers were concise, relating the facts as she knew them. She handled Gerrity's questions like a true professional, some of which had to be embarrassing to her. She had ample opportunity to take potshots at Joe Galetti but she didn't. One thing was clear. Gerrity had preempted any chance Saxe had of springing the affair on the jury as a surprise tactic. As I got up to walk out of the courtroom, I was only sure of one thing. Jerry Saxe was probably rethinking his strategy for cross examination.

When Judge Matthews reconvened the court, he had just finished a conversation with a very attractive, young female who was taking notes as he spoke. I'd learn later that she was Helen Cortez, his law clerk. Jerry Saxe was up and pacing in front of Maria Galetti. He said, "Now, Mrs. Galetti, let's go back to this affair you mentioned. You knew the man you were having this affair with wasn't separated, didn't you?"

"I took him at his word that he was separated," Maria said.

"Oh, c'mon, you didn't just fall off the turnip truck. You can't tell me, at your level of sophistication, that you hadn't heard that one before, can you?" Saxe said.

"No, I can't," Maria said. "It crossed my mind that it might not be so, but I wanted to believe him," Maria said.

"Do you think Joe Galetti was unjustified in taking the action he did?" Saxe asked.

"I thought it was a harsh penalty," she said.

"Answer the question, please," Saxe responded.

"Objection," Gerrity said. "He's bullying the witness. She answered the question, Judge."

"Judge, she didn't say whether Mr. Galetti's decision was justified or not," Saxe said.

"I'll sustain the objection. She answered the question," Judge Matthews decided.

Saxe continued to question Maria right up until lunch, but neither side gave an inch. Jerry Saxe built a solid base, as he did with Trip, concerning Joe Galetti's reputation as a surrogate father to Maria's children and as a man who gave generously to the community. Maria was on the stand for nearly three hours, and I knew she had to be mentally exhausted, but when she walked off the stand at the lunch break, she looked fresh and crisp and every inch the lady I thought she was. I was no expert, but Maria enhanced her case as a witness with the jury. I don't think they felt any real sympathy for her, but they did think she was credible; and, in an odd way, I think the women on the jury liked the way she handled the questions about her affair. She was straightforward about it and didn't try to duck the issue. In hindsight I believe Ned Gerrity was right to put that one on the table before Saxe could have a field day with it. Just as I was leaving for lunch, Helen Cortez touched me on the arm and said, "Mr. Riley, I'm Helen Cortez, Judge Matthews' law clerk."

"Hi," I said. "Nice to meet you."

"Nice to meet you," she said. "I just wanted to let you know you're on the stand this afternoon."

"Thanks. That'll limit my calorie intake for lunch," I said.

"I don't know," she said, smiling, "you don't look like a guy that would be easily intimidated."

"Thanks, I'll see you this afternoon."

As I walked outside, who should be standing there but my gorgeous wife. "This is a very pleasant surprise," I said as I gave Holly an extra long hug.

"Geez, I'll come down here every day if I'm assured of a greeting like that," Holly said.

"Take it to the bank. Where are the kids?" I asked.

"Happy as pigs in that stuff with Claire," Holly said. "Hey, I brought a couple of sandwiches and a cold drink. Are you hungry?"

"Starved. Let's go sit by the water and eat," I said.

We drove down to the water in Hingham and set up shop, sitting on a bench facing the Hingham Yacht Club. We ate and gabbed and I told Holly I was up next on the stand. She looked at me and said, "Are you nervous?"

"I have to admit I have some butterflies. But you know this visit with you for lunch has served as a perfect reminder to me," I said.

"What does it remind you of?" Holly asked.

"If we ever have a squabble about money, just tape my mouth with duct tape and send me to the basement for an hour."

"But the basement has the pool table in it. What kind of punishment would that be?" Holly asked.

"Good point," I conceded. "Okay, the attic," I said. "It just isn't worth it. Maria being asked about an affair in front of strangers. Can you imagine the headlines tomorrow? If I get to be an asshole, promise me you'll take me out in a field and shoot me."

"I promise," Holly said as she leaned over and kissed me.

Holly dropped me off at the courthouse, and I wasn't exactly on time. Luckily for me, people were still milling around when I entered the courtroom, but then I saw Helen Cortez nod at the clerk of courts and the proceedings began. Helen walked by me and said, "I was just about to send out the posse."

"Sorry. Thanks for milling around until I got back," I said.

I was sworn in and Ned Gerrity quickly established who I was and where I lived. Ned's first questions dealt with my affiliation with Galetti-Pantry Place and then he said, "What's your relationship with the defendant?"

"He's my boss," I replied.

"How do you get along?" he asked.

"We disagree often on issues but it's nothing personal," I said.

"How would you describe Mr. Galetti?" he asked.

"He's bright, authoritative, and maybe a bit of an introvert," I said.

"Anything else?" Gerrity asked.

"Yes. He's a man of his word and he's very principled. Integrity would be high on that list of principles," I remarked.

Gerrity ran through the same list on Maria Galetti, and I responded very positively to include how innovative she was.

Then he asked, "What were your thoughts when Maria Galetti was removed from her job?"

"I was angry. In fact, Joe and I had a knockdown, drag-out fight about it. Figuratively speaking, of course."

"But weren't you named to replace her?" Gerrity asked.

"No, I wasn't," I responded. "I was named executive vice president, and Joe assumed Maria's title of president."

"But her loss was your gain," Gerrity stated.

"Not really," I said.

"Why not?" he asked.

"Because when the announcement came out, I had either quit or been fired; I wasn't sure which it was," I said.

"You felt that strongly about the termination of Maria Galetti?" Gerrity asked.

"I did," I said. "I gathered up my stuff in a cardboard box, and I took a cab home."

"What happened after that?" Gerrity asked.

"Joe and I sorted it out, and Maria called me and said, although she appreciated the support, she didn't want me to quit."

"Didn't you harbor bad feelings about Mr. Galetti after that incident?" Gerrity asked.

"It's a good question but the answer is no. This business is an emotional one, and the three of us—four, including Dom—worked together for over fifteen years. Frankly, I think the case could be made that this was a family disagreement, and I probably had my nose where it shouldn't be. We have a small executive committee, which is good for communication, but sometimes we get on each other's nerves," I said.

Gerrity wheeled away from me, not all that happy with my answer, and said, "Your witness."

Saxe was on me quickly. He said, "Mr. Riley, just a reminder, you are still under oath. Did you ever have an affair with Maria Galetti?"

Gerrity leaped to his feet and said, "Objection, Your Honor. Relevance."

Saxe responded quickly. "I'm trying to establish that Mr. Riley is not riding down the middle of the highway as he portrays himself. He's not a neutral witness, but prejudiced against my client, Your Honor."

"I'll allow the witness to answer the question."

"What was the question?" I asked. I knew what the question was, but I wanted to see Saxe's reaction. I could tell he thought I was playing with him a little, as a smile escaped from his lips.

"Did you ever have an affair with Maria Galetti?"

"No, I never did," I responded.

"Did you ever think about it?" Saxe asked.

"Objection, Your Honor," Gerrity said, "calls for speculation."

"Overruled," Judge Matthews said.

"Yes, I did. She's a very attractive woman," I said. I was expecting Saxe to follow up on this attraction to Maria, but he moved immediately to a new area.

"What have you got to gain from this case, Mr. Riley?"

"Not much but we could lose a lot. This case is a distraction to our business, and I'm sure, as we sit here, that our competitors are thinking of ways of taking business away from us."

"But we heard in earlier testimony that you are a likely candidate for CEO if Mr. Galetti should lose this case," Saxe said.

"I think that is purely speculation. And if I were named CEO, it would only be until the board deemed that a family member was ready to take over the job."

"So you would be a caretaker of sorts," Saxe said in kind of a disparaging manner.

"Your words, not mine, Counselor," I replied.

"What would your words be?" he asked.

"I'd say that being president of a billion-dollar business didn't define me as a caretaker," I replied.

"I'd agree," Saxe said. "Is it not true that you own some family stock?" he said.

"It is true," I said.

"So if this becomes a Mexican standoff between the Galetti families, you might have the swing votes. With that in mind, you could hold up both families for ransom," Saxe said.

"Is there a question in that diatribe?" I asked. The audience laughed at my question, but it seemed to really annoy Saxe.

"The question is, would you use your shares to leverage your current position?" Saxe asked.

"I guess I would have to talk to an attorney. But I only hold twenty-five shares, and the shares are derived equally from each side," I responded.

"Your Honor," Saxe said, "I'd like to make sure, for the record, that Mr. Riley is listed as a hostile witness. He refuses to answer my question," Saxe said.

"Frankly, Mr. Saxe, I think he answered your question, and it has already been established that he is a witness for the plaintiff in this case. So let's stop wasting the court's time," Judge Matthews said.

"Yes, sir," Mr. Saxe replied.

Saxe kept hammering away. "Isn't it true, Mr. Riley, that you resigned your post some years ago in a dispute with Mr. Galetti?"

"It is true," I admitted. "In fact, I've already testified that it was true."

"Isn't it also true that you and Mr. Galetti will yell at each other in board meetings to the embarrassment of the others in attendance?" Saxe asked.

"Mr. Galetti and I have been yelling at each other since I was thirteen years old," I replied. "As to the feelings of the other board members, I'm afraid you'll have to ask them."

Saxe kept me on the stand all afternoon, but, finally, he was done with me. Judge Matthews closed the proceedings for the day, and as I left my seat to head home, Helen Cortez came by me and said, "Riley ten, fat lawyer zero."

I laughed out loud and said, "Thanks. I'll tell you, being on the stand is no day at the beach."

Gerrity grabbed me on the way out and said, "Good job. I think the jury reads you as an impartial working stiff who wants to save the business."

"You know, Ned, I wasn't really concerned about the jury so much as I was Saxe. I was sure he was going to lead me into some type of trap, and, as a result, I'd be backing and filling for an hour or two," I said.

"I can tell you, he was frustrated with you. The tip-off came when he wanted you declared a hostile witness when you really hadn't said anything really offensive," Ned Gerrity said.

"Well, that's disappointing; I wouldn't have minded being somewhat offensive," I said. "See you later."

* * *

What a tangled web we weave…where were we so far? Nowhere, really. Maria and Trip established that they felt there was a clear case of fraud, and I think I was window-dressing. Gerrity had established that Joe was hard-nosed, egocentric, and that he could be ruthless. But Saxe came right back and showed him as an extraordinary family man and a great supporter of the community. True on all counts.

So, in truth, Joe was the swing vote here. Only he could unlock the mystery of where the stock was now and how and why it got there. The next week or two would be critical.

My mind was in a whole different place, really, particularly after I had testified. What was the competition thinking? If my biggest competitor was locked in a court battle, what would I do to steal share of market? What tricks would I have up my sleeve if I knew my competitor had taken his eye off the ball? For one thing, I'd turn up the heat. Slowly turn up the GRPs on radio and TV and run some gangbuster ads. Hey, wait a minute, screw the competition…that might be a great defensive strategy. Just when they think they have an advantage, we beat them to the punch.

I was driving home when these thoughts struck me, so I pulled over to the side of the road and called my assistant, Mary. I asked her to have the media buyers in my office at nine sharp, and the head buyer and merchandiser there at ten-thirty. Damn, this business is fun. I didn't know how much fun until I had to spend some time on the witness stand.

The headlines the next day in the metro and local newspapers were all about the Galetti trial. WIDOW ADMITS AFFAIR; DAY ONE: GALETTI FAMILY SQUARES OFF OVER A BILLION; JOE GALETTI: JEKYLL OR HYDE?

The affair got the most ink—along with pictures of Maria from just about every camera angle. I actually learned a new word from the stories. Internecine as in "internecine court battle over ownership." When I looked it up, the definition was mutually destructive: ruinous or fatal on both sides. Perfect. I'd never run across a word before that so accurately described the Galetti court battle.

Joe was on the stand in the morning, but I was in the office with the media folk. They had some fine commercials, and I was about to tell them something that would be music to their ears. As the two media folk peered at me from across the desk, I said, "Gentlemen, I want to take those commercials and turn the gross rating points up to saturation. I want ninety-five percent of the homes to see these commercials at least once a week."

"That'll be about two hundred twenty GRPs a week," Larry Barnes said.

"What will it cost me?" I asked. I really didn't want to hear the answer, but I knew we had a war chest that would sink the USS *Constitution*.

"Plenty. We'll get you the best rate available locally, but nationally, we're going to have to buy on-the-spot market because of the lack of lead time," Barnes said.

"Do it. But don't buy me *Gomer Pyle* reruns. If it's going to cost big bucks, then get me prime-time stuff. And, Larry…"

"Yes, Russ?" he asked.

"If you run these ads on *Laverne & Shirley*, I'll know it. Larry, I've got kids that watch that crap, so don't think I won't be looking."

"Gotcha. Thanks, Russ. We're out of here. Thanks to you, we've got a lot of work to do."

Next came the head buyer, Shirley Macober, and the head merchandiser, David Williams. My God, if they weren't total opposites—Shirley Macober was black and came up in the system starting as an aisle clerk. She'd been with us for 23 years, and she knew her stuff. I think a lot of people were afraid of her because she was big, over six feet tall, and she weighed about 180 pounds but she wasn't fat. She was just big. I thought she was attractive, and I loved her sense of humor. She had married her high school sweetheart, who was a long-distance freight hauler, and they didn't have any children. In a secret recess of my mind, I was wondering what it would be like to make love to this woman. Would I be bouncing off of the ceiling? God, I was a pervert. But I knew one thing: in arm wrestling she beats her husband three times out of five.

David Williams was in his early 30s, a graduate of Darden School of Business at Virginia, balding, married, had four children, and he was about 5'8" and weighed 160 pounds. But looks can be deceiving. I'd played golf with him, and he drove the ball 280 yards consistently...and, more importantly, straight. He was the perfect fit for people such as Shirley and me because he was always talking about "business planning" and "organizational strategy," while we had a tendency, if you grew up in the industry, to fly by the seat of our pants.

I opened the meeting with Shirley and David by saying, "You're looking particularly ravishing today, my dear."

"Oh, fuck, this opening means I'll be working over the weekend," Shirley said.

I laughed hard at Shirley, and she was grinning as well. "And how are you, David?" I asked.

"Relieved that 'my dear' was meant for Shirley and not me," David said.

I laughed at that too. Thankfully, David had a business mentality, not a bean counter's mentality. "I'm going to make this short and sweet. Sunday's newspaper is already in print, but I want to pull Wednesday's and redo it," I said.

"Oh great," Shirley said. "And while we're at it, why don't we have a frigging fish fry in every supermarket parking lot and invite all our customers?"

We hadn't been five minutes into this meeting when I lost complete control. But I continued anyway. "Let me tell you why I'm upsetting the applecart." I brought them around to my little video TV screen and played the commercials for them. Their reaction was immediate. Shirley said, "Jesus, those are good. You've even got a couple of 'sisters' in them. Is diversity coming to the Ice Age?"

David spoke for the first time. "They're excellent. Memorable and hard-hitting. But, Russ, is anybody going to see them?"

"Everybody who has a TV. We're running a saturation campaign. Ninety-five percent of homes at least once a week," I responded.

"What the hell did you have for breakfast?" Shirley asked.

"The competition," I said. "These guys are licking their chops over this court case, so I thought we'd slip a grenade into their pâté du foie."

"That brings us to the reason for this meeting, I assume," David said.

"Bingo. I want an ad that compares prices on the top twenty-five selling items with our two top competitors."

"But we aren't the lowest price chain on the majority of those items," Shirley said quite correctly.

"We will be next Wednesday," I said.

"I can change the prices, and David can redo the ad, but we won't have any product in the store," Shirley said. "David Pondorf, in the warehouse, will never go for it."

"Leave Pondorf to me. I've known him since I was thirteen years old. Your job is to order the product, Shirley, and, David, your job is to get the price right and get it in the papers by Wednesday. And, Shirley, you'll need to bulletin the stores today," I said.

I sat with them for another hour while we picked the items, and they took off to get it done. I called Pondorf. He had worked with me in the original store, and people were more scared of him than they were of Shirley. He was literally a giant, slightly over 6'3" and well over 300 pounds before he put his other foot firmly on the scale. And he was fat. He chewed big stogies and he ran a hell of a warehouse. But I was one of the few people who knew he was a big pussycat. One of the little-known secrets in our business was that the buying department and the warehouse rarely saw eye-to-eye. They should work in tandem like a hand and a glove. One department buys the stuff, and the other ships it. Right? Wrong. They fought almost every day over something. Turf war at its worst, and, unfortunately, our organization was no different than the industry.

Pondorf came on the phone and said, "What the fuck do you want?"

"Hello to you too, you douche bag. Don't piss me off or I'll come down there and kick the shit out of you," I said.

"Not on your best day. I'll throw you around like a sack of meal," he said.

"Better than having you eat one, you big son of a bitch. We'd have a profitable warehouse if you'd stop eating up all the food down there."

Pondorf laughed hard and said, "To what do I owe this personal phone call from the exalted president of the company?"

"I need you, in the next two weeks, to stand on your hands and not knock down the building," I said. Pondorf and I talked for 10 minutes, and he agreed that he could not only do the job, but he could do something that would help the cause. He had a machine that could assemble prebuilt pallets, and once he saw the quantities Shirley was ordering, he could start putting the pallets together for shipment to the stores. The advantage was that the store could pull the blister wrap off the pallets and put them directly on the floor. Time was money. We had the money but we were a little short on time.

I think it was an advantage having grown up in the system. I'd known David Pondorf before we ever had a warehouse, and, like me, he had a lot of loyalty to the Galetti corporation. He wanted to get the job done right the first time; it was just his size and demeanor that scared people away. As soon as I hung up from Pondorf, I called Joey Jr. and asked him to come to my office. Joey Galetti Jr. was younger than his cousin Trip by two years, and the two boys had been close ever since either could remember being aware of the other. They were a study of contrasts. Trip was big, charismatic, quick to come to a conclusion, and very confident. Joey was slight, a bit unsure of himself, bright, and he pondered things endlessly. I'd put them through the same training program, and they both excelled but in a different manner. Trip was a big-picture guy, while Joey studied every detail of a business plan. They had one thing in common with their dads; Trip always started a question with "how," and Joey always started his with the word "what." The other thing the boys had in common was that they liked to win.

Joey came to my office promptly, and I asked him to take a seat. I said, "How are you, Joey?"

"Good, all things considered. I make specific reference to the current Galetti range war," he said.

"Yeah, things could be better. How is your mom these days?" I asked.

"Quiet. She doesn't approve of this fiasco, and I think she misses her daily walks and chats with Maria."

"How about your dad?" I asked.

"He's holding up his end. If anything, he's a little more intense than usual...if that can be believed," Joey said.

"How about you and Trip?" I asked.

"We're doing okay but I think we both have come to realize that our plans for the future may be in jeopardy," he said.

"What do you mean?" I asked.

"Well, depending on the outcome of the trial, we may or may not be fifty-fifty partners. If we aren't, we won't be able to operate the way our dads did before Uncle Dom died."

"I see what you mean," I said. "For the record, I'd bet the two of you would be a pretty formidable team."

"Thanks. Frankly, we think so too, but right now everything seems to be in suspended animation," Joey said.

"Right. While you're feeling so light on your feet, I've got a job for you," I said.

"Okay," Joey said.

I took about 40 minutes to explain to Joey the action plan I had just initiated with buying, merchandising, and the warehouse. And then I said to Joey, "I've just spent several million dollars to surprise our competition and jump-start our business. I think it's a good plan because it has the element of surprise, and it will be well-executed. That's where you come in, Joey. I've got to watch other things while your dad is in court, so I'm turning this over to you. Don't screw it up."

"And if I do?" Joey asked.

"It's back to dairy," I said.

"Oh, Jesus. I better make this work."

"You'll do fine. First thing I'd do—"

"Is alert Arnold Cable," he said as he finished my thought for me.

I took a second and said, "Yeah, that's what I was going to say. But since you're a mind reader, I'll let you go…"

Joey got up and waved as he left. The phone was ringing, so I picked it up, and the voice on the other end said, "Russ, it's Elsie Barden."

"Just the woman I wanted to talk to," I said.

"How come?" she said.

"Because I need an opinion from a veteran businessperson," I said. "What would you do if your boutiques were under the pressure we're under right now?"

"Cry," she said.

"After a good cry what would you do?"

"I'd run the goddamned biggest sale you ever saw," she said.

"Great. That's just what I'm going to do. I'm glad you called. What can I do for you?"

"Great minds," she said. "I just wanted to get your feel for how it's going so far," she said.

"I don't know, really. I'd say both sides are scoring points, but Joe's side won the battle of the headlines."

"I agree," she said. "But I loved the way Maria handled herself under very difficult circumstances," Elsie said.

"How'd it go this morning?"

"Pretty mundane. Gerrity is circling the wagons around Joe, but Joe seems evasive to me. He doesn't answer anything directly. It would annoy the shit out of me if I were on the jury," she said.

"I'm about to head over for the afternoon session," I said.

"Okay, see you there," she said as she hung up.

* * *

As I pulled into the court parking lot, I saw Ed Rollins, the *Supermarket News* reporter I'd met in Bermuda some years ago. As I approached the entrance to the courthouse, Ed greeted me by saying, "Who would have thunk it?"

"Who would have thunk it indeed," I replied. "How are you, Ed? This must be a big-time event if you're covering it in person."

"None bigger. It's not every day that you see a family squabble over a billion dollars. Frankly, this is a lot more interesting than reporting the most recent price of barley in the Southeast."

"I hear that. What's your take on this morning with Joe on the stand?" I asked.

"Pretty peaceful this morning but I think Gerrity will be touching some nerve endings this afternoon," Rollins said.

"So I arrived for the good part," I said.

"Your timing is impeccable. My mind keeps wandering back to Bermuda now that this fiasco is brewing," Rollins said.

"Why?" I asked, knowing exactly where he was headed.

"You and Maria at a table for two and this affair we've just heard about. I keep asking myself, since neither of you were married at the time, if there was something I missed," Rollins said.

"Keep it in your pants, Ed, will you? For God's sake, it's ancient history, and her husband had only been dead for two days. I hope you factored in a little common decency while your mind was wandering," I said.

"Yeah, you're right. It's ancient history and it's not really germane unless I was writing for *Star* or some other Hollywood gossip rag," he said.

"See you later," I said. I could have done without that exchange, but at least I gave Rollins credit for saying what was on his mind. That was a strange time, with the passing of Dom and Maria sleeping in my bed because she couldn't sleep alone after all those years of sleeping with Dom.

Gerrity was just starting the questioning of Joe in the afternoon session. I sat in a seat fairly close to the back of the room as Gerrity asked his first question. "Mr. Galetti, how much is Galetti-Pantry Place worth in today's dollars?"

"I couldn't say. You'd have to ask my chief financial officer, Lenny Hirshberg," Joe responded.

"Roughly, one dollar, one hundred million, a billion? Give us a ballpark figure," Gerrity asked.

"Over a billion," Joe said.

At this point Gerrity went to the side of the room and slid a generated chart over near the witness stand but facing the jury. Joe could see it clearly as well. I was on an angle to it, which made it hard for me to see it, but it was still partially facing the audience in the courtroom. "Now, how many shares of stock were issued for the business?"

"One thousand shares," Joe responded.

"So, if I did the math right, and that's always a question, each share is worth one million dollars if your firm is valued at over a billion dollars."

"You did the math right," Joe said.

"Who holds what amount of stock today? That is, how many shares does your family hold, and how many shares does Maria Galetti's family hold?"

"I built this business. We only had sixteen stores when my brother died. Seventy-five percent of the current business has been added since the death of my brother. It's been sixteen years since he passed away. I've never cheated anybody in my life. Why would I have to? I don't need the money. I drive an eight-year-old car, and I work seventy-five hours a week. Do you believe me?"

"Mr. Galetti, your record precedes you. But the question I asked is, how many shares of the original stock does each family own now? When you and your late brother became executors of each other's wills, you also agreed to share the business equally. That means each family should have five hundred shares."

"That's how it was originally, when Dom died, but I've had expenses incurred for taking care of his family. And at least one of that family has asked me to sell his shares to support his lifestyle in Europe. That money doesn't grow on trees. But that family still has twice as many shares as they have earned."

I was starting to see what Elsie Barden's frustration was all about this morning. Joe just wouldn't answer the question. Maybe the answer was in there somewhere, but I couldn't find it. Gerrity remained very calm but he was like a bulldog that had seized the cuff of a good pair of trousers. He just wasn't going to let go. "Mr. Galetti, I don't think it's a complicated question; how are the original one thousand shares allocated today between the two Galetti families?"

"You'll have to ask my comptroller and the tax lawyers," Joe finally said.

"You have no idea what the answer to the question is?" Gerrity asked.

"I'm not sure," Joe responded.

Gerrity turned to the judge and said, "Your Honor, I need to ask the witness to step down, subject to further recall, and call his CFO to the stand to obtain the answer to the question that Mr. Galetti can't answer."

"Is this witness available, Mr. Gerrity?"

"I don't know, Your Honor. His name is Lenny Hirshberg."

The judge looked at Joe and said, "Do you know if Mr. Hirshberg is in the courtroom, Mr. Galetti?"

"He is not, Your Honor," Joe responded. "He's back at our headquarters in Bridgewater."

"I see," Judge Matthews said. "The court is dismissed until Monday morning at 8:00 a.m. We will begin on Monday with Mr. Hirshberg, Mr. Saxe."

"Yes, Your Honor," Saxe responded.

"Would you please ensure that Mr. Hirshberg is in court on Monday?" the judge asked.

"Yes, sir, I will," Saxe responded.

I left the courtroom and headed for my car. As I was backing out of my spot, I saw Jerry Saxe talking to the reporters while Joe made his getaway in his automobile. I put my window down just in time to hear Saxe say, "It's a travesty that anyone would even think to bring a man of Joe Galetti's reputation for integrity to court. This is a man of principle, a leader in the community, a devoted family man, and an entrepreneur without peer, whose reputation is being dragged through the streets like a common guttersnipe without a scintilla of hard evidence. Thank you, ladies and gentlemen, have a nice weekend."

Chapter 12: Poor, Pathetic Little Turd

Nobody was home that Friday afternoon when I walked into my house, but the phone was ringing. I picked it up and said, "Hello."

"Russ, sorry to bother you at home but this is important."

"Who is this?" I replied.

"It's Ed Rollins from *Supermarket News*."

"Hey, Ed, the workweek is over. Give it a rest," I said.

"Look, I've picked up a tip that Joe Galetti and his wife, Alfie, are separated, and she's filing for divorce."

"What's that got to do with me?" I asked.

"I'm looking to confirm the story," Ed replied.

"I don't know anything about it, and I'm pretty certain I would have heard something if it were true. But why are you interested?" I asked.

"Because it could have a major bearing on this case," Rollins replied.

"How so?" I asked while starting to see where Rollins was going.

"Well, it doesn't have a direct bearing on the case, but I'm assuming if they divorce that Alfie would receive some stock in the settlement."

"Okay," I said. "But doesn't the jury need to determine who owns what before this could become a factor?" I asked.

"I suppose," Rollins said.

"So what's your hurry?" I asked.

"A guy in the food business has to ask me that question?" Rollins said.

"I got it. Competition. You want to break the story first."

"Bingo."

"Sorry, Ed, I really don't know anything, but if I did, I still wouldn't tell you anything," I said. "But a word to the wise. If Joe is willing to go to court over billions of dollars, I'm thinking he wouldn't hesitate to drag you and that rag of yours into court if you report something that isn't true."

"Don't worry, Russ. I'll have it pinned down before I go to press. Have a good weekend."

"You too, partner," I said as I hung up.

Normally, I wouldn't put any credence in a report like this, but these weren't normal times. I hit the refrigerator for a Corona, changed out of my business clothes, and headed to the backyard to try and wrestle with this new turn of events.

But after one sip from my beer, I was out of my seat, back in the kitchen, and dialing another number. Maria Galetti answered and I said, "Hi, Maria, how are you holding up?"

"Well, thanks, and I'm glad it's the weekend. I'm going to get a book, curl up in a corner, and just enjoy being by myself," Maria said.

"The reason I called is I just got a call from Ed Rollins of *Supermarket News*," I said.

"Our Bermuda friend?" she asked.

"The same," I responded. "He called me to confirm a story. He had heard that Joe and Alfie were separated and that she was filing for divorce."

Maria hesitated and said, "It's true but I can't understand how he'd know about it."

"It blows me away. I didn't have an inkling, and I'm guessing Joey Jr. doesn't know either."

"He knows. But in his case, I'm guessing it's not something he'd talk about at the watercooler at work. Alfie called me and said Joe has been seeing somebody and that she got wind of it. When she confronted him he didn't deny it."

"Jesus. This is turning into a prime-time soap opera," I said.

"Yeah, life imitating art," Maria said. "You're not going to confirm it with Rollins, right?"

"No way," I said. "I told him even if I knew something, I wouldn't tell him."

"Good," Maria said.

"Well, have a good weekend with your book," I said.

"You as well; and Russ?" she said.

"Yes?"

"It took a lot of guts to tell the world on the stand that you were thinking of having an affair with me," Maria said.

"Hey, I was under oath," I said. "I just hope Trip doesn't beat the crap out of me."

"No, no, he's okay. In fact, he's been kidding me about it, although I think he's wondering how anybody would be attracted to his old mom," Maria said.

"Get that boy some spectacles, but I know what you mean. See you later," I said.

I walked outside to the backyard and took a long pull on my Corona. The next thing I knew, Holly was poking me and saying, "Wake up, it's the middle of the afternoon."

"Hey, how you doing? What time is it?"

"Four-thirty," she said as she leaned down and kissed me.

"Where are the kids?" I asked.

"In the TV room," she said.

"What's going on?" I asked.

"Well, we've got dinner reservations at our favorite place at seven-thirty," she said.

"Great. How was your day?" I asked.

"We spent almost the whole day at the pond. Those kids of yours love the water. They'd stay in all day if I let them. What did you do to entertain yourself today?"

"Let's see; I spent a few million this morning and went to court in the afternoon," I said.

"How did that go?" she asked.

"I'll tell you at dinner," I responded.

We were on our way to dinner after I had picked up and delivered the sitter to our house. I learned on the way that Claire was at the pond with Holly and the kids, so I had missed a real family outing and a picnic Claire had pulled together that was fit for a king. As we entered Pier 4, something looked familiar to me as I passed the bar on the way to the dining room. Sitting in the far corner were Joe Galetti and Diane Dunbar. I was so shocked that I took a second look to confirm I'd really seen what I thought I'd seen, but I at least had the presence to keep walking.

After we were seated I said to Holly, "I think I just saw something quite unbelievable."

"Joe Galetti and Diane Dunbar by chance?" she asked with a smile.

"Wow, nothing gets by you," I said in utter amazement.

"It would be a good thing for you to remember," she said, laughing.

"Okay. But what the hell do we do if they march in here and sit at that table?" I asked, pointing to the table next to us.

"We say howdy and eat our dinner," Holly said.

"Jesus, you're some kind of cool cucumber," I said.

"Hey, we're the married couple, remember?" Holly said.

"Okay, okay, but I need to tell you something," I said.

"What?" she asked.

"Maria told me this afternoon that he and Alfie are separated," I said.

"Well, that certainly makes the cheese more binding," Holly said. "But my question is, what is your lawyer doing playing footsie with Joe Galetti?"

Just then the waiter came by for the drink order, and I ordered a double martini straight up, and Holly ordered a wine spritzer. "Good question," I said, thinking to myself that I was somehow being compromised.

As it turned out Diane and Joe never made it to the dining room, and if it hadn't been for the fact that Holly had seen them too, I would have doubted what I'd seen with my own eyes. No matter what they were doing together, it just seemed too bizarre to me. I don't know what was worse. If it was business, why would Diane be talking with Joe Galetti when she already represented me? And if it wasn't business, why in the world would Diane be tangled up with a married guy? Joe Galetti was just smarter than that. Why would he take the chance of being spotted in a very public place when he was fighting for his business life? I held Holly's hand all the way out to our car. She could tell I was distracted, and that's why she probably said to me, "Russ, sleep on it for a couple of days. I know you think the inmates are taking over the asylum, but you're on the periphery of a situation that may have a rational explanation. And if it doesn't, we just have to move on."

"I know you're right," I said. "But I've known most of these people all my life, and right now I'm feeling as if I don't really know them at all. In business, even our nutty business, logic usually helps to sort things out, but I just don't get any of this."

"Well, sometimes life is a lot more complex than business. Maybe it's a series of midlife crises, and they all hit at once. Joe's lost his brother, his sister-in-law is suing him, and maybe he's just cracked under the pressure. I don't know about Diane. She's successful, isn't married, and maybe she's a moth drawn to the flame. You've known her for a long time but not well for the last twenty years or so."

"You may be right," I said, "but the next thing I expect to hear is that Claire ran away with the bearded lady from the circus."

Holly laughed at that and said, "Now there's a stretch. But don't stay up at night trying to figure out stuff that's out of your control."

It was good advice. I spent the rest of the weekend fooling around in my workshop, trying to build a Soap Box Derby car. We were never going to make the finals in Akron, Ohio, with the machine I had built with the kids, but I sure had a good time running it down the driveway until we hit a rock and busted an axle. Claire had invited us over for a burger cookout with the kids on Sunday, and we all had a ball at Gramma's house.

On Sunday night I was going through my closet, looking for something to wear for the next day, when the phone rang. It was Arnold Cable, who almost never called me on the weekend. "What's up, Arnold?" I said.

"I was playing poker with a couple of pals last night, both lawyers, and they told me that Joe Galetti will be indicted on RICO charges concerning the way the pension fund has been handled by the board."

"When?" I asked.

"Within two weeks," Arnold said. "In truth, the indictment on the pension plan and the labor department investigation doesn't add up to a hill of beans monetarily; but it's a lethal blow to Joe's reputation as a model citizen and casts doubt on his character at a very inopportune time."

"Why doesn't it add up to a hill of beans?" I asked.

"Because the worst thing that can happen is that the court will tell the administrators of the pension fund to sell the risky holdings and convert the money to more conservative instruments. Hell, when I was at A&P and we were doing poorly, the executive committee tried to disband the pension fund and feed it back into profits for the company. The courts stopped them from doing it, but nobody went to prison. And that's all that will happen here. But Gerrity has to be dancing in the street; terrible timing for Jerry Saxe and Joe Galetti."

"Jesus, what a mess," I said.

"It is that," Arnold said and he hung up.

I couldn't get away from this case even on the weekend. And it was growing more complex by the minute. I sensed for the first time that the empire Joe Galetti had built over a lifetime was about to slip through his fingers. I was saddened by the news of his divorce and what looked like another high-profile court case concerning the pension fund. But, in truth, I was fighting mad about Diane Dunbar's role in this, and, as it turned out, I couldn't heed Holly's advice of sleeping on it for a few days. At eight o'clock on Monday, I was in her waiting room, without an appointment, awaiting her arrival. She appeared 20 minutes later, and I could tell by her facial expression that I was the last person she expected to see in her waiting room. "What are you doing here, Russ?" she asked.

"I need to see you, Counselor," I said.

"Okay. Follow me," she said as she made her way to her office, with me close behind. As pissed as I was, I still couldn't help but notice what an extraordinary physical specimen she was. She was dressed in a matching skirt and jacket, very conservative, really, but it was, at the same time, an alluring look. She'd look good in anything, and maybe, I thought, that was part of my problem. I should have hired a very smart, ordinary-looking guy; our history was in my way.

"Coffee?" she asked.

"No thanks," I said. "Let me get right to it, Diane; what in the fuck were you doing having dinner with Joe Galetti at Pier 4?" I asked.

"We didn't have dinner; we had drinks. I made dinner for him at my place," she said.

"Oh, even better," I said.

"I don't see that it's any of your business whom I socialize with," Diane said.

"None of my business, none of my business," I said as my voice started to rise. "How about he's married, he's my boss, and my lawyer is fucking him," I replied.

"When did you become my keeper?" she asked as her voice started to rise.

"I'm not your keeper. But at the very least, it seems inappropriate to me. He's already hired every lawyer east of the Mississippi, and if it were business, it seems as if it is a conflict of interest, since I'm already your client. And if, as I suspect, it's something else, it's even worse. If it's romantic, the man's married and he's fighting for his very existence right now. The last thing he needs is to be in the gossip columns with a pretty woman, who, by the way, isn't his wife and is young enough to be his daughter."

"Are you done?" Diane asked.

"No, but I'm out of breath," I responded.

"You don't know the whole story," Diane said.

"If you are referring to his separation and possible divorce, I know that part of the story," I replied.

Diane seemed surprised at my revelation but asked, "How'd you find out?"

"It's none of your business but I'll tell you. A reporter I know from *Supermarket News* called me."

"Jesus," Diane said.

"What could you be thinking about?" I asked.

"Don't take that tone with me," she said.

"Tone? What tone would you take if your lawyer were whispering sweet nothings to your boss while getting laid in some intimate setting?" I asked.

"We don't talk about you when we're making love. By the way, I'm usually on top while we're doing it," she said. "He's a powerful man and he chased me down, not the other way around. I have some empathy for his wife, but the breakup was inevitable," Diane said.

"I didn't get it until now," I said. "You are one coldhearted bitch."

"You're just jealous," she said. "God, you're a naive asshole. You think we should be back in the backseat of your car, humping each other like we did it in high school. You poor, pathetic little turd. You're just a bit player in this action. I didn't get to where I am today without stepping on a few toes."

"I've got two words for you, you miserable excuse for a human being: You're fired," I said.

Diane Dunbar just laughed at me and said, "Get lost before I call security."

As I began to leave the office, I said, "You can expect a call from a real lawyer concerning your ethics in this case."

"Oh, I'm all atwitter with trepidation," she responded.

I barged out the front door of the building, running into a man and knocking him to the ground. I picked him up, dusted him off, mumbled "sorry," and walked to my car but not before I heard him say, "Asshole, look where you are going."

He was right. I didn't look where I was going when I hired the eminent barrister, Diane Dunbar. She was right about one thing. I was naive; Jesus, I didn't have a clue. When I sat in my car, I was shaking with rage. But I think I was really madder at myself than Diane. How did I not see this one coming?

After leaving Diane abruptly, I returned to the office without a lot of motivation and thumbed through my messages. Bill Hartman had called, so I picked up the phone and returned the call. After saying hello, Hartman said to me, "How are you holding up? It's been a crazy couple of weeks for you."

"You can say that again. What's the reaction out there to our most recent marketing and merchandising moves?" I asked.

"A couple of things. You guys did such a good job of coordinating the TV and newspaper stuff that it didn't escape any of your competitors. What I mean by that is, sometimes you can turn up the tube and run hot advertising in the paper, and the competition will notice the newspaper stuff but not pick up the 'heavy-up' on TV right away. But this campaign is so well-coordinated between copy and feature pricing that it's pretty obvious. That's a good thing, by the way," Hartman said.

"Good perspective. That was Joey's idea and it seems to be working, as the initial volume has been super," I replied.

"How's the battle going inside the building?" Hartman asked.

"It's a little disjointed. In fact, I could use your good ear to bounce a couple of things off if you have some time." Hartman agreed to meet me after work for a beer.

Arnold Cable walked into my office, sat down, and just looked at me. "What?" I said.

"I just got a call from some of my old A&P buddies who work this market," Arnold said.

"And?" I asked.

"Man, they are stunned at what we did this past week. They had this big plan to blow us out of the water this coming Sunday, but that was before our stuff hit."

"Are they readjusting?"

"Trying. One of my friends says it's chaos over there. They are readjusting their prices and working with no lead time. Further, they have to get approval from New York to spend the kind of dough they need, so that's slowing the process. My guess is that they'll match us on Sunday, but they won't have anything in the stores to back them up. So they'll be issuing rainchecks like confetti, and, at the same time, they'll be pissing off a lot of their consumers."

"Hear anything from Stop & Shop?"

"Very quiet, ominous even," Cable replied.

Arnold took off and, at the end of the day, I visited Hartman at our pre-designated watering hole. But before I left I called Holly and told her I'd be late. She had a mild objection but didn't lay too much guilt on me. I was only two miles from my destination, so I thought I'd beat Hartman to it, but when I opened the door of the bar, he was already ensconced at a barstool with a draft that looked like it needed a refill.

I sat down next to him and said, "How long have you been here, big fella?"

"Just long enough to wash down a little of that road dust," he said. "How was your week, Bill Buckner?"

"Jesus, it wasn't that bad, but it was close," I said. "But at least I had fun at work."

"As soon as I saw the newspapers, I knew you were behind it," Hartman said. "I'll tell you, it's working. In case you haven't had a chance to be in the stores, I can tell you they are doing brisk business."

"As opposed to brisket of beef?" I asked.

"You know, I see that advertised all the time, and I still don't know what it is. It sounds like something that should be hanging in a broom closet or maybe that office you had when I first met you," Hartman said.

That made me laugh; I was feeling better already. I'll say one thing for Hartman—he was steady. When I was around this guy, I just felt as if things were going to be okay. "What a weekend," I said almost to myself.

"First, Ed Rollins calls me and tells me Joe and his wife, Alfie, are separating."

"True?" Hartman asked.

"It's true," I replied. "Then, when I'm out at dinner, I see Joe and Diane playing footsie at Pier 4."

"I'll tell you this," Hartman drawled, "it sure is boring on my side of the desk when I hear your tale of woe and I'm glad."

"Of all the things, the most troubling to me is Joe and Diane Dunbar."

"Personally or professionally?" Hartman asked.

"Both. Ain't it beautiful? My lawyer is representing me, with Joe being the potential adversary, and they're discussing every little thing while they frolic under the covers."

"Man, this smells of soap opera. A made-for-TV flick at the very least," Hartman says.

"Yeah, but who plays me in the flick?" I asked.

"Yogi Berra!" Hartman immediately responded.

I laughed so hard that I started to cough while tears were running down my face. I said, "Jesus, Hartman, I've got to give it to you. You are one funny son of a bitch."

"Well, you know what Yogi said when a reporter at spring training asked the usual inane question. The reporter said, 'What size baseball cap do you wear, Yogi?'"

"No, I don't. What did he say?" I asked.

He said, "I don't know. I'm not in shape yet."

Ten minutes with Hartman and my troubles seemed to be diminishing rapidly. He looked at me and said, "What are you going to do about the good ship USS *Dunbar*?"

"Break a frigging bottle over her neck, to use a ship-launching metaphor—and let the bow line off and let her drift out to sea," I said.

"Good move. What a fucking Jezebel. You know what I think?" he said.

"Do I have a choice?" I asked.

"No," he responded. "I think she couldn't fuck you, so she's going to fuck your boss. But don't get too carried away. After what you just told me, I think every pig on the planet has porked her."

"Jesus, talking about going up the chain of command," I said.

"Yeah, but just make sure it's not your chain that's getting yanked," Hartman said.

"What do you mean?" I said.

"Well, you've dumped her as your lawyer, so now she whispers in Joe's ear that you were planning to use your shares to aid and abet Maria, the enemy. By the way, were you boinking Maria?" Hartman asked.

"I'm pretty sure she's already done that. And no, I wasn't boinking Maria," I said.

"Pity," Hartman said. "I don't know how old she is, but man, those pictures in the paper this week were flat-out juicy. She's right up there with Natalie J."

"Actually, I'd have to pick Natalie, but Maria wins the battle of legs, hands down. I knew you'd have a good slant, Hartman. I come to talk serious shit with you, and we end up talking about broads."

"My absolute favorite subject, except, of course, P&G," Hartman responded.

"You Proctoids are all the same…mean bastards," I said with a smile.

"Hey, listen, I know our industry is a royal pain in the ass, but would you rather be doing anything else for a job?" Hartman asked.

"Center field for the BoSox?" I said.

"Naw, get real. Who the hell wants a multimillion-dollar salary when you can be out there busting your hump in the food business?"

"That's the first thing you've said that makes any sense," I responded.

"Even a blind squirrel finds a piece of poontang every once in a while," Hartman said.

"You don't want me to mention that little bon mot to Jenny, I'm sure," I said.

"Hell no. I don't want to be sleeping in the Hotel Camaro," he said. "What's up in court tomorrow?"

"Lenny 'Listen' Hirshberg," I responded.

"What's that mean?" he asked.

"Our CFO is going to tell everyone where the stock is now. But when he gets nervous, he starts every sentence with the word 'listen,'" I said.

"What a mess," he said. "I got to get going, or Jenny will put me on the charcoal grill," he said.

"Hey, have a good week. Seriously, thanks for sitting down and giving me your slightly bizarre point of view," I said.

"You're welcome. Anytime. Best to Holly; tell her she's a saint for me," Hartman said as he rolled off the stool and headed for his car.

I picked up the tab…as usual. It was role reversal. I was the customer but I always picked up Hartman's tab. Among other things, Hartman made me realize that my problems weren't insurmountable. My problems were molehills, not mountains.

Monday I was back in court, listening to a very nervous Lenny Hirshberg on the stand. "Now, Mr. Hirshberg," Ned Gerrity said, standing next to the generated chart that he had placed in the courtroom on Friday. "Who owns the thousand shares today that once were split evenly between the Galetti families?"

Lenny looked right at Gerrity and said, "Seven hundred fifty shares are held by Joe Galetti and two hundred fifty by the late Dom Galetti's family."

The courtroom started to buzz. Gerrity had pounded away with the previous witnesses that the stock was originally split 50-50 between the families. Gerrity had gleaned from Hirshberg more information in one question and answer than he had received in all of the testimony given by Joe Galetti so far. Everyone in the room, for the first time, sensed that all was not on the up-and-up in the Galetti Empire. I tried to read the faces of the jury, but they remained fairly stoic. Helen Cortez, the law clerk, perhaps being young and inexperienced, showed the most body language. Her face told me she thought this was a breakthrough and that sentiment had shifted to Maria's team.

Gerrity pressed Hirshberg. "But, Mr. Hirshberg, isn't this stock supposed to be equally held by both families?"

"I don't know. I'm not a lawyer," Hirshberg responded.

"Well, tell me this, Mr. Hirshberg. How did two hundred fifty shares of stock move from Maria Galetti's family to Joe Galetti's family?"

"You'll have to ask the tax lawyers," Hirshberg said.

"I remind you, Mr. Hirshberg, you are under oath. I hope you don't expect the jury to believe that, as chief financial officer of a corporation doing in excess of a billion dollars, you don't know how the assets are split between families and how they got that way."

"Listen, I know some of it, but I had nothing to do with the family will, and my department has been audited every year by an outside accounting firm. You can check the records yourself, Mr. Gerrity. We are as clean as the driven snow," Hirshberg said.

"Oh really, Mr. Hirshberg?" Gerrity asked. "Is it or is it not true that, as we speak, the labor department has asked a grand jury to look into your real estate practices concerning the company pension plan?"

Jerry Saxe was on his feet, yelling, "Objection, Your Honor. Mr. Gerrity is referring to something that hasn't even transpired. There are no indictments. There is no case. This is just a sham, it's a wooden horse, and it's tabloid sensationalism with no facts behind it that have any place in a court of law."

Judge Matthews' response was immediate. "I will sustain the objection, and I'll ask the jury to disregard anything remotely involved with this case. And I'm also warning you, Mr. Gerrity, that I will declare you in contempt of court if this subject is broached again."

"Yes, sir, Your Honor," Ned Gerrity said in a somewhat chagrined tone. Gerrity may have been admonished by Judge Matthews, but, in my view, he was very effective. Certainly to me there seemed to be some "pee holes" in the freshly driven snow Mr. Hirshberg had alluded to.

Hirshberg was practically twitching in his seat. I knew Lenny pretty well, and I thought he was an honest man, but he was an introvert, and it was clear that he didn't like confrontation. "Let's get back to the two hundred fifty shares, Mr. Hirshberg," Ned Gerrity said. "How did they get from Maria Galetti's family to the possession of Mr. Joe Galetti?"

"Well, family members of the late Dominic Galetti sold their shares to Joe Galetti so they could live in the style they were accustomed to," Hirshberg said.

"Which family members?" Gerrity asked.

"Maria and Arthur Galetti," Hirshberg responded.

"But, Mr. Hirshberg, we've already heard testimony from Maria Galetti that she was unaware of any stock being sold," Gerrity said.

"Listen, listen," Hirshberg said. "I don't know anything about that. I'm just telling you what the facts are as I know them. The stock does not provide dividends, so if someone in the Galetti family wanted money, they would have to sell shares."

"No further questions, Your Honor," Gerrity said. As the judge was turning the witness over to Jerry Saxe, Gerrity noted on his chart in the front of the room that Joe's family had 750 shares and Maria's family had 250 shares.

Saxe was on his feet immediately with a number of papers in his hand. "Mr. Hirshberg, I show you a series of transactions that indicate how the two hundred fifty shares moved from Maria Galetti to Joe Galetti. Can you verify these for me?" Hirshberg looked at the papers and said, "Yes, this is the paperwork that caused the shares to be transferred to Joe Galetti."

"I ask you, sir, are these the signatures of Maria and Arthur Galetti?" Saxe asked.

"They are," Hirshberg said.

"No further questions," Saxe said as he returned to his seat.

Hirshberg was excused and Joe Galetti was back on the stand. "Mr. Galetti, I presume your memory is now refreshed and that you are aware that you own seven hundred fifty shares and Maria Galetti's family owns the remaining two hundred fifty shares," Gerrity said from his seat at the table.

"I am," Galetti responded.

"But, Mr. Galetti, in earlier testimony you indicated that only one member of Maria Galetti's family had sold stock. We've just heard Mr. Hirshberg say there were two members of that family who had sold stock. Which one were you referring to when you testified last week?" Gerrity asked.

"Arthur Galetti," Joe said. "Look, he was living in Europe with no viable means of support, and he wanted to sell his stock to accommodate his lifestyle."

"But why would he have to sell stock if there were no dividends?" Gerrity asked. "Wouldn't he be entitled, as a shareholder, to receive a share of the ongoing profits?"

"Look, I built this chain with my own hands by working eighty hours a week. The kid never did a lick of work in his life. Why should he share in the profits?"

"Because he was a stockholder," came the lightning-quick answer from Ned Gerrity.

"Objection, Your Honor," Saxe said, "the witness answered the question."

"Sustained," said Judge Matthews.

"I'll rephrase, Your Honor," Gerrity said. "Mr. Galetti, was Mr. Arthur Galetti aware that he was selling his stock in the corporation and not receiving ongoing profits?"

"He signed the paperwork," Joe Galetti said, responding to Gerrity's question.

"But, Mr. Galetti, you just said yourself that Arthur Galetti never worked in the business and, in fact, wasn't even living in the United States. Is it your judgment that he knew what he was signing?" Gerrity asked.

"I don't know," Joe Galetti said. "He certainly wasn't a businessman, but the boy could read."

"Okay, let's move on. Why had it slipped your mind that Maria Galetti had sold stock?"

"Because it was a long time ago," Joe Galetti said.

"How long ago?" Gerrity said.

"About three months after Dom died?" Galetti responded.

"You're telling us that you sold some of your brother's stock to yourself three months after he died?" Gerrity asked, his voice rising ever so slightly.

"I am," Joe Galetti said.

"But why would she do that?" Gerrity asked. "She was a widow with four children."

"That's precisely why," Galetti responded.

"So you're saying that all this benevolence that we've heard about was really a business deal. You supported your dead brother's children and his family by selling their stock to your side of the family," Gerrity said.

"I didn't look at it that way," Joe Galetti responded.

"Tell the court how you did look at these circumstances," Gerrity said.

"I had to be responsible for the welfare of two families, and I had a successful but small business at the time to run by myself. I did what I thought best for both families. I made sure that my brother's family never wanted for anything, but there was a price in hard dollars to pay for that luxury," Joe Galetti said.

"Did Maria Galetti understand that you were selling her inheritance to accomplish these goals?" Gerrity asked.

"She signed the papers, so I assumed she did," Galetti responded.

"Did you ever have a conversation with Maria Galetti telling her that you were supporting her family by selling her stock to yourself?"

"I don't remember, but I don't think so," Galetti said.

"Tell me about Parnelli Brothers Construction Company," Gerrity said.

"They build our stores," Galetti said. "And Norm Parnelli is on our board of directors."

"Have you known them a long time?"

"Over thirty years," Joe said.

"Have you ever lent them money because they were in financial trouble?" Gerrity asked.

"I purchased certain real estate holdings from them because they needed cash at one point," Joe Galetti admitted.

"How much cash?" Gerrity asked.

"About four million dollars," Joe Galetti said.

"You lent a friend four million dollars, but you sold your dead brother's stock to support his family?" Gerrity asked.

"The Parnelli brothers had collateral that they put up for the loan, and I considered Maria's stock transfer collateral as well," Joe Galetti responded.

"So, in your opinion, there's no difference in how you look at dealing with your family and how you consummate a business deal with a friend," Gerrity said.

"Business is business," Galetti said.

"But there's one major difference, Mr. Galetti. According to the terms of the will, you were the executor of your brother's will, and all monies were to be divided equally among the families. You broke that trust, Mr. Galetti."

"They still have twice the stock in value that they would have had if our chain had remained the same size as it was when my brother died," Galetti said, responding to Gerrity's statement.

"Mr. Galetti, the evidence is starting to pile up describing you as not only not a nice man, but one who only uses integrity if it's convenient. Let's see if I can count the ways. You not only fired your sister-in-law from the board of directors, but obtained affidavits from two people indicating the details of an affair. You barred your nephew from the company via court order, you've fired your president on at least one occasion, and sold your sister-in-law's stock without her knowledge, after being turned down by her when you proposed marriage to her. And yet you have loaned money to friends because they had a cash flow problem. Blood would seem to be thinner than water in this scenario," Gerrity said.

"Objection, Your Honor," Jerry Saxe said. "These accusations are scurrilous and beg the point, which I'm having a tough time trying to decipher among these innuendos."

"Your Honor, I'm just trying to establish the total lack of character and integrity with Mr. Galetti. He's a ruthless human being who would run over anything or anyone who is in his way and back up the truck to be sure he got his intended target," Gerrity fired back.

"I'll allow this testimony in spite of Mr. Gerrity's colorful remarks. I happen to agree with Mr. Gerrity in that this trial has everything to do with character, trust, and integrity."

I had to leave the courtroom at noon, but Gerrity hounded Joe Galetti for the rest of the week, questioning almost his every act of decision over the past 20 years in spite of frequent objections by Galetti's lawyers.

When I returned to the office, I had a message from Shirley Macober that said, "We've got a business to run, and you're pulling your pud at the trial." I called her right away, and she steamed into my office under full sail. As she plunked down in a chair in front of my desk, I said, "Hi, Shirley. I got your message."

"What message?" she asked. I turned the pink phone message around and she read it. "Jesus Christ, I didn't mean for Mary to quote me directly."

"Why, Shirley Macober, I do believe you are blushing," I said.

"It's just high blood pressure," she said with a laugh. "First, my compliments to you; I don't know what you said to David Pondorf down in the warehouse, but he's doing a hell of a job. Everything is working perfectly and we are having a hell of a week, if my withdrawals mean anything."

"Super. What's the emergency?" I asked.

"It has to do with our wholesale arm of the business. As you know, about twenty percent of our volume comes from shipping independent stores as a secondary supplier."

"Okay," I said.

"Well, I got a huge order today for a number of good items from guess who," Shirley said.

"I give up," I said.

"A&P," she said.

"You're kidding me," I said.

"Dead on the level," Shirley said. "What do you want me to do?"

"What do we make on those orders?" I asked.

"Cost plus five percent," she responded.

"Hell, ship them," I responded.

"But I'm sure the product we ship them will be used against us and our current merchandising plan."

"I'm sure you're right. But they'd do the same for us."

"In a pig's ass they would," came Shirley's very quick response.

"Hell, ship them one of those too!" I said.

"I can't. You're busy," Shirley responded.

I laughed at Shirley's remark. "Listen, check with legal to make sure there is no conflict of interest, and if there isn't, let them rip," I said.

"Aye, aye, Captain," Shirley said.

"And, Shirley, don't ship them anything that we may need ourselves. If we're in short demand, ship it to our stores first," I said.

"You know, you're kind of a cute honky when you get all businesslike," Shirley remarked.

"Why, Shirley, I do believe you are sexually harassing me," I said.

"I certainly hope so," she said. I could hear her laughing all the way down the hallway as she left.

I spent the rest of the day with a never-ending bunch of people wanting my attention about one aspect of the business or another. In the middle of all this foot traffic, I suddenly realized that some of these people would have gone to Joe Galetti's office for advice, but he wasn't available and it didn't look like he would be for a while. But people such as Lenny Hirshberg had to have decisions approved, and I, as the guy who had the authority, let them move ahead. It's strange in business, even in a small business, people try to cover their butts in case something goes wrong. They need to tell someone that they had permission from a higher authority. It was the same way in our company, although Joe Galetti had told me on more than one occasion that I often begged for forgiveness but hardly ever asked permission.

As I left the building for the day, I saw Joey Jr. walking toward the parking lot, and I hollered at him. "Hey, Joey, hold up."

He stopped and waited for me, and, as I drew closer, he said, "How goes the battle?"

"Thanks to you, pretty darn good," I said. Joey smiled and we fell into step together. Joey was built like his dad but he was shorter. He was a good deal better-looking because, fortunately for him, he looked like Alfie, his mother. He really was coming into his own as a businessman. It was just lately that I started to notice his formidable skills because I was always comparing him to Trip.

"You mean our preemptive strike on the competition?" Joey asked.

"Exactly," I said. "They don't know whether to crap or go blind. Shirley Mac told me that A&P is in such disarray that they came to our wholesale arm with a very significant order."

"No way," Joey said.

"Oh yeah, and we're shipping to them at cost plus five," I responded.

"Wow, what a crazy fucking business. Aiding and abetting the enemy while making plus five," Joey said.

"Yeah, and Shirley says we're moving product at a very rapid rate. Joey, you've done one hell of a job working all the elements of this plan. You should be proud of the work you've done," I said.

"Thanks, Russ, I really appreciate the feedback. But I was just the arms and legs; you did the strategic part of this surprise attack," Joey said.

"Maybe so but, clearly, the strategic part wouldn't have meant squat if we hadn't executed it flawlessly," I said. Changing the subject, I asked how things were on the home front.

Joey hesitated for a second and said, "You know Mom and Dad are separated."

"Yes. I'm sorry to hear it, because your mom is just a top-quality person. She was so nice to me when I was coming up in the business. I don't say this very often, and I know it sounds old-fashioned, but she's a real lady," I said.

"I certainly don't have an impartial view in these matters, but I think my dad is having a belated midlife crisis. And this court case isn't helping any. Were you there today?" Joey asked.

"I was and your dad was holding up okay. It makes me cringe to see the families ripping each other up. How's your relationship with Trip lately?" I asked.

"Strained," Joey said. "We were always close as kids, so that is helping us to get through it. We agreed when it started that it was going to be a nasty situation, and we're doing our best to ignore the acrimony, but it hasn't been easy."

"Anything I can do?" I said.

"Just what you have been doing. I know someday that someone from my generation, depending on how the case comes out, will be running this operation. But what Trip and I are in total agreement on is that we'd like to have something to run when this is all over. So you'll be doing your part by maintaining and even building the business while this fiasco is ongoing," he said.

"I'll do my best," I said.

"That's plenty enough in my view. See you, Russ," Joey said.

"You bet," I said.

When I arrived home Holly greeted me at the door, and I saw Claire sitting in the living room. It was great to see some friendly faces who had absolutely nothing to do with business or a courtroom. Holly said to me, "Your mom and I had some business to transact, so I invited her over for supper."

"What a great idea! How are you, my little butterfly?"

"I'm doing great," Holly said.

We had a wonderful dinner together. Claire was climbing up on 70 years of age, but I'd guess people would think she was 55 until they learned she had a son my age. But it was more than that; I think she was enjoying life more than anytime since my dad died. She had grandchildren to spoil and kids that she really enjoyed being around. After Claire left I showered and got into a pair of shorty pajamas that Holly had tried twice to throw away. I had to admit they were a little shopworn. We both arrived at the bedside at the same time, and we propped up our respective pillows as we both plunked on the bed.

"Man, does that feel good. I'm pooped all of a sudden," I said.

"I know what you mean," Holly said. "How was your day?"

"Busy. I'm Joe's fill-in while he's at court, so my office is a swinging door of people looking for guidance," I said. "Our little sneak attack on the competition is a sensational success, but I wanted to talk to you on an entirely different subject."

"Okay," Holly said. "Fire away."

"Diane Dunbar," I said.

"You know, Russ…in the last week I've learned you were thinking about having an affair with Maria Galetti, and now I have to listen to you talk about Diane Dunbar," Holly said.

"Wait a minute," I said. "Timing is everything. I had my fantasy about Maria long before I met you, and my discussion about Diane will be very brief."

"Good opening gambit, Mr. DA," Holly said with a smile.

"I fired Dunbar yesterday," I said.

"What?" Holly asked. "Tell me more."

"I thought you told me that you were tired of talking about this subject," I said.

"Not when there's potential dirt to be spread around!" Holly said as she adjusted the pillows and sat up in bed.

"Something's falling out of your nightie," I said.

"There's more where that came from if this is really juicy," she replied.

"How about Diane calling me a poor, pathetic turd and a naive asshole?" I asked.

"Get out of here," Holly said.

"Yup, and she told me that, when she and Joe were doing it, she was on top," I said.

"Eww…disgusting," Holly said. "He's old enough to be her father."

"My line exactly," I said. "It ended with me threatening to sue her over an ethics violation and then knocking one of her clients flat as I barged out the door."

"Unbelievable," Holly said. "I can't lie, I love it. But where does that leave you?"

"Hartman says in a made-for-TV flick, starring Yogi Berra as me," I said.

Holly laughed and said, "Really, how are you feeling?"

"Vulnerable, naive, and wondering when the next shoe will fall."

"For what it's worth, I think the person that is pathetic in this scenario is Diane. Nothing is important to her except power. She's consumed by it. I mean, just think about it. Do you think she'd give Joe Galetti another look if he weren't worth a billion or two and one of the most powerful men in the state? No way," Holly said.

"I guess but boy, do I feel like a jerk. You know, six months ago we weren't in court, Joe and Alfie weren't separated, our pension plan wasn't under suspicion, and I hadn't talked to Diane Dunbar in twenty years. Nirvana."

"Yeah, but you seem to be rolling with the punches okay," Holly said.

"Thanks to you," I said.

"Say good night, Russ," Holly said.

"Good night, Russ," I responded.

Chapter 13: The String Runs Out

The irony of the headlines looking back at me in bold print at the checkouts in our stores was inescapable. One of the gossip rags that usually has a headline such as "World's Biggest Baby Born—28 Pounds" ran a front-page story about Joe Galetti's separation from Alfie. In the text it stated that Alfie was seeking a divorce, and there were pictures of "the other woman" on Joe's arm leaving the theater. The "home wrecker" was identified as Diane Dunbar, a successful trial lawyer. The local media had latched on to the story and just wouldn't let it go.

The trial, meanwhile, was about to conclude. After Ned Gerrity had finished questioning Joe Galetti, his own attorneys kept him on the stand for another four days, and Jerry Saxe ran witness after witness to the front of the room to attest to the credibility of Joe Galetti as an honest and fair man. Suppliers, local businesspeople, politicians, and the heads of major charities marched up to the stand on behalf of the beleaguered Joe Galetti. On the day the last witness was attesting to his sterling character, *The Boston Globe* broke the story that Joe Galetti was being indicted by a grand jury regarding the company's pension plan. So the tip Arnold Cable had received from his poker-playing pals turned out to be accurate. Arnold had told me that it wouldn't amount to "a hill of beans" when all the dust cleared, but, like everything in life, timing was everything. And the timing could hardly be worse for Joe Galetti. The press already had a story, and now this news of the indictment just compounded the situation.

The media had hooked these two stories together by concentrating on the future position of Joe Galetti. If Joe lost some of his stock as a result of the impending divorce and if he were found guilty of doing inappropriate investing with the pension fund, he could find himself a minority stockholder with a series of numbers running across his tunic as he served time in a local penitentiary. I was conflicted by these events. I knew the pension indictment was more air than substance. At this point, if my 25 shares counted, I'd still want to see Joe Galetti running the business. We'd had a winning formula for a long time, and, from a selfish point of view, I didn't want to change something that wasn't broken.

These were the thoughts that kept running through my mind when it wandered off whatever task I was working on at the time. Working was actually great therapy, and it seemed like weeks since I'd been to the courthouse. But I was drawn back there almost against my will for the closing arguments. The night before the last day of the trial, Holly read me Shelley's "Ozymandias," and I remembered it from high school vaguely. But it seemed apropos somehow. The king, Ozymandias, brags about the riches of his city and that this level of splendor may never be reached again by mankind. But by the time the traveler reads this proclamation centuries later, there is nothing left of this opulent kingdom but "lone and level sands [that] stretch far away." And that is how I was thinking about our company, once the different factions of the Galetti family had spent millions of dollars chopping each other up for public consumption.

Both attorneys were up to the task of closing arguments. Ned Gerrity stuck to some very simple facts. His was brief and impactful, and his concluding statement was as follows:

"Ladies and gentlemen," Gerrity said. "We've put you through a long and arduous time. Weeks and weeks of trooping witnesses in front of you like livestock at an auction. But that all ends now. The facts are these. Joe Galetti was the executor of Dom Galetti's will, and the major stipulation in that will was that the business, Galetti-Pantry Place Supermarkets, would be split fifty-fifty among the two families. Period. Not for one year, three years, or five years, but in perpetuity. That trust was broken by Mr. Galetti, and we are asking that you right this injustice. Further and specifically, we are asking that the two hundred fifty shares of stock that Mr. Galetti usurped be returned to the family of Maria Galetti and that Mr. Galetti return the profits that have been garnered over the last fifteen years to her family as well. Thank you, ladies and gentlemen of the jury."

Jerry Saxe spoke for an hour. He reviewed Joe Galetti's business-building skills, his work in the community, and his reputation with the people he dealt with day in and day out. His concluding statement, at least to me, was a surprise because it dealt with a specific point of law regarding the statute of limitations. Jerry Saxe's concluding statement began as he said, "Maria Galetti knowingly signed a document selling her stock to Joe Galetti almost fifteen years ago. Now that the chain has grown to a billion dollars or more, she wants the stock back. It doesn't work that way. No more than if you sold a hundred shares of stock, saw it had gone up five dollars a share, and called your broker back and said, 'I was only kidding; I didn't want to sell that hundred shares after all.' A deal is a deal. I remind you also, ladies and gentlemen of the jury, that this transaction happened long ago and that the statute of limitations has long since passed. I have to agree with my worthy adversary. You've listened to a plethora of testimony. I'm sure the transcript of this trial could fill a small-size room. But I ask you to remember that every witness I put in front of you—every single one of them—attested to the integrity and character of Mr. Joseph L. Galetti over a very long time. Mr. Galetti has spent a lifetime being a solid citizen who has lent a helping hand to all in need. I ask you to dismiss these charges for what they are— scurrilous and based on innuendo. Thank you, ladies and gentlemen of the jury."

The judge instructed the jury. As I understood the charges, the jury had to determine if there was fraud committed by Joe Galetti and then they had to determine damages.

I left the courtroom that day strangely relieved. The verdict, of course, wasn't rendered, but I was happy that at least the trial phase had concluded. The point Saxe brought up about the statute of limitations had a strange effect on me. If this point of law was upheld and the jury found for the defendant, I sure wish it had come up at the beginning of the trial and not the end. Maybe it was my supermarket mentality, but what a colossal waste of time, energy, and money. In my mind's eye I saw Saxe standing up on the first day of the trial, bringing this point to the attention of the judge, and the judge making a favorable ruling for Joe Galetti. End of trial. I guess that's why I'm not in the legal system.

When I returned to the office, Lenny Hirshberg was waiting for me in my office. "We've just received an order from the court. Judge Matthews has frozen our assets at the request of Ned Gerrity."

My first question was, "Why?"

"Maria's family is afraid Joe will transfer more assets to his side of the family before the jury renders a decision."

"Can we still operate?" I said.

"I've sent the lawyers to court to ask for relief for everyday operations."

"Good thinking," I said. "Keep me informed, Lenny."

"Will do," he said.

This seemed like a last straw. Finally, the family bloodletting had officially crossed the line and was now effecting the business directly. I walked back to my office and locked my desk. I left the building and headed to an industry function at the Four Seasons.

We were honoring four people in our industry who would be enshrined in the Food Association Hall of Fame. These were always interesting events because it brought together all the dignitaries of the industry, and, for one night, we celebrated our collective good fortune over drinks and dinner. This particular night we were enshrining the daughter of Stop & Shop's founder and her husband into the Hall of Fame, and Joe Galetti would introduce them. I had to blackmail Hartman into coming because this particular woman had been the consumer advocate for the chain, and she continually assaulted Hartman's company for one practice or another. They had too many SKUs of toothpaste, their toilet paper was a "cheater" roll because, instead of taking the price up, they cut the sheet count. At one point this toilet tissue had 650 sheets on it, now had 400 sheets, and she told the press that his company had filled the roll with "bicycle air" instead of sheet count. Hartman would have rather been in a rat-infested cellar tied to a chair with water dripping on his forehead than this event, but, God love him, he showed up anyway. As soon as I arrived at the event, I saw him with a drink, trying to hide in a corner of the room. From about 10 feet away, I said, "Hey, Hartman, let's talk toothpaste. I understand you guys are adding seventeen mashed potato-flavored SKUs to the line."

If looks could kill, I would have dropped on the spot, but Hartman couldn't help but smile when he said, "Shut the fuck up, will you? Isn't it bad enough that I feel like a bull's-eye waiting for an arrow…and now I have to suffer humiliation from you as well."

"Don't worry. Hang with me. I won't let her beat you with a stick," I said.

"Why do I feel like I'm face-to-face with Benedict Arnold?" Hartman asked.

I had to laugh at Hartman. Just as we were turning to head for the bar, she was standing in front of us. Sylvia Gottleib herself. Consumer advocate extraordinaire. Even I was a little ruffled by her sudden appearance. She was in her early 60s, short, plump, and in a dress that had more cloth than a mainsail on a Beetle Cat. She was heavily made-up and she was dripping in jewels. She said, "Well, if it isn't the arch enemy, Bill Hartman."

"Mrs. Gottleib," Hartman said.

"What evil are you and your company up to now?" she asked.

"Well, we're thinking about reducing our sheet count on toilet tissue again," he said.

"You can't be serious," she said.

"Oh yes," Hartman said. "We're going to call it the 'one-dump roll'—just enough sheets for one turn in the bathroom. It won't look like much, but it'll turn over in the warehouse like gangbusters."

Simultaneously, Sylvia and I burst out laughing uncontrollably. Finally, when we stopped laughing, Sylvia said to Hartman, "You know, Bill, you're all right for a manufacturing type. Thanks for coming tonight. I'll be sure and relay that story to my husband, because I know he'll kill himself laughing."

"Thank you, Sylvia," Hartman said as he leaned over and gave her a peck on the cheek.

And she was off to see other people. I sat with Hartman and enjoyed the festivities. I told him that it took unbelievable balls to tell one of the most powerful people in the industry a story as insane as the "one dump" toilet tissue, and he replied by saying something that was profound. Hartman said, "You know, you and I didn't get where we are because we pussyfoot around. And we've been around long enough that we have the right to speak our minds. What the fuck are they going to do, fire us? And if they did, so what? We're survivors. I always want to be respectful, but I'm not going to take any shit from anybody."

Not a bad philosophy and it was curious to me that, although I'd been unable to articulate it to myself, I felt exactly the same way.

When I arrived home that night, I related the day's happenings to Holly. She was stunned by the things that I witnessed in one day. The chain had a serious cash flow problem, we were under court indictment for possible pension fund improprieties, the U.S. Labor Department had suddenly taken an interest in us, our stores were doing sensational business, and I witnessed not only a Hall of Fame enshrinement, but one of the funniest exchanges between manufacturer and customer I had ever heard. But with the diversity and scope of the day, Holly's first question surprised me. "Was Diane Dunbar with Joe at this function?"

"Are you nuts?" I replied.

"After listening to what happened in your day, I thought anything was possible," Holly said.

"Good point. If she had showed up, it wouldn't have seemed out of the ordinary with everything else that was going on."

"I think you would have noticed," Holly said. "What else are you thinking about?"

"The trial ended today and I had two reactions. The first was that I was glad it was over, but the second was that it made me go all the way back and reflect on my life, and that led me to thinking about the future," I said.

"I thought I smelled some wood burning," Holly said.

I smiled at her. What a breath of spring air she was. It made me ask her, "Don't you ever get down about things? You know, when I drive up our street every night and turn into that driveway, I feel as if I've entered a haven where the gremlins can't get me. I'm safe. And it's because of you and your attitude, I'm convinced of that," I said.

"Oh, sure I do. I get moody. Sometimes the kids drive me nuts. Or the bank will call and ask why I invested in a stock in their portfolio that lost thirteen cents today. So I roll my eyes a lot, but overall I feel blessed to be absolutely surrounded by people who love me, which, of all rare occurrences, includes my mother-in-law. How many people can say that?"

"Not many," I said.

"And you know, Russ, you're no small part of that. We've been married a long time, and I love you with an almost embarrassing passion. In all the years we've been married, I can't remember the last fight we had over anything. And I know whatever it was, it was settled before we went to bed that night. So give yourself a little credit too," Holly said.

"Thanks, I really appreciate that. And the feeling is mutual. I just want you to know about a thought I had for the first time today."

"Fire away," Holly said.

"I'm thinking about quitting."

Holly just looked at me and then she said, "This thing has taken more of a toll on you than I would have imagined."

"Well, I think I'm getting better at looking at things more objectively. Usually, if something bothers me, I tuck it away somewhere and conveniently forget to revisit it. But you know I never did this job for the money. I did it because I loved it and believed in the integrity of the Galetti family. I have to think that Dominic is looking down on us and seeing a scene from the Tower of Babel. I think he'd be greatly disappointed at the most recent turn of events, and you know what…I am too."

"Listen, honey. I'm totally supportive. Don't stay because you feel you have to support your family. We'll be fine," Holly said.

"Thanks. It may be nothing. But I wanted you to know what I was thinking so that it wouldn't be a surprise," I said.

"You're a good man, Russell Riley. And as long as I'm in your life, whatever you do is okay with me," she said.

"I've got news for you, my friend. You're not in my life, you are my life," I said.

"C'mon, let's hit the sack," Holly said with a smile. "And while we're at it, let's count our blessings."

When I was riding to work the next day with the radio off, I felt as if a 1000-pound anvil had been lifted off my shoulders. I hadn't really resolved anything, but I was looking at alternatives to what had become a way of life for almost 30 years. At about noon Lenny Hirshberg came to my office to report that the judge had relented on his order to freeze assets and would allow us to spend funds "to operate the business in a normal manner." That was a relief to me because I'd already gone to Hartman to see what our suppliers would say if we needed extended terms for a period of time. He had checked with his credit department, which led the industry in these types of matters, and they said they would be willing to extend terms but that we would lose our two percent discount for prompt payment. This was a two-edged sword because I'd committed the chain to a very aggressive merchandising plan, and we needed every discount we could lay our hands on. After Lenny left my office, I called Hartman to tell him that the judge had relented and that we would not be having a cash flow problem. The reason I did it was I knew Hartman would immediately call his credit department and give them the update. Past experience with our suppliers' credit departments was that they talked to each other, and I didn't want any rumors circulating to the effect that we couldn't pay our bills.

After lunch Joe Galetti, making one of his infrequent visits to his office, called me into his office. He looked old. Joe was even thinner than usual, and his complexion was pasty. I opened the conversation by saying, "Welcome back, Joe. It's lonely here at the top."

"Russ, I know I've been preoccupied by the trial, but what the fuck has been going on here?"

"What do you mean?" I asked as his tone and his question really caught me off guard.

"I've been looking at the numbers, and our volume is good but our profit sucks, and we've paid our ad agency more this month than we did in the last year," he said.

"Okay. I took the offensive and decided to launch an all-out attack on our competition before they did something similar to us," I said.

"What evidence did you have that they were going to strike us?" he asked.

"None…just a gut feeling," I said.

"You spent several million dollars in lowering prices, buying TV spots, to say nothing of turning our warehouse upside down on a gut feeling?" Joe asked.

"Yep."

"That's just irresponsible, Russ. I didn't authorize any of this," Joe said.

"You weren't here, Joe, and I made the decision. As a piece of hindsight, at least one chain was gearing up to kick up our butts, but we beat them to the punch."

"What chain?" Joe asked.

"A&P," I replied.

"How do you know?" he asked.

"Because they are ordering a shitload of products from our wholesale arm," I said.

"You're selling stuff from our warehouse to a competitor?" he asked.

"Sure am, at cost plus five percent," I replied.

"I thought I told you and the board that we were retrenching, not expanding, and that we would be working with a consultant to study our consumer more closely."

"You did but it was my view that we wouldn't have any consumer to study if we didn't go on the offensive," I said.

"Russ, you weren't authorized to make that decision without talking to me," Joe said in a very steady voice.

"Joe, I'm the president of this organization, and you seemed more than normally occupied on several fronts," I said.

"What's that supposed to mean?" he said.

"It's pretty obvious, isn't it, Joe?" I said.

"Let's keep it professional, not personal, Russ," he said.

"How the hell can it not be personal when you're testifying in court, being indicted over pension fund irregularities, getting divorced, and running around with Diane Dunbar? Jesus Christ, Joe…professional, my ass. I can't pick up a paper and not read about one or more of those items every day."

"You don't approve?" Joe asked.

"I'm not here to approve or disapprove. My job is to keep a pretty good business afloat while family members tear each other limb from limb. And I think I'm doing a pretty good job of it."

"Well, Russ, I don't happen to agree. And as long as you've put her name on the table, I'm particularly upset by how you treated Diane the other day," Joe said.

"Frankly, Joe, I don't give a shit how upset you are about it. In fact, I think it's an outrage that you even know about it. For Christ's sake, she's supposed to be my lawyer, not your playmate of the month."

"Watch it," Joe said. "You're skating on very thin ice."

"It's your show, Joe," I said.

"You're damn right it is, and you seem to have forgotten that recently," he said as he stood up from his desk and walked over to the window. "Given the circumstances, I think it best if you resign, effective immediately."

"I'm not going to quit, Joe," I said.

"Okay. Russ, you're fired," Joe said. "I expect that you'll be out of here by the close of business today."

I stood up and left Joe's office and returned to my office next door. I put on my coat, picked up my business bag, and walked out of the building.

Thirty years working for an organization "man and boy," as my dad used to say, was down the chute as the result of a five-minute conversation with Joe Galetti. I didn't expect to be such an accurate prognosticator. I'd told Holly the night before that I was thinking about quitting, but, frankly, I didn't envision it happening quite so quickly. Joe had given me the chance to resign, but in the end I couldn't do it. Don't ask me why. I thought I was doing the right thing, and somehow I wanted to go out on my shield. As I drove out of the parking lot of headquarters, I thought to myself that Joe's dad, Dominic, would have sided with me. I hated leaving a sinking ship, but Joe really had no alternative in mind, and I was quite confident that my earlier tirade with Diane Dunbar played a major role in my termination.

As I drove in our driveway, I saw Holly standing in the driveway washing her car. She was in a sleeveless shirt and a pair of short shorts. Pretty typical behavior; she could afford to have the car washed, at least through today, but she just wouldn't do it. She looked at me with some concern and said, "What are you doing home? Are you sick?"

"I'll give you a buck three eighty to wash this one," I replied.

"Russ..." she said.

"Well, you know that conversation we had last night about maybe quitting the job," I said.

"You quit," she said.

"Almost," I said.

"You were fired," Holly said.

"Yeah, by the man himself," I replied.

Holly dropped the hose she was holding as I opened the door and stood in the driveway. She came over and gave me a hug and didn't say anything. Finally, she said, "It was time."

We both went in the house and, for a short time, went our separate ways. I changed into shorts and a golf shirt, grabbed a beer and the paper, and headed out to my favorite chair in the backyard. Holly joined me with a tall iced tea in her hand, and we talked for the better part of an hour. I told her about the conversation with Joe, how I thought Diane had been a major influence in the decision, and that, at the moment, I couldn't even think about next steps for me. Holly's end of the conversation followed a familiar theme.

We had good financials, she could go back to work at any time, and that I ought to cool it for a while. And that's exactly what I intended to do.

The only thing we talked about in any detail was how to handle the next few days, as, usually, the termination of a senior employee at a large local business would only be a story on the second page of the business section of the major papers. But this circumstance was different. With the highly publicized trial now with the jury, Joe's divorce, and the pension plan indictment, we were pretty sure that this would be seen as another link in the ongoing saga of events swirling around Galetti Supermarkets. We thought time would be on our side because the news media wouldn't pick up the story until the next day. As we were finishing this conversation, I said to Holly, "If Natalie calls, I'll take it."

"In a pig's ass," Holly snapped. "I'll handle Ms. Jacobson."

"Pity," I replied.

Holly laughed and said, "Hey, don't lose that in the next few days."

"Lose what?" I said.

"Your sense of humor," Holly said as she gave me a hug and headed for the kitchen.

Interestingly, the phone didn't ring at all the rest of the day. I was a little surprised by that because I felt sure that Joe Galetti would have put an announcement out internally.

There was nothing in the papers the next day either. Holly had contacted a lawyer to represent me concerning my remaining severance pay and the larger issue of my 25 shares of stock in the corporation.

Reality seemed to grip me the next day. Although we were financially sound, I really needed to find work for any number of reasons, not the least of which was that, over time, I'd drive Holly nuts being under her feet at home. More importantly, our two children were moving into the all-important formative years, and I think we both thought it was critical to have Holly at home and accessible to them. It's weird when your routine is broken and you are no longer leaving the driveway every morning. I read the paper, jogged, worked in the garden, made lunch, and took a nap. About midafternoon the phone started ringing, and the first call was from Ed Rollins at *Supermarket News*. After exchanging pleasantries, he said, "I have a release from your headquarters saying that you have resigned to seek other opportunities."

"Not exactly, Ed," I said.

"What then," he said.

"I was fired by Joe Galetti," I responded.

"Can I quote you?" Rollins asked almost immediately.

"Yes," I said.

"Can you tell me why?" he asked.

"I can't, Ed," I said. "I think it's more appropriate for my former employer to handle this kind of thing."

"I understand," responded Rollins. "I want to wish you well. You've always been a straight shooter, and, in doing background checks, I don't think you'll be unemployed long."

"Thanks, Ed, I really appreciate that."

As soon as I hung up, I called upstairs to Holly and told her that the news was out. She had agreed to screen my calls. She did a great job of it. All the major papers called, and she handled them herself. I talked to Trip, Arnold Cable, Bill Hartman, and Elsie Baden. Maria didn't call, perhaps on the advice of her lawyer; and then the shocker of the late afternoon, when Holly came into the den to tell me that Diane Dunbar was on the line. I told Holly to tell her I wasn't available. Jesus, the unmitigated gall of this woman had reached new heights as far as I was concerned. Maybe to rub a little salt in the wound.

The most interesting call came from someone I wasn't expecting a call from at all. Ed Pondorf, the 300-pound warehouse supervisor whom I had grown up with in the business. He opened with his usual kindly sentiment. "Hey, shit for brains, they finally figured out what your contribution was around here, eh?"

"Fuck you, Pondorf, and the horse you rode in on. Not that a horse could carry you for long," I said. "But you may be right. I fooled them for thirty years. What are you up to?"

"I got trouble asshole high to a ten-foot Indian," Pondorf replied. "Here, let me put you on the blower; I got company."

"Hey, Russ, it's Shirley Macober, the best buyer in these here United States."

"Hey, Shirley, great to hear your voice, even if I don't approve of the company you keep," I said.

"Well, that's what we're calling about. Thanks to you and the alliance you forged between buying and warehousing, we are kicking some major butt. I haven't been this happy since the hogs ate my brother," Shirley said.

I could hear Pondorf laughing in the background when I said, " So, I don't get it. What's the problem?" I asked.

"The grapevine has it that this sale you dreamed up got you canned," Pondorf explained.

"It played a minor role; Joe and I just weren't seeing things eye-to-eye, and, at the end of the day, he's the boss," I said.

"Well, we just wanted you to know that this afternoon, our respective departments are holding a sit-down strike in your honor," Shirley said. "It seems appropriate since you spent most of your time sitting on that cute little tush of yours while you were here."

"You heard that, Pondorf; clearly, that was sexual harassment," I said.

"Yeah, and you'll give her twenty minutes to cut it out, right?" Pondorf said.

"Right," I said. "Seriously, guys, you're joking about this sit-down thing, right?"

"Dead serious," Pondorf said. "And don't make Shirley and me come over there and kick your ass either."

"Come to think of it, I don't think anyone has ever seen you two guys in the same room together, leading some to believe that you are one and the same person," I said. "But, honestly, I'd prefer you didn't do anything to disrupt the organization."

"Listen, douche bag, and I say that with all intended respect, it's too late. We've got signs made and the whole ten yards," Pondorf said.

"Okay, you guys…great talking to you. I have to tell you this phone call made my day," I said.

"Don't get too choked up, Russ," Shirley said. "We're only doing this because we're afraid your replacement will be worse than you, if that's possible."

"I love you guys too; so long," I said.

I had the strangest emotional response as I hung up the phone. Tears were rolling down my face as Holly moved over to where I was sitting. "Are you okay? Who was that?" Holly asked.

"Pondorf and Macober telling me that they are staging a sit-down strike on my behalf this afternoon," I said.

"That's so cool," Holly said.

"I tried to talk them out of it, but they weren't having any of it," I said.

The next day there was a picture of this little ragtag group of about eight folks marching around in front of headquarters. It was a small effort as protests go, but I felt good that our management, or part of it, wanted to express their displeasure at my canning. To tell the truth, I wasn't that crazy about the decision myself. Even though it was a very minor deal, it didn't stop a lot of people from calling me to express support or poke fun at me. Almost without exception people I talked with who didn't know Pondorf wanted to know who the monster was in the picture of the demonstration.

As my 15 minutes of fame were fading me back to obscurity, I noted that nine days had passed since the trial had concluded. The jury was still locked away, trying to decide the case. Two days later the verdict was handed down. Joe Galetti's side had reason to hope because it had taken almost two weeks for the jury to return a verdict. Their optimism was short-lived.

It turned out to be a stunning victory for Maria Galetti. The first thing the jury did was throw out the statute of limitations question, because they felt the first time Maria knew her stock was being sold was earlier in the year, when she received the tax form in the mail. They further stated that Joe Galetti did fraudulently maneuver the stock to his advantage. They awarded $500 million to Maria and asked that 250 shares of stock be returned from Joe Galetti to Maria Galetti. So, in total, Maria's award amounted to three-quarters of a billion dollars. There were tears of relief from Maria Galetti's side of the courtroom and hugs from her lawyers but no outward celebration. Joe's lawyers were clearly depressed, but outside the courtroom they vowed to fight on, indicating that this was just one step in a long series of courtroom battles between the two sides.

They may have been right, but, to me, it was one hell of a giant stride for Maria Galetti. Further, the court ordered that Joe Galetti be removed as CEO. It also left me in a very interesting position. I held the swing shares that would determine who would be the majority owner. At first, I didn't really think it mattered, because Joe had been removed as CEO. But I was wrong. Maria Galetti called me the next day, and I immediately said to her, "Congratulations, Maria. That was a stunning victory for you, and I'm sure you're very happy about it."

"Russ, I'm very happy about the decision, and I think justice has been served, but it's not something to celebrate on the whole as far as the Galetti family is concerned," Maria said.

"I see your point," I said. "What's your first order of business?"

"To try to establish a board of directors and a CEO," she said.

"Good move," I said.

"I'm going to need your support to do what I want to do," Maria said.

"How can I help?" I asked.

"Well, first of all, I need your proxy of the twenty-five shares you hold. At this point each family has four hundred eighty-seven point five shares, not five hundred, as reported in the paper. There are a number of scenarios that may transpire. Joe may have to sell shares to me to pay the five hundred million he owes me, and I could pick up the voting rights to shares that Alfie may garner from the divorce, but that's all in the future, and we need to act now."

"Not to be crass, but what's in it for me if I throw in with you?" I asked.

"Well, for one thing, your old job and a seat on the board," she said.

"Who would be CEO?" I asked.

"Trip," she responded.

"What about Joey Jr.?" I asked.

"He's decided to resign," Maria stated.

"Okay, Maria," I said. "When do you need my decision?"

"As soon as possible," she replied.

"Okay, I'll get back to you," I responded.

"Russ…" Maria said.

"Yes," I responded.

"I thought you'd jump at the chance. What's the delay?" she asked.

"I want to talk to Holly about it," I said.

"Fair enough. See you later," Maria said, ending the conversation.

Before I could find Holly, the phone rang again and I said, "Hello," expecting it to be Maria trying to tell me something she had forgotten the first time.

"Russ, Diane Dunbar," she said.

"Hello, Diane," I said.

"Joe asked me to call you," she said.

"Are you representing him?" I asked.

"Not officially," she said.

"Have Joe call me," I said.

"He wanted me to talk to you about the decision of the court yesterday," she said.

"Have Joe call me," I repeated.

"This is just some preliminary stuff he wanted me to talk with you about," she said.

"Have Joe call me," I said.

"Jesus, you're a pain in the ass," Dunbar said.

"Glad to be of service," I said and hung up.

Five minutes later the phone rang again, and it was Joe Galetti. Never a man to waste words, he said, "Russ, I need those twenty-five shares to maintain a grip on this organization."

"Joe, you need a lot more than my twenty-five shares," I responded.

"Listen, kid, five hundred million isn't chicken feed, even for me, but I don't have to sell anything to raise the dough."

"But, Joe, you've been removed from the CEO spot, you've got a divorce pending and another trial looming on the pension fund," I replied.

"That's precisely why I need to keep control of this chain," he said.

"What's the deal?" I asked.

"I make you CEO. Hell, I got the idea from Trip's testimony in court. Listen, Joey has already said he's leaving the company. So Trip would be president, and I'm guessing Maria will want to be on the board."

"How does that help you? The board will be a majority of Maria's folks," I said.

"Yeah, I know. But with you as CEO and me holding a majority of the stock, I think I'll get a fair stake."

"What about Alfie?" I asked.

"Well, if she is awarded some of my shares and votes with Maria, I become a minority shareholder, but I still get a fair shake if you're the CEO," he said.

"Why would you propose me for CEO when you fired me as president?" I asked.

"Because times change. I was the boss and I made a decision to have you resign for overstepping your bounds. But now I'm potentially on the outside looking in, and I'm banking on your integrity," Joe said.

"Joe, all in, all done, I think you're a good man. But I think it's time for you to take a backseat," I said.

"Will you consider this offer?" he asked.

"Certainly," I responded. "And, Joe…"

"Yes?" he asked.

"Don't have Diane call me again," I said.

"Okay," he said.

In less than an hour, I'd gone from the ranks of the unemployed to having two job offers. One as president and the other as CEO. I sat down with Holly at the kitchen table, and we just kicked around what I'd been told by both sides of the Galetti family over the past hour or so. Her only comment was, "Aren't you the most popular kid in class all of a sudden?"

I spent the next two days at home, thinking about my future. Surprisingly, the most relevant factor to me was Joey's resignation. To me it signified that the family business, as I knew it, was over. No matter which offer I took and no matter when the appeals ended, it was never going to be the same as it had been. I'd spent 30 years in this family business avoiding whatever politics transpired, but in the future the pride of ownership and pulling together to be successful was no more. Don't get me wrong, I wasn't complaining. I'd started as an aisle clerk in a one-store operation. To say I'd been lucky to ride this gravy train as long as I had would be a vast understatement.

But having Joey resign and not take his place in the hierarchy led me to how I would resolve my future.

The following Monday I asked Maria, Joe, and Trip if they could join me at headquarters and reserve a conference room where we could talk. I'd made my decision. When I arrived the three combatants were waiting for me in the main conference room. As soon as I stepped into the room, I could feel the tension as Maria and Trip studiously avoided eye contact with Joe. I poured a cup of coffee, said hello to Trip and Joe, and received a hug from Maria. Just for a minute it reminded me of a happier time, when we were, for all practical purposes, the board of directors at this once thriving company.

I went to the front of the room, took out three index cards with my notes on them, and began to talk. "First, I want to thank you for all agreeing to meet with me. Under the circumstances, even meeting in the same room has become an onerous chore for this family. I promise to make this brief, but I would be negligent if I didn't thank the people in this room for my employment with this company for the last thirty years. Your dad, Joe, was an idol to me, and, as you know, he put me through college at no expense to me or my family. In addition, his two sons really took me under their wings and taught me the business, as well as making me a shareholder in a very successful corporation, Galetti Supermarkets, Inc. I, in return, tried to do the same type of mentoring for Trip and his cousin, Joey Jr., when they were coming through the system. And what I was trying to teach the boys was basically what Dominic taught me. If I could sum up his lessons to me, they would be one, integrity, first, last, always; two, treat your customers and suppliers as you want to be treated; and three, his favorite, I think…cash is king.

"I have to tell you that I feel as if I'm one of the luckiest stiffs on Earth. For thirty years I literally jumped out of bed because I wanted to go to work. Couldn't wait to start the day. How many people can say that about their career? It never felt like work to me. And you know what? I think a lot of people in this organization felt that way. Arnold Cable, Dave Pondorf, and Shirley Macober, to name three off the top of my head. This company built loyalty in its people.

"But we're in a new era now, and that fact was crystallized for me when I learned that Joey Jr. has left the organization. In my own mind I always saw Trip and Joey running this organization, as the third generation of this remarkable family, just as you and Dom ran it years ago, Joe. I remember Trip asking me, when he was thirteen years old, if I'd be working for him someday, and I remember telling him that it was a distinct possibility.

"In the most recent days, I've gone from the unemployed to being asked by the two sides of the family, in separate conversations, to be president or CEO. And I thank each of you for your consideration. What I've decided to do is neither one of those jobs. The time has come to make a break. Frankly, this wrangling between the families has become more than personal, to the point that it's interfering with the business. Another way of saying the same thing is, I'm not having any fun, not enjoying what I'm doing under the current circumstances.

"Here's what I'm recommending. I will sell my shares at fair market value, to be determined by an independent accounting firm, back to the family as I received them. Twelve and a half shares back to each side of the family. In so doing, all of the stock will be back where it belongs, in the Galetti family. That's it, folks. What do you say? And, Trip, now we know the answer for the question you asked me so many years ago. No, I won't be working for you someday, although, under different circumstances, it would have been a pleasure."

Nobody said anything at first as I stood at the head of the conference table, with my index cards in my hand.

Maria was the first to speak. "I feel as if I just lost a close friend. What will you do?"

"Thank you, Maria, I appreciate it. I have no idea what I will do at this point," I said.

Joe looked at me and said, "If we do this, Russ, you'll have to sign a no-compete clause."

I responded to Joe by saying, "The bean counter right to the end. In all due respect, Joe, I don't think you're in a position to demand anything." Joe glared back at me but said nothing.

Trip stood up, came around the table, put his arm around me, and said, "I wish it were different, and we all wish you'd change your mind. But if that's not in the cards, speaking for my mother and myself, we will accept your terms without a no-compete clause."

I shook Trip's hand and, as I was leaving the room, I said, "Thanks, Trip. See you later."

I walked out the front door of the building, knowing I'd never reenter the headquarters as an employee.

Epilogue

Five years have passed since I walked out of the Galetti headquarters building as an almost employee of the firm. In looking back at the trial that split the Galetti empire, there was one winner. The legal community. In all, they collected over $100 million from the Galetti family, and Ned Gerrity, Maria's lawyer, has become a household name here in New England. The board of directors changed dramatically; as Trip became CEO, Maria was named president, Alfie was named to the board, while Joe Galetti and Norm Parnelli were removed from it. Joe married Diane Dunbar but they divorced 17 months later. Joe still has an office in the building but is rarely seen. Joey started his own computer software firm and, last year, sold it to Microsoft for $30 million. Helen Cortez landed a job in Brussels with a prestigious international law firm. She's now ready to come back to the States, and it is rumored that she and FBI agent Larry Nelson are talking merger. If she settles in Boston, they will save a boatload of money on flights between Brussels and Boston.

The business is still ongoing, but there are signs that it is not growing. Galetti Supermarkets has built four more stores, but they have closed nine. The current rumor is that a Dutch-based supermarket company is planning to acquire Galetti as yet another tentacle of supermarket chains that they have purchased up and down the East Coast. Galetti markets are showing further signs of decline. They are losing share of market, and they have turned away from national brands and begun to push their own private label. Not a good sign. To an insider it means volume is slipping, and they are trying to make up corresponding profit loss by selling a more profitable private label.

The reason I know their business condition is that I'm in their stores quite often. After leaving Galetti, I had a number of decent offers from larger competitors but felt that it would be just too weird to work for another supermarket chain. If I were going to work for a chain, I suppose I would have taken one of the two jobs the Galetti family offered me after the trial. But I stayed in the industry, as Bill Hartman and I went into the food brokerage business together. We started with a few lines, and we have expanded slowly. We don't want to be the biggest, but we do want to be the best. Importantly, I'm having fun again, even though every other Tuesday, at 10 a.m., I'm trying to wrestle another big order out of Shirley Macober, and most times I lose that battle. She's good but I already knew that; after all, I hired her.

I see Maria every once in a while, and I think she likes being back in the business. I always thought she'd find that special someone after Dom died, but it hasn't happened yet. Claire is 75 years young, and her grandkids still can't stay up with her. Our kids are both in high school, and Holly is working part-time at her old firm. We shouldn't have to worry too much about paying college tuition; I cashed in my 25 shares of Galetti Corporation and had to pay Uncle Sam $13.3 million in taxes.

I keep turning it over in my mind, trying to think what lessons I learned from this family in turmoil that eventually cost me my job and a decent livelihood. I guess part of it is that there is no such thing as status quo. Conditions change, people change, and what seemed vital yesterday could be irrelevant tomorrow. Certainly, money doesn't guarantee anything, including happiness. But, most of all, it all boils down to a very personal philosophy. If you have a family that loves you and a job you love, it probably doesn't get any better than that.

THE END

DATE DUE

OC 02 '14			
OC 14 '14			
OC 31 '14			
DE 03 '14			
JA 07 '15			
MR 26 '15			
			PRINTED IN U.S.A.

CPSIA information can be obtained at www.ICGtesting.com
Printed in the USA
LVOW04s0913280814

401204LV00032B/1302/P